THE BOY I HATE

TAYLOR SULLIVAN

GOOD HOUSE
PUBLISHING

To my niece, who has always been my biggest fan. And my sister, who I will love forever, no matter how far a distance separates us.

CHAPTER ONE

SAMANTHA ELIZABETH SMILES sat across from her boyfriend of the past six years and blinked. A slow, sloth-like blink, as she simultaneously filled her lungs with just enough air to keep her heart from jumping out of her chest. "Wha-what do you mean you can't go?"

Her voice cracked with the question, but she couldn't help it. In only two days they were to leave on their trip, a three thousand mile journey across the US. Yet here he sat in the middle of the restaurant, telling her, in the nonchalant way he did everything, that he couldn't make it.

She searched his deep brown eyes, desperately looking for any sign she'd misheard him, but there was nothing. Not a hint of remorse that he was breaking a promise. Not a bit of understanding that he was leaving her with little choice but to make the drive from Los Angeles to New York alone.

But it was more than that; it wasn't a broken promise that left her breathless. It was the fact that he didn't realize how important this was. He didn't realize that everyone on the planet expected him to be there. That everyone would expect her high-school sweetheart to be there for her best friend's wedding. But they did, *she* did, and her cheeks heated at the thought of trying to explain his absence.

Steven leaned back in his seat, taking the folded-up napkin and tucking it neatly into his lap. "I didn't say I couldn't go, I said I couldn't drive with you; big difference."

She choked, trying to keep the panic in her throat from bubbling to the surface. "What do you mean?"

His face softened, and he leaned across the table to take her hand. "I wouldn't miss seeing you in your bridesmaid dress for the world." He played with her fingers, turning them over in his to see the dark stains beneath her fingernails. "But Renee is your best friend, not mine. She doesn't need *me* to be there. She needs you."

The room began to spin slightly, and Samantha took back her hand to reach across the table for her glass of wine. "*I* need you, Steven. Doesn't that matter?"

"Samantha…"

"Everyone expects you to be there."

"I'm sure they'll understand."

"It's not just that." She took a large gulp of chardonnay, closing her eyes for a second before opening them again. "I've never driven cross-country before. I really don't want to do it alone."

He sat back, his face hardening with a disapproval that wasn't foreign to her. "Where's my strong, independent girl? Where's the Samantha who's not afraid of anything?" He adjusted in his seat, rolling his shoulders back in the way he always did when they argued. "This internship is a once-in-a-lifetime opportunity. You can't expect me to give it up for a wedding. You can't expect me to give it up to drive a slab of concrete across the US."

She cringed. "Slab of concrete?" Though truthfully, the insult wasn't a big surprise. He'd been growing impatient with her sculptures for months… She'd never expected him to use such derogatory words to describe her art. Slab of concrete?

"Sammie." He closed his eyes, setting his napkin softly on the table. "That's not what I meant, and you know it." His voice softened, and he waited for her to look back up again. "I love your work. I know Renee will love it too, but why don't you fly, honey, give it to her when she visits this summer?"

Samantha took a calming breath and shook her head. "I'm not flying. I promised Ren—" But she stopped herself, realizing the argument would fall on deaf ears. "You know what, never mind. It's obvious you don't understand."

His brows furrowed and he tilted his head to the side. "Sammie, I support you in everything. I thought you supported me, too. This is my future. This is for *us*, baby. For *our* future."

She whipped her eyes up.

Us.

Our.

Future.

There it was again. The words that sent her heart racing like a stampede of wild cattle. Though it wasn't the words, per se, it was the meaning behind them. It was the talk of finality. The end. Forever. Because marriage, to Samantha, was what her parents had. The laughing so hard at the kitchen sink you peed a little. About something no one could understand but the two of you. The eternal kind of love that didn't even end with death. And it wasn't even that she was opposed to that future with Steven. She could see it. He was the perfect catch. He did everything right... But he was all she'd ever known. All she'd ever been with...

She took a calming breath, chanting in her head that this was just Steven. The planner, the man who knew every step he would make ten steps before he actually made them. Her friend. The guy who'd been by her side since junior high, her boyfriend since junior year...

3

"But if it means that much to you…"

She raised her hand, cutting him off before he could say more. "No. No—you're right." Her brows pulled together and she looked down at the table. "This is a big deal." It had been his dream forever. She couldn't bear the thought of taking that away from him. "I'm being selfish. You can't pass this up. You can't."

He took her hand, pulling it forwards again until she rose slightly from her seat. "Are you sure?"

She swallowed, looking him dead in the eye. "Positive."

He lifted her fingers, pausing briefly before kissing each one. "I already have my pinstriped suit at the cleaners and a flight booked for Friday afternoon. You won't miss me, baby. I promise."

He finally released her hand, allowing her bottom to settle comfortably on the soft, cushioned chair. She took a deep breath, hoping the action would cause her heart to slow to a normal speed, then opened the menu. "Good."

———————

THE REST of the evening went by without any surprises. It was filled with conversation, mostly about Steven and his news about the new position: the recognition, the honor. And like before, he reminded her of how rare an opportunity his internship truly was.

Connor and Associates was the most prestigious Law Firm in Los Angeles, representatives of the rich, the famous, and the top secret. They allowed exactly five openings outside of Ivy League schools per year. *Five.* Which meant that Steven, who graduated summa cum laude out of UCLA's law program and would have a bright future ahead of him no matter where he went, had just had the granddaddy of opportunities fall into his lap. This opening would never come again. There was no question about it.

The more he spoke, the brighter his eyes became, and Samantha loved it. To watch his face glow. To see him actually giddy with excitement, like he'd gotten an autograph from his boyhood idol—or better yet, been asked to play in a game with his favorite team. It was awesome, because she'd practically grown up with Steven…and he was her best friend outside of Renee. Samantha was proud and excited for him, and she wouldn't let her disappointment diminish that.

———

It was late that evening when Steven finally pulled alongside the curb outside of Samantha's apartment. She leaned forward, fetching her bag from the floor of his Prius where the long strap had somehow gotten tangled around her foot.

"Are you sure you're not mad at me about the trip?" Steven asked.

He normally wasn't so considerate, and the fact that he was made her glance up, finding him subdued and contemplative. She untangled the strap of her bag, took her time slowly rising in her seat, and narrowed her eyes "You mean about the internship? No, why would I be?"

He lifted his shoulders. "You said everyone was expecting me."

She bit her bottom lip, looking down to her lap before responding. "They'll get over it."

"Will you?"

She met his kind brown eyes that were honest and sincere. "It's a gift, in a way."

His eyes narrowed, but he adjusted in his seat to humor her. "How so?"

"Ammunition."

"Ammunition?"

"Yep. I'll be able to hold this over your head for all eternity."

He laughed. "Is that right?"

"It will go something like this: 'Honey, I want a new car… Oh, and do you remember that time you ditched me?', or 'Steven, go get ice-cream, oh yeah, and do you remember that time you forced me to drive cross-country alone?'" Samantha beamed. "See, it's a gift that keeps on giving."

Steven shook his head, leaning forward to take her chin between his thumb and forefinger. "And I'll give you everything, Sammie," he whispered. "Not because I ditched you, but because you're the best thing that's ever happened to me." He gave her a quick kiss on the lips, reached for the automatic locks, and unlocked the door. "Now get out of my car so I can get some shut-eye!"

She smiled and leaned back in the seat.

"You think I'm joking," he began again, "but I need to be at work in eight hours." He leaned across the passenger seat and shoved the door open.

"On a Saturday, really?"

"They're working on a big project and I said I'd help." He raised his chin to the door and widened his eyes.

"Okay, okay…" Samantha laughed, dragging the strap of her messenger bag over her head before climbing out of the car. "Call me tomorrow and let me know how it goes."

"Will do." He smiled. "Now get your cute butt upstairs."

She rolled her eyes.

"I'm serious!"

She straightened her back, throwing her hand to her forehead in a salute. "Yes Sir! Whatever you say, sir!"

"Smart-ass." He lifted his chin. "Go."

CHAPTER TWO

Samantha grabbed a can of sparkling water out of her fridge and looked around her apartment. It felt... empty. Even though it was smothered in drawings, and cluttered with a mishmash of furniture. She pulled in a breath, downing half the can as she kicked her shoes to the center of the room.

In a way, she was grateful Steven wasn't going on the trip. Not that she wouldn't cry with relief if he suddenly changed his mind- but she could really use some time to think.

Her gallery opening hadn't gone at all as planned. A month had passed, yet she still didn't feel herself. Sure, plenty of people had attended, making it appear to be a huge, beautiful success to all who were watching. Reporters were sent out to cover the event, even a local photographer who was highly regarded for his skill. They were all singing her praises, taking pictures, and telling her how much they admired her creativity. But not a single person had actually wanted to purchase her art. Sure, there were a couple of offers from passersby—a couple of lowball offers that would barely cover the cost of the materials it took to create them... But each piece took more than a month to complete. More than a month of all the free time she could spare after her waitressing job at Donovan's. She needed more than that. More than a lowball offer and some flattery... She needed real money, a huge "fuck you" in the form of a paycheck, to everyone who doubted her and her work.

Her worth.

Even Steven. She'd known for some time that he didn't agree with her chosen career... and granted, he'd been the ear to her frustrations for the past two years...but a slab of concrete? The words still pinched at her heart and made her feel ill.

Without thinking, she set the half-drunk can on the table and walked down the hall to stand at the door to her studio. She turned the handle, letting the door crack open before giving it a firm shove to swing wide on its hinges. Her eyes landed on the clay-spotted sheet that hung over the sculpture in the center of the room. The one she'd worked on for three months without coming up for air.

It began the day her best friend called to say she was getting married. No hello, no greeting of any kind before the words exploded like a bomb through the receiver. "We're getting married!"

The news hit Samantha in a weird place. That grumpy, raw spot in the middle of her chest that she never wanted to admit existed. The place where jealousy, hurt, and discomfort twisted in intricate knots. She didn't know why, because it wasn't as though she begrudged Renee's happiness, but she would be lying if she said the first emotion that rolled around in her stomach wasn't sadness.

Renee and Phin's engagement happened so fast. Renee had only moved to New York six months before, and now she was getting married. Which meant that, as Samantha knew all too well, Renee was never coming back to LA. Their friendship would dwindle, the way relationships always did when people moved apart, and Samantha would lose the only friend who ever really understood her. The one person she could be herself with, who knew her battle with a wild heart, and all the things she dreamed of doing.

She hung up the phone that day in shock. Almost with grief, as she made it back to her studio. But she didn't pick up the pieces where she'd left off. No, she started something new. The sculpture took on a life of its own. Samantha's hands moved through the clay with a passion she hadn't felt in years, and the fire inside her didn't stop for months.

Every day she continued to work. Adding, sculpting, and perfecting it…and working through all the emotions and disappointments that had been churning through her blood for the past year.

She spent more time on that one sculpture than she any other piece she'd ever created. *Slab of concrete.* She pushed the words down to her stomach and flicked off the light.

Her home, which was once filled with the constant commotion of her best friend's personality, was now empty. Renee's bedroom across the hall would never again be filled with laughter, nor the stinky ballet shoes Samantha always complained about. It was funny how the thing she thought she disliked most about Renee could be one of the things she longed for most when she was gone. But in her heart of hearts, she never thought they'd be apart. Never thought she'd be more than a thirty-minute drive away from resting her head on her best friend's shoulder.

Samantha grabbed the suitcase out of the closet and dragged it down the hall, determined not to think about it anymore. Sulking wouldn't bring her friend back, and in truth, she was happy for Renee. It was time to face the sad reality that at the tender age of twenty-three, her childhood days were over. Her best friend was gone, would be married in a couple of weeks, and Samantha's dreams of supporting herself through her art were fading.

She needed to come up with a plan for her future, a real plan—because making a living doing something she loved was a fool's quest. She never believed it before, but after last month's opening, she realized her sculptures were a fluttering dream, and when she came back from NY she would pack up her studio and begin working on a real career… The thing that would pay her bills, 'something grown up and respectable.'

"It's time to grow up, Samantha." She squeezed her eyes shut as moisture threatened to seep from her faulty lids. "It's now or never."

She unzipped her luggage, muttering under her breath that she should be happy. She had a boyfriend who loved her. A hard working, driven man who'd been dedicated to her happiness since middle school. But there was a sort of loss that settled deep in her gut when she thought about this being the end.

Steven was her first boyfriend. Her first love, her first date. She knew all there was to know about him, and he knew most things there was to know about her. She loved all those things about their relationship. She loved the sweet expressions that came on people's faces when they heard they'd been together since high school. She loved his stability. His dedication…

But there were times she hated all those things. Times when she longed for what Renee had. That sweep-you-off-your-feet, irresponsible love she'd seen in movies. The love she heard in Renee's voice every time her friend spoke about her fiancé.

A soft breeze washed across Samantha's face, causing the sheer white curtains to flutter and the tears to cool and dry in place on her cheeks. She placed her bag on the center of her bed, wiped over her face, then fished her cell from her pocket. She needed to call her best friend and break the news. It was late, yes, past one in the morning in New York, but the news would eat her alive if she didn't tell.

She dialed the number, dreading the conversation ahead of her. Dreading the fact that she'd have to defend Steven's choices—even when she wasn't sure she liked them herself.

"Sam!" Her best friend answered on the third ring. "Hang on! Let me get to someplace quiet."

Samantha nodded, thankful for her best friend's fast-paced life so she could compose herself. "Sure." She walked across the room, listening to muffled noises that sounded like they came from inside a bar. Laughter, clinking glasses, and chatter. She toyed with the tattered edge of her dresser, as her heart fluttered with anticipation of how this conversation would go.

"Hey!" Renee finally said, out of breath. "Sorry. Opening weekend, things are crazy here! How are you? Your dress finally came in! I can't wait for you to try it on!"

Samantha smiled as the words flew from her friend's mouth. Loving, enthusiastic, even so early in the morning. She sat gently on the side of the bed and took a breath. "It's good! I'm packing right now, getting everything ready for the long trip." She licked her lips. "But that's actually why I'm calling. There's been a change of plans." She squeezed her eyes shut, hoping the action would give her strength. "Before you go all crazy on me—I'm still coming—I mean, of course I am. I wouldn't miss it for the world." She pinched the bridge of her nose, rising from the bed before she lost her nerve. "It's Steven. He got an internship with Connor and Associates. It's a dream come true. A once-in-a-lifetime opportunity—"

"Sam, what are you trying to tell me?"

Samantha cringed, biting her nails. "I'm coming alone." The line went silent, and she could almost feel Renee gritting her teeth. "I wanted to tell you so you could change reservations."

"Are you kidding me?"

11

"He won't miss the wedding. Don't worry about that!"

"You think I'm worried about the wedding?"

"Renee, this is a big—"

"Does this mean you're *driving* here alone?"

Samantha looked up to the ceiling, trying not to let the tone in Renee's voice make her emotional again. "I'll be fine—"

"When did this happen?"

Samantha shrugged. "Tonight."

"Tonight? You mean he gave you two days' notice?"

"Yes, but—"

"Sam! I'm pissed for you! Who does that? Who cancels two days before a three thousand mile road trip? I can't believe he's being such a dick—and I also can't believe you're going to take it!"

Samantha rolled her eyes. "He's not a dick, Ren. This internship is a big deal. He's been working on it for twelve months. If he passes on this now, he'll never get it again."

"There are other firms."

"Not like Connor and Associates."

"So?"

"He'll be at the wedding; that's the important part, right?"

"It's just... He always does this to you."

A dull ache began to pound behind Samantha's eyes, and she pinched her brow trying to ease it. "No he doesn't."

"Yes. He does. Remember prom?"

She threw herself back on the mattress, unable to believe Renee was bringing this up again. "Prom was five years ago."

"You're right. But Bali was just last year."

Samantha closed her eyes, because until this moment, Renee had never said anything at all about the long-lost trip. It had been Samantha's graduating wish all throughout college, her dream for as long as she could remember. But somehow Steven had convinced her it was frivolous. That it was a waste, not only of money, but of precious corporate ladder climbing time. They ended up in some stuffy hotel in Los Angeles, sipping flat, generic "champagne" and rubbing elbows with pretentious people who could "take them places."

"He always puts his job ahead of you; that's what I'm saying. It's just the same shit. Him putting his life above yours."

"I don't see it that way."

"And I thought he was going to propose?"

Samantha stared up at the ceiling, wild cattle taking over her heart again. "That was your theory, not mine." She rose to her feet, walked toward the window, and pulled in a calming breath. "Honestly, I'm glad I'm driving alone. I could use some time to think."

Renee paused a moment, silent in a way that told Samantha she was worried. "About what?"

"I don't know. Life. Career choices." Sam brushed aside the curtains and pulled the double-paned window firmly shut. "Maybe mom was right."

"Sam, it was your first gallery, you can't expect—"

"Expect what? To sell something, after five years of trying?"

"Look, I don't want to fight you on this, but driving across country to figure out your life is crazy. We're talking three thousand miles. And my beautiful blond girlfriend who always seems to attract the creepiest of men when out alone."

Samantha laughed, staring out the window to the street below. "Yeah… Well, I'll keep the doors locked." She walked toward the closet and pulled more clothes from the hangers. "Besides—my mind's made up."

"Sam…"

"I'll be fine. Really."

"Why don't you drive with Tristan? He's leaving tomorrow, and I'm sure he could use the company."

"Ha!"

"What's so funny?"

"I am NOT driving with your brother."

"Why not?"

"Because I'd rather eat poop." It was a gross analogy, but it was mostly true. "I can think of a million other things I'd rather do than be held hostage with Tristan. It's bad enough you invited him to the wedding."

Renee laughed. "He's my *brother*. Or course he's going to be there. And he's not that bad. He's had a rough year—I think he's finally growing up."

"Tristan Montgomery, grow up? I'll believe that when I see it."

"Good. I'll have him pick you up tomorrow at ten."

"No no no, that's not what I—"

"I have to go." Renee sing-song yelled into the receiver, "Be ready by ten! I LOVE YOU!"

CLICK.

Samantha looked at her cell, her eyes bulging with shock and terror before redialing the number.

The line went quickly to voice mail. "Hi, this is Renee. You know what to do. BEEEEEP."

"Shit!" Samantha hung up the phone. An image of Tristan popped into her mind and she closed her eyes. "Like hell!" She moved across the room, pulled her chair from her desk, and sat down upon it. If Renee wasn't going to answer, she'd be forced to send an email.

RENEE,

I'm sure you're expecting this email. I mean, why wouldn't you, after dropping that bombshell of a bad idea in my lap? Tristan? Really? REALLY?

And since when is he "Not that bad?" It's hard to believe those words actually came from your mouth!

SAMANTHA PAUSED IN HER TYPING, drumming her fingers on the mouse pad before continuing.

Tristan Montgomery was *that* guy. The guy every girl wanted and every guy wanted to be. The boy who made even grown women blush when he walked into a room.

He was also the guy who was handed everything on a silver platter. The one who worked hard for nothing, yet had everything. Tristan was everything she stood against, yet girls used to befriend Renee just to get closer to him.

Everyone except Samantha.

In fact, Renee and Samantha's relationship had blossomed over their mutual hatred for Tristan Montgomery. Samantha was the only girl outside of Renee who didn't like him. No, correction, didn't LOVE him.

There wasn't anything in particular about Tristan that left a bad taste in Samantha's mouth, it was *everything*. The fact that teachers turned a blind eye so he could stay on the varsity football team. The fact that he said nothing, did nothing, was no more than a high school jock, yet every girl in high school bowed at his feet.

You're worried about my safety Renee, and you think driving with Tristan would make things better? He had his license suspended senior year for too many speeding tickets. He jumped off your parents' roof and into your neighbor's backyard pool on a dare! This isn't a guy who makes the best decisions regarding safety. He doesn't think about how his actions could affect other people.

SHE CLOSED her eyes as memories flooded her. Tristan was a risk-taker and never thought about the consequences of tomorrow. He did whatever he wanted, whenever he wanted, without thinking about the future. And he was the only boy who held one of Samantha's firsts outside of Steven.

She cringed.

He was the only part of Samantha's life she couldn't share with her best friend… and that scared the shit out of her.

CHAPTER THREE

Six years earlier

Samantha adjusted the pillow behind her head, glancing up the stairs at the sound of Renee's cough rattling from the loft of the cabin. She cringed at the wicked sound of it, certain the Montgomerys should come home from their party to take her to the hospital—but as soon as she sat up to reach for her phone, the dull snore of her sleeping friend came drifting down to comfort her.

She smiled, sure it would keep her up all night, and picked back up her book. She'd been reading all week, catching up on her ever growing list. This was their last trip before junior year, but poor Renee was stuck in bed with a bout of pneumonia. Fevers, body aches, and a prescription for antibiotics and rest. The trip had become remarkably uneventful as a result, but Samantha really didn't mind. She was just happy to be away. From chores, too much heat…and Steven.

Mostly Steven.

The pressure to become his girlfriend was beginning to annoy her. He'd been at her house almost daily, hinting about needing an answer before school started. It was no secret that he loved her. He'd confessed to as much in front of their entire sixth grade band class. Everyone knew how he felt, but until now they'd been just friends. The best of friends.

Samantha loved Steven with all her heart, but she didn't like him *that* way. He was her best friend outside of Renee—and she was determined to keep it like that. Dating him would only mess things up. But how could she tell him no without hurting him? To say no, and not have him push her away completely? It was a catch twenty-two in the worst kind of way. No matter which way she said it, her words would be a rejection. A rejection she wasn't sure their friendship could recover from.

She nestled down in the couch, determined to get lost in her book and not think about tomorrow, but bits of sun steamed in through the tall picture window, reminding her that the day was almost over. That they'd be returning home in the morning. To school, to homework, and big fat decisions.

The front door slammed open, and Tristan strolled lazily into the cabin. He'd just come back from a run and his hair was slightly damp, his shirt off—revealing his perfectly sculpted chest and abs. She swallowed. She didn't much like him, but she wasn't blind. He was hot. More than hot. Broad shoulders, washboard abs, with that bad boy messy vibe that everyone loved.

She glanced back at her book, ignoring him like she always did, but before she could read the first line, something heavy settled down at the other end of the couch. She glanced up and found him sprawled at the other end, arms braced against the back cushions, feet up on the coffee table. She cleared her throat, making herself smaller on the other end—because this was odd. Normally Tristan didn't stick around for this long. Normally he had a crew of people vying for his attention that would pull him away. She knew for a fact there was a cabin full of girls just across the lake who would volunteer for the job. She'd seen them with her own eyes. Splashing around all week, practically naked, obvious in their attempts to grab Tristan's attention.

Before she knew what he was doing, he leaned forward and snatched the book right out of her hands. "Let's go swimming," he said, leaving her mouth open, and heart pounding.

She blinked a few times, not knowing what to say as he placed her novel on the coffee table.

She was so confused by his behavior she had a hard time breathing. "I'm not going anywhere," she replied, pushing herself to the edge of the couch to grab her book again.

He quickly blocked her. "You haven't done anything all weekend."

"So?" she replied, not attempting to hide her irritation. "Renee's sick—if you haven't noticed."

"Oh, I noticed." He smiled before leaning back in his seat again. "Renee snores like a jackhammer." A loud grumble came bellowing down the stairs again and Tristan raised his brows in response. "See?"

Samantha laughed, but then shook her head and hit his arm. "You're mean."

He shrugged. "Just because she's sick doesn't mean we shouldn't enjoy ourselves. This is our last night of vacation. Monday morning we leave for home. I pack for college, and you get ready for another year of high school. Don't make me look like a loser splashing around in the lake by myself."

She grinned at the imagery, but couldn't help glancing over. "You won't be alone." She lifted her chin to the west end of the lake. "Those girls have been dying for your attention all weekend."

He set his feet to the ground, leaned forward and laughed under his breath. But it wasn't a laugh of happiness or humor; it was something else.

19

"What? Are half naked women not your type?"

"It's not that."

"Then what?"

He glanced over at the kitchen, as though contemplating ending this conversation, but he met her eyes again, offering the bluest storm she'd ever seen in her life. "I wanted to spend my last night with you."

Her heart squeezed. Like the air had been sucked from her body. She wasn't sure why, but for some reason he sounded serious.

Samantha forced herself to keep breathing, disgusted by the fact he affected her so easily. She didn't think it was possible, but she felt even more uncomfortable than before. Why would Tristan want to spend his last night at the lake with her? Why would he want to spend his last night with her *alone*? And why did the fact he said so cause a conflicted feeling to form in her stomach? A mixture of butterflies, adrenaline, and nausea.

She looked toward the cabin door, battling her wild heart and the parts of her that wanted to let it loose.

"Come on," he said, bumping her arm with his shoulder. "I promise to be a perfect gentleman."

She crossed her arms at her stomach, wondering if she was about to throw up.

"What? You don't believe me?"

"It's not that. I'm just surprised the word 'gentleman' is a part of your vocabulary."

His blue eyes danced with amusement and he started laughing. "Go upstairs and change, Sammie. I'll meet you outside in five minutes." He pushed himself off the couch, not waiting for a reply, and headed to his bedroom in the basement.

She waited for the door to close before taking a much-needed breath. For some reason, he assumed she would meet him, even without an answer. But she knew why. Because requests like that were all it ever took from Tristan Montgomery. He had the body of a God, all six foot something of him, and his wild surfer boy hair was the blond icing on top of the beautifully sculpted cake. She knew she should ignore him and continue reading, but her heart had never pounded so hard in her life. In spite of herself, she was curious about what it would be like to spend an evening with Tristan Montgomery. Curious to see if what everyone said about him was true…

She smoothed her hair behind her ears and headed upstairs. Renee was buried under a mound of blankets, and rolled on the mattress toward the door when Samantha entered the loft.

"Hey," Renee said in a hoarse whisper. "Have I been sleeping long?"

"Hey," Samantha replied, smiling as she sat softly on the side of the bed. "Just all day. How are you feeling?"

Renee shrugged. "Eh, could be better." She frowned. "Sorry I ruined your weekend."

"You didn't ruin anything." Samantha shook her head. "I finally caught up on all the reading I've been wanting to do this summer. For what it's worth, I'm team Edward."

Renee wrinkled her nose and flashed a sleepy grin. "What time is it? Are you coming to bed?"

"No…" She looked away. "Tristan actually asked me to go to the lake with him—for some reason I'm actually considering it."

Renee's eyes narrowed, analyzing her in a way that made Samantha fear she could see her heart. That she knew Tristan had affected her downstairs, and Samantha's stomach rolled with the thought of it.

"You should go," Renee finally stated.

Samantha looked down to her hands, her heart flipping with discomfort. "I don't know—"

"It'll make me feel better. I feel bad you've been stuck in here all weekend when you could have been home having fun."

"I haven't been stuck—"

"Go, Sammie. It's our last night. I know it's Tristan, but maybe you'll meet some other guys. There *are* guys here; I've seen them walking around through the window." She turned back around. "And you need to get out—if only for a little while."

Samantha looked down at her fingers, thinking it would be so much easier to turn Steven down if she was able to tell him she had met someone else. "Okay." She looked up at Renee again, then reached out to adjust the blankets around her friend's shoulders. "I'll go, but only for a little while."

CHAPTER FOUR

SIX YEARS EARLIER

IT WAS ALMOST eight thirty when Samantha walked out on the back deck to look for Tristan. The night was warm, but the breeze off the lake offered just enough relief to make the August evening pleasant. Her long blond hair was braided over one shoulder, and she clasped a red-striped beach towel firmly at her chest.

She found him sitting on the steps, looking out to the water. His body was splayed out in gray swim shorts and a white t-shirt, but he didn't notice her right away. His focus was directed to the lake, as if deep in thought, and the soft glow from the back porch light allowed her to see his features.

She leaned against the log siding and watched him. She'd known him for as long as she could remember, but this was the first time she'd ever seen him alone. Normally, he was surrounded by groupies, both the male and female variety, and it was odd to see him like this. Like a wolf away from his pack, or a white iris in a field of purple. Out of place, but beautiful nonetheless. It intrigued her.

"You came," he said, his voice quiet and contemplative. But he didn't turn around to face her. He continued to look out to the lake, as if he saw something out there she couldn't. "I didn't think you would."

She pushed away from the wall, wondering how long he'd noticed her there without saying a word. "Why's that?"

He rose to his feet and dusted off his shorts before facing her. "Just a hunch." A slow smile transformed his features as his gaze swept her up and down. "I'm glad I was wrong, Sammie Smiles."

He walked down the steps, the name from her childhood barely audible on his lips. Low and soft...but incredibly sexy. She didn't like it, didn't like it at all. Because for some reason, the way he said it made her stomach flutter. She wasn't sure if it was the fact they were alone, or something else, but he sounded honest. Like he really was happy to see her.

She cleared her throat and looked out toward the lake. "Where are we going?"

"The dock," he replied, jetting his chin out to the lake before glancing back up at her. "You okay with that?"

"Sure," she said, adjusting the towel at her chest before walking down the steps.

The dock sounded safe enough. Out in the open, visible from almost every cabin. She followed him down the path to the beach, closely watching her step as they made it down to the sand. Then his footsteps slowed, and he began walking right beside her. She knew it was intentional, because he was almost a full foot taller than her. But his strides matched her short ones perfectly—step after step—and she realized he was trying to do what he said he would. To be a perfect gentleman. And he was actually succeeding.

Their walk continued, neither saying a word as they headed in the direction of the dock. Which gave Samantha plenty of time to reprimand herself for being so nervous. She wasn't quite sure the reason, because she knew nothing would ever eventuate between her and Tristan. He could have any girl he wanted, literally, and she had no interest in him whatsoever. But Tristan Montgomery had this way about him. A presence so big the whole world would miss it the moment it was gone... and she was feeling it right now. All around her, over every inch of her skin.

They made it halfway to the dock before either spoke again, but then he turned to her, as if he'd been repressing the words for so long they exploded from his lips. "I leave for Austin next week," he said, standing in front of her.

It wasn't a question, but a statement. She wasn't sure what to do with it. Congratulate him, or give him a high-five. Instead, she looked at him, wondering where all this was coming from. "Are you excited?"

He raised his shoulders, but said nothing as he began walking backward.

Nervous energy shot through her heart and she looked down to her feet again. "Well you should be," she said with a nod. "An acceptance to UT is an honor."

He remained quiet, and she continued. "They have one of the best football teams in the US. It'll be a great opportunity for you—"

He spun around, cutting off her last word as he picked up the pace again. She paused for a second, wondering if what she'd said offended him. Personally, she'd always thought of college as some big, exciting experience. The beginning of the future, the first step toward adulthood. And she knew from Renee that Tristan had a full scholarship—and like always, a whole plethora of new women were out there waiting for him to charm their panties off... But for some reason, he didn't seem excited. Or happy about it at all, actually.

"I can't wait to go to college," she said, to fill the awkward space. "Though I probably won't move away like you. Not that

I don't want to. But CalArts is my top choice, and it would be foolish to spend money on room and board when I could live at home for free." She could hear Steven's voice when she said it, but he was the smartest person in her life, and she was sure it was true.

He looked her over, his brows furrowing, and his feet slowing. "Don't you ever do anything foolish?"

She lifted her chin. "Not really. Not like you do."

He laughed. "You think I'm foolish?"

She shrugged. "You do foolish things."

"Like?"

"Like jumping off your parents' roof into the neighbor's pool."

He grinned. "That was one time."

"And taking Suzy Baker to senior prom even though you knew her boyfriend was out to get you."

His grin widened. "I never thought you paid that much attention, Sammie Smiles."

She cleared her throat. "Well, you're kinda hard to miss—I mean, the stuff you do. It always causes so much drama, and everyone can never stop talking about it. You're like our local celebrity."

They came to a full stop and he turned to face her. "Will you miss me?" he asked. But it wasn't in that flirtatious way he used with other girls. He wasn't even smiling when he looked up to meet her eyes; he was dead serious. His eyes held hers, his lips formed in a straight line as though he was holding his breath.

She looked into his clear blue eyes, her breaths becoming shallow and uneven. She shook her head. She didn't know what was happening to her, but she didn't like it. "No," she finally said. "How could I? I hardly know you."

He laughed, but it didn't seem a happy one. Then, before she could recover from the whiplash conversation, he pulled his shirt overhead and began running toward the dock. "Maybe I can change your mind."

Without waiting for her reply, he jumped off the dock and landed with a large splash in the water. He spun around, the light of the moon reflecting off his wet hair, glistening down his bronzed skin and bare chest. "Come on, Sam. Are you gonna swim with me or what?"

PRESENT DAY

SAMANTHA STARED at the bright computer screen, her eyes glassy and aching, as she focused on the cursor in the middle of the page. Tristan terrified her. Not because of who he was, but because of how he affected her. He set the wild heart of hers free, and he did it in a way that was so subtle she didn't even notice it happening until it was over.

But Renee was right. It would be silly for her to drive alone. Foolish to drive three thousand miles just to avoid the boy she hated. But it was also selfish. Because she knew Renee would worry if she tried to make the trip alone, and Renee already had enough to worry about. A whole wedding's worth of worry.

Samantha held her finger on the delete key and erased the whole email before grabbing her phone from the mattress and opening up her texts.

SAMANTHA: Tell your brother I'll be ready at 10:00 a.m. sharp.

REPLY DOTS CAME RIGHT AWAY, as though Renee had been waiting.

RENEE: Swwweeee! I will. Thank you!!!!

SAMANTHA GRINNED.

SAMANTHA: You're welcome.

SAMANTHA SET the phone back on her desk, exhausted, and pushed her half-empty suitcase to the side of the bed and climbed in beside it.

"Seventy-two hours," she whispered. That was all she had to survive to get to NY. Seventy-two hours with Tristan Montgomery.

God save her soul.

CHAPTER FIVE

Present Day

"He's late, Ren. Are you sure he's coming?" Samantha let the curtains slip between her fingers, allowing them to fall closed as she turned back to pace across the living room floor.

"He's coming, Sam. I called him ten minutes ago, and he said he's on his way. He'll be there. Relax."

"We're going to hit traffic."

Laughter came from the receiver. "Lunch time traffic?"

"Be quiet!" She held back a tiny grin and leaned against the wall. "I've been dressed for over an hour, I hardly slept, making sure I had everything ready, and his being late really pisses me off. I thought you said he'd changed?"

"He overslept, Sam, he'll be there. Look, if he isn't there in thirty minutes, I'll buy you a coke."

Samantha closed her eyes. "A rum and coke."

"Whatever you want," Renee agreed. "But I have to get back to practice. Can you call me when he gets there?"

Samantha sat down on her couch and clicked on the TV.

"Sure. But if he's not here in an hour I'm leaving without him."

"Fair enough," Renee replied. "I'll see you in a few days."

"Okay."

"Bye."

"Bye." Samantha placed her cell beside her on the couch and leaned back to switch the channel to Judge Judy. She'd been so stressed about this morning's trip that she'd hardly slept at all. She kept having dreams about Tristan. About him hanging by his fingertips on the edge of a cliff and calling her name. "Sammie! Sammie!"

She would try to go to him, but the closer she got, the faster her heart would pound, because she couldn't make her feet move. Even though she could see he was falling, she couldn't go to him. She was afraid that if she did, she'd go over the cliff with him.

The dream was dark and disturbing to say the least, but there was so much truth to it. She was afraid of seeing Tristan again. Afraid that seeing him would pull her wild heart right out of her chest. Just like he had in the middle of the lake six years earlier.

SIX YEARS EARLIER

"JUST JUMP, ALREADY!"

Samantha stood at the water's edge, looking down from the dock as Tristan waded in the darkness of the lake below. A shiver raced through her. Not because it was cold—if anything, it was a hotter than usual. She shivered because suddenly she wasn't sure she wanted to be there. She looked back over her shoulder. Toward the cabin where her best friend was still sleeping, sure she was making a huge mistake. But the evening was perfect, the sky crystal clear, displaying a plethora of stars too many to count, and the smells of the wilderness mingled with the scent of freedom.

"How deep is it?" she finally asked, as she dropped her towel to the edge of the dock. Her black bathing suit was simple, nothing too sexy or revealing, though she still had to stop herself from crossing her arms at her chest for more protection. Samantha had a curvaceous body. Large breasts and hips to match, but she was incredibly self-conscious. She'd been aware at an early age that her curves were a distraction. Hyper-aware, even in sixth grade, when the boys started ogling.

"Not deep." He stood up in the water, indicating it hit him mid-stomach. "Jump, already!"

Before she could talk herself out of it, knowing she'd be much more comfortable shielded by the dark water, she held her breath and jumped out as far as she could manage. But instantly, she started sinking. Her eyes bulged and her arms flailed about in panic. She desperately tried to get back to the surface, but the more she struggled the deeper she sank. She couldn't get her head above water—not high enough to take a full breath.

Before she knew what was happening, Tristan's arms wrapped around her belly and he jetted them both toward the surface. He wrapped one arm around her neck, his body like a floatation device, keeping her above water as he swam on his back toward a large fallen branch.

He helped her up to sit, where she coughed and sputtered, the water she'd almost drowned in expelling from her throat and lungs.

"You can't swim, can you?" he asked, out of breath. "You can't fucking swim!"

She coughed out the last bit of water, clinging to the branch and pulling in as much air as she could manage. "You

31

lied to me! How did you do that? You were standing, I saw you!"

"There was a branch—" But then he smoothed the wet hair from her cheek and examined her face. "I didn't know, Sammie. Are you okay?"

She pushed at his chest, startled by his closeness, startled by the fact that she thought he'd be laughing, but he wasn't. He looked worried, if anything, almost scared.

"Are you okay?"

She didn't answer. She glanced in the direction of the cabin, barely able to see the light of the front porch. She couldn't believe she'd come out here. That she'd convinced herself it would be okay, even though the voice in her head had been screaming for her not to do it.

"I'm sorry," he said again, bracing his arms on either side of the branch to pull himself up to sit beside her, making the whole thing shake under his weight.

They were both silent, his eyes fixated on the open water before he spoke again. "Why would you come out here when you don't know how to swim?"

She clenched her jaw, unable to share the answer that sprung to her mind. Because she was curious. Because she liked the way she felt when he was close to her. "I asked you how deep it was. I trusted you."

His head tilted slightly to the side and he looked at her. "Why? You don't even know me."

He was throwing her words back in her face and she didn't like it. "'Cause I'm an idiot!" she yelled. She began scooting down the branch, determined to get away from him by any means possible. To get back to the shore, to her best friend, even by the most humiliating way she could think of.

But he lowered himself to the water, blocking her off on the other side. "Where are you going?"

"Back to the cabin. Far away from you."

"Why? Because of that?" He gestured to the spot where she'd nearly drowned. "Why do you hate me so much, Samantha? You've hated me for as long as I can remember, and I don't know why. What did I ever do to you?"

She stopped moving, too shocked by what he was asking to even look at him. It was true; she'd hated him forever, but the fact that he'd noticed made her heart hurt a little inside. She didn't know what to say. "I—"

But he stopped her. "You know what, I don't want to know." He reached out to tuck the last bits of hair behind her ear. "I'm sorry, Sam. I really am. If I—" But he stopped, as if not allowing the words to leave his tongue. He looked back up at her, his expression somber and dark. "Forgive me?"

PRESENT DAY

BOOM BOOM BOOM

Samantha startled out of sleep, the sounds of banging reverberating through the walls and floor. She threw her feet off the side of the couch and sat forward to turn off the television. The pounding came once again. BOOM BOOM BOOM.

The front door.

"Hang on," she shouted. "I'll be there in a second!" She grabbed her cell phone off the coffee table, and realized it had been almost an hour since she'd gotten off the phone with Renee. Tristan Montgomery was on the other side of that door, and she had no idea how long he'd been out there.

She pushed hard against the couch, forcing herself to stand, then walked over to the entertainment center to check her reflection in the television screen. "Oh God," she whispered, taking in the long strands of hair stuck to her face and smoothing them behind her ears. This was the first time she'd seen Tristan in six years, and a red imprint of her couch cushion was etched into her cheek. No. She shook her head at her reflection. It wasn't the first time. She'd seen him a handful of other times as well. In passing, when he came home for visits from college...but he never seemed to notice her. Never again after that night.

When she finally opened the door a minute later, unsure if he'd left because he was so quiet, she found him resting in the stairwell, his back against the wall, laughing into the receiver of his cell phone. He stood there so casually, it seemed as though he did this every day, as though he hadn't just been beating down her front door with his bare fists.

"Yeah, I got it." He smiled. But not to Samantha—he was speaking to whomever was on the phone. "Talk to you later."

When he finally turned around, he placed his cell phone in his back pocket. "I thought I was going to have to break the door down." He lifted his shoulders. "Either that or you changed your mind."

He brushed past her, not waiting for an invitation before stepping into her apartment. "I have to piss. Where's your bathroom?"

She made a face at his choice of words, but decided quickly against making a comment, and turned swiftly toward the hall. For the next three days, she was stuck with him. Three thousand miles, and she was determined not set off on the wrong foot. "It's down the hall."

She wrapped her arms around her belly and walked in the opposite direction toward the window. This was a bad idea, she could feel it in her bones. Renee had said he'd changed, but she thought in a good way. If anything, he was worse! Gruff, callous, entitled. Though maybe a bit rougher. His jeans were a weathered blue, roughed up in the way that was fashionable these days, and his shirt was gray, form fitting, and indicated that he still had the body he was known for in high school. But now he had a scruffy shadow of a beard that matched his messy surfer-boy style.

Though it wasn't his looks that made Samantha uncomfortable. It was the way he acted—as though he owned the place. As though it was his world, and she just existed in it.

He walked out of the bathroom some time later, wiping his hands on his back pockets, even though she knew she'd hung up a towel that morning.

"Is this your luggage?" he asked, gesturing to her suitcase in the corner of the room.

She nodded, but before she could add that it was only the beginning, he lifted the bag up to his shoulder and headed for the front door.

"Wait!" she shouted, maybe a tad more frantically than she'd intended.

He turned on his heels, his eyes wide open with a "what the hell is wrong with you?" expression.

"The sculpture," she finally managed to spit out. "I need help getting it downstairs."

"The sculpture?" he repeated slowly, as though he didn't quite understand what she was telling him.

She turned on her heels, not bothering to explain, and headed for her studio. "It's this way."

A minute later, they stood in the middle of the room, Tristan's eyes wide, taking in the three foot tall, two foot wide, bubble-wrapped creation. It was the best she could manage given its shape, but she had to admit, wrapped up like this, it did look rather crazy.

"And we're bringing that with us?" he managed to ask.

"Yes." She nodded.

He bit his lip, as though trying to make his mind up about something, and shrugged. "Well, okay." He set her suitcase to the ground, stepped toward and lifted the sculpture a few inches. He quickly set it back down and stepped backward. "Shit. What's in there? Steel?"

She scrunched up her nose, knowing it was heavy. But seeing that it was too heavy for Tristan made her nervous. How the hell would they get it downstairs? "Here, let's lean it on its side. I'll grab one end, you grab the other."

SIX YEARS EARLIER

"WHY ON EARTH would I trust you, Tristan? I know who you are; I've seen what you do!"

His eyes narrowed, but he wouldn't budge from his spot blocking her on the branch. "For someone who doesn't know me, you sure know a lot."

She rolled her eyes. "I don't have to know *you*. I know all the people you've hurt, and that's enough."

"Like who?"

"Veronica Ward. Jenny Chavez. Sophie Miller. Need I go on?"

"Do you always believe what people tell you, or only when it involves me? I'm curious."

"What's that supposed to mean?"

"It means, check your sources, sweetheart." He pushed back off the branch, causing the whole thing to rock backward and cover her in water.

She held on for dear life, watching him swim away toward the center of the lake, damning herself for coming out here at all. "Are you just going to leave me here?" she screamed.

"I haven't decided," he said, stopping ten feet away. "What did they tell you?"

"You're holding me hostage now?"

He shrugged.

She clenched her jaw. "Fine. If you must know, I'll tell you. But it's the same thing every time: you stringing them along, making them think they have a chance with you, then turning around to be a complete dick! And for your information, Tristan, I don't need to check my sources. I've seen it with my own eyes. It's not like it's a big secret; you display your dirty laundry out for everyone to see!"

He swam toward her, taking only two strokes to cross the distance. His bare chest pressed against her legs, his eyes wide as though he needed her to see him. "You're wrong. You think just because someone gets hurt that's my fault? It may sound arrogant, but I can't prevent a girl from falling in love with me." He shook his head. "I can't prevent her from climbing in my bed, loving me. But they only think they love me, Sam. They don't. Just like you, they hardly know me… They love the idea of me. The fairy tale version that'll never exist. They convince themselves they love me, and that's not my fault."

His arms relaxed a little, but he stayed right there, looking into her eyes, never faltering. "If I'm nice, if I smile the wrong way, or God forbid give them my phone number, I'm suddenly leading them on, and it's bullshit."

He pushed off her legs, turning to lean his back on the fallen branch. "Jenny and I kissed one time at a party. We were both drunk and I kissed her." He looked over. "Does that mean I owe her my future?"

She swallowed. She'd never been spoken to this way before. Yet she'd never thought of it from his perspective either. She didn't even know any of these girls, but she'd believed everything they'd said without question. She'd believed everything passed around the gossip circles she normally tried to stay out of. But now, hearing his side of things, all he had told her that she'd never considered, she couldn't even blame him for being angry.

She thought about Steven, about him declaring his love

four years ago, after knowing her for two weeks. How he wanted more, even though she'd only been a friend to him. That wasn't her fault. Yes, you can't help the people you fall in love with, but you also can't help the people who fall in love *with* you. She looked down at her fingers, shaking her head both at the fact she'd judged him unfairly, but also because she agreed with him. "No," she finally whispered. "You don't owe her anything."

His brow lifted as though her admission surprised him, and he turned to face her, studying her, as though wondering if what she said was what she really believed. When he finally spoke again, his voice was low and rough, almost a whisper. "Do you forgive me?"

She tilted her head to the side, the corner of her mouth lifting involuntarily because after all that, he'd brought it back full circle. After all that, he wasn't asking her for the apology he probably deserved. He was asking for her forgiveness. Because he didn't dwell on who wronged him. He worried more about how he'd wronged her.

"Yes."

* * *

PRESENT DAY

"Do you want to go first, or should I?"

Samantha's face was red with exertion, her back already aching under the weight of the sculpture. They'd only just made it into the living room, which meant they still needed to make it down the stairs, through the courtyard, and to the front of the building where his car was parked. "You," she said on a winded breath. "I'll follow."

He nodded quickly, silently agreeing with her decision, and turned around, carefully easing his back into the stairwell. He adjusted his grip on the bubble wrap, lifting the sculpture around a sharp corner like a professional furniture mover, and took the first step backward down the stairs. "Easy now."

She followed after him, her jaw flexed with the weight pulling at her shoulders. But she wouldn't let him see her struggle. Not now, not ever. Even it if ripped her arms right out of their sockets.

They shuffled down the steps one at a time, through the courtyard, and to the front of the building. He finally lowered the sculpture to the ground a few feet away, where Samantha released the weight, maybe with a little more oomph than she'd intended, and stepped backward.

She pulled in a few deep breaths before standing, replenishing the oxygen she'd lost on the flight downstairs.

"You're stronger than you look, Smiles." He grinned, pulling his keys from his front pocket and hanging them on his finger. "I wasn't sure you'd make it."

Samantha straightened, resisting the urge to snatch the keys out of his cocky hand. She looked down the row of cars, inwardly cringing at how much farther they still had to go. "Which one's yours?"

His lips lifted. He stepped forward shaking his head and unlocked the door to the light blue '67 Ford Mustang just in front of them.

She vaguely remembered it—from long ago. "You're kidding me, right?"

"About what?" he asked.

"About that." She gestured her chin toward the car. "We're not driving all the way to New York in *that*—are we?"

He moved to lean his hip against the taillight, and placed a pair of aviator glasses on his face. "That's the plan, sweetheart. Is that a problem?"

She pressed her lips together at the endearment. "We're

driving over three thousand miles," she stated. *Reasonable. Let's all be reasonable.* "In a car that's fifty years old?"

"And?"

"Don't you think it would be wise to take a more reliable form of transportation?"

He shrugged.

Oh, dear God! She turned toward her apartment and wiped her hand over her face. "You know what—here, let me get my car. It's not very big, but—"

"Greta"—he tapped hard on the back fender of the Mustang—"hasn't let me down yet." He popped the trunk, lifting it all the way open. "I'll ignore the fact that you insulted her."

Samantha narrowed her eyes, her heart pounding with the need to punch him. "You're just as sweet as I remember."

He huffed out a laugh, pulling the glasses from his face, and resting one finger on his bottom lip. "Oh yeah? And what do you remember, Samantha?"

CHAPTER SIX

Six years earlier

"Hang on, Sam, a little bit longer, we're almost there."

Samantha clung onto Tristan's neck, their heads bobbing up and down from each pull of his breaststroke. How he'd convinced her to do this was beyond her. She'd never even touched Tristan before, and now only the thin, wet fabric of her bathing suit separated them from being skin to skin.

Maybe it was guilt that made her agree. Guilt over believing every bad thing she'd ever heard about him since middle school. Or maybe it was because the thought of making it back by means of the tree branch made her bottom ache... But if she was being honest with herself, being this close to Tristan Montgomery made her feel alive. He did something to her, something exciting and nerve racking. But it wasn't just that. He made her think, he challenged her in every way possible, and she loved it.

As they approached the small, rocky landing of the shore, she set her feet on the ground, making the rest of the ten or so feet on her own. Tristan was right beside her, his tan back glistening in the faint light of the moon.

Tristan sat down on the rocky beach a few feet away. Long wisps of his hair clung to his forehead before he pushed them back, revealing a soft, contagious grin. He leaned back on a large rock, using it as a pillow, and looked up at the stars.

But he said nothing, just lay there, looking into the sky. Samantha stood beside him, her arms wrapped around her middle, wondering what to do. Going back to the cabin was an option, back to Renee and dry clothes, but for some reason, she didn't want to. She didn't want this night to end—not yet.

Gazing up at the sky, she marveled at the millions of stars that were normally impossible to see. She glanced down at the spot beside him, knowing it was a bad idea, but finally picked an area to sit.

They were both quite for a time, absorbed in the magic of the evening when he finally spoke. His voice soft, breathy, mysterious. "This is my favorite," he whispered.

She turned to look at him, puzzled by this new side of him she'd never noticed before. "What is?"

"This. Seclusion. The quiet... I can actually hear myself think."

She swallowed. "And what are you thinking about?" She laid her head beside his. Too close. Not touching, but close enough that the pounding in her heart increased a little.

"Not much." But the way he said it, with the heaviness in his voice, she knew it was the opposite. Tristan Montgomery was thinking about a lot. She only wished she knew what it was.

She turned back to the sky, where the night was so dark it offered a narrow patch of privacy, but she said nothing at all for a good ten minutes. It wasn't awkward though, even though she thought it should be, lying next to the boy she'd hated for as long as she could remember. She couldn't figure it out, because sometimes she felt uncomfortable with Steven, and they'd been friends for nearly four years. She played with a rock with her fingers, rubbing the soft edges against her palm. Maybe her calmness was because Tristan affected her more than she cared to admit. Maybe for the first time in her life, she was enjoying herself without the worry of tomorrow.

Tristan finally turned to her, adjusting himself sideways on the rock until he faced her. As if they were lying on a bed, instead of the beach of the lake they'd crawled out of. "You have a good vibe about you, Sammie Smiles. You relax me, and that doesn't happen very often."

Her stomach tightened, and she took a deep breath before speaking. "I relax you?" she asked, reluctantly turning her head to face him. She hated the effect he was having on her, but loved it at the same time. He causes a delicious bundle of contradictions to roll around inside her. A push and pull like she'd never felt before.

"Yeah." The corner of his mouth lifted, but he didn't say anything else. He just lay there, so close she could feel his breath on her face, so close she could feel the heat radiating off his skin.

She turned back to the sky, needing to put distance between her and the boy she wasn't sure if she hated any longer. She needed more than that; she needed to get up, go back to the cabin, and put herself to bed. But she couldn't make herself do it. She couldn't convince her body to move, no matter how hard she tried. No matter how loud her internal voice yelled, she couldn't move. Even though she knew she should, even though no good ever came of girls who sat too close to Tristan Montgomery. Because she knew that if she did, if she got up and walked back to the cabin, this moment would never come again.

"I have the same problem as you," she stated. She wasn't sure why, because there was no reason to share such a thing, but her voice came again, uneven and vulnerable. "With a boy, anyway." She hesitated for a moment, her fingers playing with the rocks by her side. She wasn't sure why she felt the need to talk about Steven, but she did. "He wants to date me. I just don't know what to tell him. All our friends expect us to get together. I mean, he's so persuasive—even I expect us to end up together, some days…" She turned to Tristan, too curious about his reaction to keep the distance any longer. "But at the same time, I don't know what to say."

His brows furrowed, and he reached out to brush a strand of hair back behind her ear. The action caused goose bumps to run the length of her body, but he acted like it was something he did all the time, like it wasn't the most intimate thing she'd ever experienced in her entire life. "Do you like him?"

She swallowed, because a tight ball of something had lodged itself in her throat. "Sometimes I do, and sometimes I don't."

"Why's that?"

"Because—" She shook her head, unsure why she was confessing all this. "Because he's my best friend. He's been there through everything. I just…"

"You don't like him like that."

She bit her lip, wondering how he'd known what she was going to say before she said it. "Yeah… I guess that's it."

"Don't sell yourself short, Sammie Smiles. Don't settle for anything less than what you want." He ran his thumb across her chin, touching her in such a comfortable way you'd think they'd been friends for years. "Tell him the truth."

"I can't. I don't want to ruin our relationship."

"So you'd rather give up on what you want to make him happy?"

"No, that's not what I'm saying."

"Then what are you saying?"

"I just don't know what to say."

"Tell him…" His eyes trailed down her face, stopping at her lips. "That you met another guy. A guy who's trying damn hard to be a gentleman right now."

He met her eyes again, as though trying to read her thoughts. "Have you ever been kissed before, Samantha?"

She turned away, too shocked by the turn in conversation to get her mind to focus. "Why does that matter?"

"Because I need to know."

"Why?"

"Because." He touched her cheek gently with his fingertips, easing her face back toward him. "If this is your first time, I want it to be unforgettable."

Her chest rose and fell with each breath. She was sure it was visible, but there was no point in trying to hide it now.

He smiled. "You have no idea, do you?"

"No idea about what?"

He pushed himself to his elbow. "How goddamned sexy you are."

She covered her face, wanting to hide away with embarrassment, but he reached out softly and brushed her hands aside. "You're beautiful, Samantha, but I think what amazes me most is the fact that you don't know it."

He leaned over, his forearm baring all his weight. "I normally don't ask, I normally don't have to, but I'm trying damned hard to keep my promise. I want to kiss you, Samantha." His mouth moved slowly toward hers. "Now's your chance to tell me you don't want me to."

She looked up into his eyes, her heart pounding like a wild stallion, but no matter what she did, no matter how hard she tried to make her lips form the words, she couldn't do it. She couldn't say no. She wanted Tristan to kiss her, even though an hour earlier she would've been horrified by the thought. But in this moment, right now, it seemed like she couldn't live if he didn't.

His lips moved closer, her silence inviting him in, telling him it was okay, that he could take the thing she'd built up to fairy tale proportions, because this moment felt like one. A fairy tale.

His mouth came slowly, settling upon hers, warm, soft, and full. But he didn't move at all after that, he just stayed there, right there, perfectly still. Their breaths mingled together, both hard and soft. Breaths that were full of excitement and anticipation, and made every nerve in her body abundantly aware of his every move.

It was erotic. Invigorating. Made her whole stomach tighten with tiny flutters. Just the simple act of breathing the same air as someone else, not touching, or even really kissing. When she exhaled, he sucked it in, taking so much more of her than a breath. He was taking her girlhood, her hope and her dreams, and leading her down the path she'd never been before. Making her think she'd never really known her body, because it was doing things she'd never felt in her life.

When his lips finally moved, her body melted. Like she'd been frozen, too afraid to do anything but breathe for fear she'd wake, but his lips were there, warm like a fire, slowly heating her from the inside out. He kissed her bottom lip, pulling it into his mouth slightly before letting it go. "Are you okay?" he whispered.

Because goddammit, he was being a gentleman. Being everything she never thought he could be. Being everything she always wanted but never knew it until now. She nodded, her grip on the rocks loosening.

He smiled against her mouth and took both her hands, relaxing them with his. "Relax," he whispered, then slowly moved her hands until he laced them up around his neck. "Hold on to me."

She felt so silly, not knowing at all what to do, but he didn't seem bothered at all. He kissed her bottom lip again, pulling a little harder until she opened her mouth. His lips were soft, full, and nothing like she thought they would be. His tongue entered her mouth, touching hers gently with the tip, as though he was coaxing her to do the same. He felt so wonderful, tasted like winter-mint gum, and she couldn't resist kissing him back.

He gripped her head on both sides, and her tongue touched his. A growl came from the back of his throat as his body shifted on top of hers. She may have been inexperienced, but she knew the reaction was a good one. She also knew his reaction was caused by her, and that made her feel more powerful than she'd ever felt in her life. His weight sank into her, anchoring her body to this very spot. His kiss grew deeper, more urgent, as his tongue pushed farther into her mouth, pulling out feelings she never even knew existed.

She couldn't think anymore; his mouth was all-encompassing, his lips soft and firm at the same time, his teeth occasionally clashing against hers, and his tongue softer than any material she'd ever felt in her life.

Tristan Montgomery was kissing her, really kissing her, and she wasn't holding anything back. The thought never entered her mind until the sounds of laughter and crunching leaves sounded from behind them.

Pushing at his chest, she scrabbled to sit as fast as she could, but it was too late. When she whipped around, the girls from across the lake were making their way through the trees, and weren't hiding the fact that they'd noticed them. Samantha pulled in a breath, squeezing her eyes shut. *Thank God it's not Renee. Thank God it's them and not Mr. and Mrs. Montgomery.*

The girls continued to laugh, making their way down the path again and back to their cabin. But all Samantha could think about was her and Tristan's kiss. About how easily it had happened, how quickly it had deepened, and what would have happened had the girls had not come along to stop it.

Samantha sat forward, wrapping her arms around her

thighs and resting her chin on her knees. All of a sudden there was a hard pit at the bottom of her stomach. One that was large, and growing rapidly by the second.

Tristan moved beside her. His arm brushing her leg as he pulled himself to sit. "You okay?"

She nodded. "Yeah." But her mind kept rolling with fear. What would've happened had it been her best friend coming to look for her? What would she have said?

"You?" she asked, trying to push the thoughts to the back of her mind.

"I'm good," he said. His voice low and textured, but there was something else. Curiosity, or maybe confusion.

She took a deep breath, trying to figure things out. Why had he kissed her? Why now? Why her? The girl he'd never seemed to notice *once* until tonight. She began playing with the rocks again, because she was too inexperienced to know what was expected after a kiss like that. Too inexperienced to know if the tingles she felt all over her body was a normal reaction. If a kiss between practical strangers was always so mind consuming and passionate.

She'd kissed her best friend's brother, something she never would've expected in a million years. But that wasn't the worst of it. What bothered her most was that she wanted to do it again. A thousand times over again.

Tristan stood, grabbing her attention as he offered his hand and pulled her up to stand beside him. She wobbled slightly, her legs like soft rubber that refused to hold her. He reached out to wrap his fingers around her waist. To steady her at the small of her back before she fell. She swallowed, not sure what to say. He'd taken a part of her. A precious piece she'd been saving for that special person, but she herself had told him there was nothing owed after a simple kiss. Nothing promised.

"We should get going," he said softly, exerting the slightest amount of pressure to pull her forward. As though he wanted her next to him. As though he wanted her lips as much as she wanted his. "Before we get into trouble."

She looked up, knowing he was right. If she stayed out here much longer, she wasn't sure what would happen. She could feel the pulsing of her body, the blood coursing through her veins in every spot where he'd touched her. She reluctantly moved away and walked steadily toward the dock, taking all her concentration to do so. She fetched her towel from the edge of the platform, only turning when she heard him move behind her. The red-striped towel clutched at her chest, her eyes vulnerable, but she didn't see the boy she hated any longer. She saw Tristan. A guy who all the girls wanted, and who was misunderstood by the masses. He wasn't the self-centered heartbreaker she'd always thought him to be. He was kind, he was thoughtful—and he was the first boy who had ever said she was beautiful.

They walked back to the cabin in silence, but it was a different silence. Because under the surface was something else. A shared secret; a kiss she vowed to remember for all eternity.

The porch light was still on, like it was earlier, but so much had changed since they left. She'd walked out that door as an innocent girl, and come back with that part of her missing.

He walked ahead of her up the steps, pausing a moment before pushing the door open. As if he was waiting for something. For her to stop him, for her to tell him it was a mistake. But she remained silent, and eventually he walked into the house ahead of her.

"Thanks for coming out tonight," he said, as he held the door wide for her to enter.

She ducked under his arm, careful not to get too close, then nodded. Because for the life of her, she couldn't think of anything else do. Her mind was still mush, her pulse still racing. She tightened her grip on her towel and chewed her inner cheek. Because God help her, she was completely unaware of what happened next. Did they talk? Not talk? She looked up to the loft, where Renee's faint snore still traveled down the staircase. Guilt washed over her and she turned back to Tristan.

He stood against the closed door, his face intense, but his body relaxed like always. She wanted to explain, to tell him she should never have let it happen. But before she could, he pushed himself from the wall and walked down the steps to the basement. He didn't say a word, and was gone from sight before she could even comprehend his leaving.

But he left the door open—just a crack, and she knew what it was. An invitation for her to join him—and she couldn't stop staring at it. Her stomach flip-flopped, and her knuckles became white where she clutched her towel too hard at her chest. It was an invitation for another kiss. To get to know the man she'd never allowed herself to truly see. But as sure as she was about the invitation, as sure as she knew he wanted her to take it, she couldn't do it.

She turned toward the stairs, not allowing herself to think about what happened. Not allowing herself to wonder what would happen if she were to follow him down to his bed.

She fetched her pajamas from her suitcase, slipped them on, all while hoping and praying Renee wouldn't wake. She climbed into bed on the queen-sized mattress, thinking she'd just made it, when her best friend turned around and grumbled in her sleep.

Renee's expression was groggy and tired, and she slowly opened her eyes. "What time is it?" she asked, with a voice full of gravel.

"Almost eleven," Samantha whispered.

Renee closed her eyes, but her lips transformed into a reluctant smile. "Those girls from the lake came over tonight," she whispered. "Just a little while ago."

Samantha's throat went dry, and her stomach churned with

sour grapes. *They told her.* They told Renee what they saw. Told her about her and Tristan.

Renee rolled to the nightstand and grabbed a red and white can of soup from the bedside table, before turning back. "They brought me this," she said, shaking the can half-heartedly in her hand. "Chicken noodle." She studied the label, tracing the words over and over with her fingertip. "Do you want to guess how long it took them to ask about Tristan?"

Samantha shook her head, her eyes shut as hot tears threatened to spill through her lids. A thousand excuses rushed to her mind, but none of them were good enough. None of them would make a difference. She'd kissed Tristan willingly. She'd kissed her friend's brother, and the only reason she'd stopped was because those girls had interrupted them.

"Do they think I don't know?" Renee asked, her head tilted to one side as her face filled with disgust. "Do they think I'm so stupid that I don't realize what they're doing?" She placed the can back on the end table, the frustration and emotions oozing from her skin. "I'm so sick of people being nice to me just to get to my brother." Her voice was harsh and broken, but there was something else there, too. She was defeated.

Samantha pulled in a sharp breath, realizing what her friend was telling her. That those girls hadn't told her what they'd seen in the woods. In fact, they'd probably come from seeing Renee when they found her and Tristan on the rocks.

Renee closed her eyes, sandwiching her hands beneath her head and pillow as she faced Samantha. "At least I have you." She yawned. "The only person I can trust."

A hundred bricks landed on Samantha's shoulders. She knew exactly what Renee was trying to say. Because up until this point, Samantha was the only girl who hated Tristan as much as she did.

"Will you get the light?" Renee whispered then.

Tears burned in Samantha's eyes, but she nodded and turned to switch off the light.

"Night, Sam," Renee said in a groggy voice.

"Night, Ren," Samantha whispered back, squeezing her eyes shut, but the tears fell to her cheeks anyway. *Right now*, she thought to herself. Right now would be the perfect time to confess. To let it out. Right now, before it festered. But she couldn't. She flipped over, facing the stairs that would take her back to Tristan's, and more tears slipped down to her cheeks and fell to her chin.

"I love you," Renee whispered through the darkness. Her voice was half asleep, so quiet Samantha would've never been able to make out the words had she not heard them a million times before.

She swallowed, barely able to contain her own sorrow. "I love you too."

CHAPTER SEVEN

Present Day

She looked into his eyes, her heart pounding. What did she remember? Is that what he wanted to know? Her eyes shifted to the pavement, where the "I dare you" in the question didn't feel quite so loud. "Not much," she said softly.

He flashed one of his panty dropping smiles and adjusted his stance. "Well that's good."

She titled her head to the side. "Is it?"

"Yeah." He tucked his hands in the back pockets of his jeans and relaxed. "I don't remember much about you, either. This trip would have been extremely awkward had you remembered *me*." He looked to the open trunk and moved his suitcase over a few inches. "The good news is, we have three thousand miles to change all that."

Her heart pinched at his easy grin and she adjusted her stance. It shouldn't have affected her. Especially when he'd confessed to not remembering her just the second before, but he was so damned attractive she couldn't help it. The reaction was much like her mouth watering at the scent of a lemon, or her nose retreating when she smelled something foul. It was one of those involuntary actions she had no control over.

But she still didn't like it.

Especially when she knew what happened when you got too close to Tristan Montgomery.

She looked back toward the sculpture, trying to regain composure. "I have a lot of reading to catch up on," she said sweetly, then turned toward the sculpture and squatted down to get ready to lift. "I'm afraid getting to know you isn't one of my top priorities."

He grinned slightly, raising his brows as he grabbed the other end. "Suit yourself," he replied, lifting, and moving the sculpture toward the trunk. But then his eyes narrowed, as though he was aware the tension between them was not one of strangers.

She followed after him, ready to be rid of this task, and on the road.

An hour later, her hair whipping around like the tail of a rattlesnake, Samantha dug through her oversized bag looking for a hair tie. The top of the convertible was down, blowing her hair in every which direction, but Tristan didn't seem to notice. His arm was braced out the open window, his aviator glasses darkening his eyes, but the rest of his expression looked very much like a man who didn't give a shit.

She heaved a heavy sigh, hoping he'd hear it and take the hint. That he'd sense her annoyance and close the top. But he seemed oblivious, caught up in his own thoughts—his own world. They'd loaded the rest of her belongings without much hassle. Filling the trunk and half of the back seat with luggage, garment bags, and pillows. But they hadn't spoken at all, beyond what was necessary. Which was just fine with her. She didn't want to talk to Tristan. He was her means of getting from point A to point B. To bring her sculpture to Renee on her wedding day. That was it.

Samantha finally found a tie at the bottom of the bag and began braiding her hair over one shoulder. Her eyes focused on the horizon as she tried to settle herself down.

Traffic was light, which allowed them to fly down the highway. She kicked off her shoes and dragged one leg into her lap before slouching forward to retrieve her audiobook. It was impossible to find comfort. To be at ease sitting next to the man who'd stolen her first kiss. Her mind had been spinning ever since the moment she first saw him. Because the night she'd come home from the cabin, she'd made a vow. To forget Tristan Montgomery, to forget the kiss that had rocked her harder than an earthquake—and to never tell Renee her secret.

She'd been successful for the most part. Because most of the time she pretended he didn't exist, and it worked. Except for those tiny moments, when a lingering snippet would sneak into her subconscious. Triggered by the oddest things: a falling star, a twig floating in a puddle of water, or even the scent of winter-mint gum. She'd always been able to stuff it down again, as effortlessly as pulling a wily hair. But now the subject of her reverie was sitting beside her, completely silent, yet very much present.

She opened her eyes and glared at his profile, unable to keep her gaze from lingering. His nose was crooked—not badly, but almost in a Matthew McConaughey kind of way. His jaw was square—chiseled, with a shadow of scruff that hadn't been there when last she'd seen him.

His hair was lighter now. Probably from driving around with the top down like this. It was about two shades darker than her own. Not brown or blond, but that shade right in between where she knew he must have been a towhead when he was little. But it was his mouth she couldn't pull her eyes from. The soft, full shape she still remembered to this day.

She closed her eyes and turned back to window. She'd be kidding herself if she said he wasn't handsome. He was honestly one of the best looking men she'd ever seen in her life. Strong features, strong body, bronzed skin, which only made his blue eyes more vibrant. But handsome wouldn't be the first word she'd use to describe Tristan Montgomery. Big. That would be the word. Not big in size. Though yes, he was over six feet tall—much larger than Samantha's five-foot-two-inch frame. But it was his sheer presence that made up the volume, more powerful than the roar of the mustang below them. More expansive than the wind blowing in her face.

But he didn't remember. His words kept whirling in Samantha's mind. The kiss that had been her first, which she'd unwillingly compared with every other kiss she'd had since, was too insignificant to take up his brain space. She leaned forward again, retrieved her laptop out of her bag, and sat it on her lap. She needed to write, to focus on anything but the man who sat beside her.

Her narrative was a diary of sorts, the way to get things out of her head so she could let them go.

DEAR RENEE,

SHE BEGAN as she always did—though Renee rarely ever received them. Samantha had hundreds of messages like this, if not thousands. Some were letters of excitement and joy, others fears and anxiety. But many were confessions. Too many. They were unedited, unanswered, unsent. Letters from a teenage girl who was confused, heartbroken, and needing someone to talk to. Letters from a drunken newly twenty-one-year-old woman, who for some reason was thinking of Tristan when on a romantic getaway with her boyfriend.

I CAN'T WAIT to see you! To see you in your wedding dress. To hug you!

I can't wait to catch up on all you've been doing since leaving LA. I know we've talked nearly every day, but it's different when I can see your face. I've missed you so much. So much more than I can say in this letter. So much—that I find myself sitting next to your brother for the next four days.

HE SAYS he doesn't remember me; is that even possible? That he couldn't remember the girl who was at his house more often than her own? But I guess that doesn't matter. The only thing that matters is that he showed up, and that I'm on my way to see you.

I MISS YOU! I miss your stinky ballet shoes! I even miss tripping over your dance bag you always left by the front door. I miss us sitting on the couch, binge watching Netflix. I worry we'll never do that again...

I KNOW IT'S SILLY, but I always pictured us growing old together. You'd live next door and come over to borrow sugar. But you'd stay awhile...so our babies would crawl on the living room floor together.

WE'D GO to cocktail parties, see romcom movies because our husbands never wanted to go. We'd always give them a hard time, but secretly we'd love it. Because it would be like old times, like sitting under blankets watching Netflix...

Six years earlier

Maple syrup dripped from the bite of waffle held midair on Samantha's fork. A sea of breakfast foods covered the plate in front of her: waffles, eggs, toast. But she'd neglected to take a bite of any of it. Breakfast wasn't her favorite meal on any given morning, but today the food was especially unappealing.

She'd tossed and turned all night long, barely able to get more than an hour's rest. Her stomach was rolling with anxiety and guilt. The feeling that still lingered now. It was guilt over kissing Tristan, but also about holding back the truth from Renee. Samantha and Renee shared everything with each other. *Everything.* Last night was the first time in their Nine-year friendship that Samantha had gone to bed knowing she hadn't told her friend the truth.

Samantha's mom had once told her that the secret to a happy life was never going to bed knowing you'd been dishonest. At the time, she'd thought her mom was trying to convince her to confess about the cookies she'd stolen from the pantry, but the advice haunted her last night. Because an untold truth felt an awful lot like a lie. Like stolen cookies leaving a sour taste in the bottom of her stomach.

Tristan sat directly in front of her now, though she hadn't looked up once. She felt bad ignoring him, because in spite of how upset she was about Renee, last night had been one of the best of her life. She was just afraid. Afraid that if she met his eyes again, even for a second, everyone in the house would know he'd taken a piece of her heart last night. They'd see the confusion whirling in her brain. Because last night she'd gone out with a boy, knowing he was the one she hated, but in just a few hours he'd made her question everything she'd believed for years.

It was like finding out Santa wasn't real, and then playing each moment you'd sat in his lap over and over, wondering how you could've not known. The fake beard, the constant change in appearance, the fact he would wear such a warm suit in the middle of summer at the fourth of July parade. Being with Tristan had shattered her sense of self, her trust in her own judgment and everything she thought she knew about everyone. She found herself piecing memories of Tristan together, trying to make sense of it all, but then pulling them apart again because it never did. Because he wasn't a dumb jock that hurt everyone like she'd always thought. That was a lie, and if anything, those lies had hurt *him*.

"Are you alright, dear?" Mrs. Montgomery's voice called from the other side of the table.

Samantha startled from her thoughts, uncrossed her feet from under the table, and glanced down the row of chairs to her best friend's mother. Mrs. Montgomery's gold hair was tied up in a messy bun on the top of her head, her long neck poised elegantly as she sipped from a large mug of coffee.

"Yeah, I'm fine." Samantha forced a small smile and shoved the piece of waffle into her mouth. "Just tired."

Mrs. Montgomery grinned, but only half-heartedly. "I hope Renee didn't keep you up all night with her coughing. I'm afraid this trip hasn't been much fun for you, has it?"

Samantha shook her head. "Oh no, it's been great." She swallowed her food. "And it wasn't Renee. I was up late…" She cleared her throat. "Reading."

Tristan made a small sound from across the table, but Samantha ignored him, not daring to look up for fear everyone would see her blushing.

Mrs. Montgomery turned to say something to Mr. Montgomery, never seeming to notice her discomfort, and eventually went back to reading her newspaper.

The plan had been to leave right after breakfast, and Samantha couldn't wait for it. She was anxious for the departure, anxious to be back at the Montgomerys' so she could talk to Renee privately. She needed to tell her what happened. To confess—and clear her dirty conscience of the kiss she couldn't stop thinking about. But she couldn't do it here, not knowing they'd be stuck in a car for five hours back to LA. She'd tell her when they got home, as soon as she got her alone, no matter how difficult it was.

A creak sounded from the other side of the room and Samantha turned around. Renee stood on the very top of the staircase, her hair a tangled and unbrushed mess, held high by a yellow scrunchy on top of her head.

"Well if it isn't my little ball of sunshine!" Mr. Montgomery shouted. "It's good to see you out of bed and alive."

Renee croaked out a word that sounded something like "morning," then came down the steps, and crossed the distance to pull out a chair next to Samantha.

"How do you feel, honey?" Mrs. Montgomery asked, as Renee sat beside her.

"Better," she answered, reaching across the table for the platter of waffles. "Do we have any orange juice?"

Everyone began passing plates and pitchers. Chatting about everything and nothing, as Samantha stuffed her face with maple-covered waffles and bacon. She hoped that if she kept her mouth full for long enough, everyone would forget she was there and not ask questions.

The plan almost worked. Until she excused herself to the kitchen. She entered the tiny room, placed her plate into the sink, then braced her hands on either side of the counter, her eyes fixed on the dark, ominous sky that had rolled in overnight. It was like a message from God, punishing her for all her wrongdoings. "I see you, God. I know what you're up to, and I don't like it!"

"What was that?"

Samantha whipped around, finding Tristan standing in the doorway with an empty plate. He moved toward her, deposited his dish in the full sink, then rested his hip on the counter beside her. Although he said nothing, there was heaviness between them that told her there was much on his mind. He looked at her, his mouth still, but his eyes full of questions. Questions that both scared and excited her. Questions she wasn't sure she could answer.

She turned back toward the window, unable to face him any longer, and picked up a kitchen rag and began twisting it between her fingers. "About last night," she began. "I'm going to tell Renee everything." She nodded. "As soon as we get home."

He adjusted his stance, and even though she wasn't looking at him, she could tell he wasn't happy. "It's none of her business, Sam."

She closed her eyes, opening them a second later to shake her head. "But it is. You're her brother and I'm her best friend. Renee and I tell each other everything, and it's killing me she doesn't know."

"Okay."

"Okay?" She turned to face him, her heart pounding.

"Yeah."

His eyes softened, and she immediately stepped backward. "What does that mean?"

"It means if you want to tell her, that's fine with me."

She grabbed hold of his shirt and pulled him into the pantry. "Why?" she whispered. "You've known me for nine years, yet last night was the first time you ever noticed me. Why?"

His brows furrowed and he looked into her eyes. "I've always noticed you, Sam."

She swallowed, her hands flat against his chest, her back straining against the shelf that held all the canned goods, but all she could think about was kissing him again.

He chuckled, deep and coarse, but with a hint of something she didn't understand. The action caused the dimple on his left side to sink into his cheek—and somehow make him look more handsome. His hands rested on the top of her arms, moving up and down in a way that made her lose her breath.

"You're crazy," he finally said. "All this time I thought you were this cute, nerdy girl who spent too much time reading."

She licked her lips. "You thought I was cute?"

"Yes." He laughed again. "Look, as much as I like being close to you, sooner or later someone's going to come in here and find us in the pantry."

Her eyes bulged and she turned to peek through the crack in the door. He was right. If Renee found her in the pantry with Tristan, there would be no explaining it. Nothing left to do but tell her the honest-to-God truth right there in the kitchen. She pushed him out the double doors, intending to follow right after him, but Mrs. Montgomery walked into the kitchen at that moment.

"Oh, there you are," she said, stopping in her tracks. "Have you seen Samantha?"

Tristan laced his hands behind his head and shrugged. "Nope." But it was not convincing. Not one tiny bit.

Mrs. Montgomery's brows furrowed, and she looked over his shoulder. She turned back and tilted her head to the side as though she knew something was up. "Your father's packing up the van and wanted to know if your suitcase was ready to be loaded."

Tristan stepped forward and placed his arm around his mother's shoulder. "Not yet, but I'll do that right now."

She looked up at him and smiled a knowing smile. "Son, why do you look so guilty?"

He laughed, throwing his head back to look at the ceiling before escorting her from the kitchen. "That's just my face, Mom."

"Uh, huh." She laughed, but a moment later they were both gone, walking arm in arm into the living room.

Samantha pulled in a much-needed breath and slouched against the pantry shelves. She needed to get out of there before she was caught, but it was another few minutes before she felt comfortable enough to make the first step. She quickly checked her reflection in the kitchen window, hoping she didn't look too flustered, and walked out to the dining room as quickly as she could.

Tristan was standing by the couch folding his clothes, but stopped as soon as he saw her. She reluctantly walked toward him, aware someone could walk into the room at any moment. "Don't tell, okay?" she whispered without stopping. It was a juvenile request, but it was the best she had, given her time constraints.

He grinned slightly, making her heart squeeze with uncertainty. Because she was at his mercy, he held all the cards, and she was simply the joker in his pocket.

"It's our little secret," he replied, picking up the last folded shirt and placing it on top of his clothes in the suitcase before zipping it shut. He grabbed hold of the handle and threw it up to his shoulder.

"Thank you," she whispered, but before she reached the top of the stairs, she turned around and looked back to the living room. He still had his suitcase lifted to the top of his shoulder, his hair shining from the sunlight that came in through the opened door, and she thought he might be the most beautiful thing she'd ever seen in her life.

PRESENT DAY

"WHAT ARE YOU WRITING?" Tristan asked, his voice breaking through the silence of the Mustang.

Samantha's heart lurched in her chest and she slapped the laptop closed. She turned to face him, panic in her face as she tried to comprehend his words. "What was that?" She put her feet on the floor, wishing the top was still down so she could stand and clear her head, but she was trapped. Trapped with the only other man she'd ever kissed besides Steven.

He doesn't remember. He doesn't remember any of it. The thought should have comforted her, but it did nothing. It did nothing at all.

He lifted his chin to her laptop, likely curious by her odd behavior. "What are you writing?" he asked again. "You've been staring at your laptop for over an hour."

She cleared her throat. "Have I?" But her voice pitched a little higher than usual and she took a drink of water. "I was just…thinking."

"About?"

She bit her bottom lip and glanced out the window. "About Renee." It was a lie, but it sounded reasonable enough.

He immediately nodded, but took his sunglasses from his face and threw them to the dashboard. "Tell me about it." But there was a tone in his voice that caught her attention—he was worried about something—what? She wasn't sure.

Samantha's shoulders relaxed a little and she leaned forward to put her laptop away. "She moved to New York only last November, and now she's getting married. It's all happening so fast…" Her words trailed off, because she'd already said more than she intended. She hadn't talked to anyone about Renee since she heard the news. Even Steven, because he was never interested in anything to do with her best friend's life. But why she felt compelled to talk to Tristan baffled her.

"I guess they're in love," he said, causing her heart to lurch before she turned around again.

She shrugged. "Yeah, I guess. Have you met him?"

"Yeah." He looked over his shoulder, changing lanes, then met her eyes for the first time the whole trip. "A couple of months ago. He's a good guy, I guess."

"You guess?"

"Yeah, I guess."

He didn't say more, and she didn't press it. She turned toward the window and adjusted her seat belt. Nervous flutters beat against the inside of her stomach, but she took a deep breath, and tried to ignore them.

"What about you?" he asked. "Are you in love?"

She squared her shoulders, surprised as hell by the question. She hated relationship talk. Hated people butting into her love life… But she lifted her head and looked him dead in the eye, almost asking him to challenge her. "Yes. Actually, I am."

He squinted slightly and reached up to pull down the sun visor. "And where is your knight in shining armor?"

There it was. The judgment that was unmistakable. She turned to the window, hating the way it made her feel. Because it made her feel insecure. Made her feel slightly angry with Steven for the first time since he'd told her about his internship. She pulled in a deep breath and tried to sound confident. "Work," she confessed, her stomach dropping a few inches.

"Well that's unfortunate," Tristan stated, but there was a tone in his voice that almost sounded like he was pissed off.

She turned back around, slightly confused. "How so?" she questioned, disturbed by the fact she'd been so consumed with the conversation she hadn't realized they'd pulled off the freeway.

He pulled into a parking space, pushed down the emergency brake, then turned to face her, his expression hard. "His priorities are in the wrong place."

She shook her head, uncomfortable with the lecture-like tone he was using. Her chest inflated and she grew a little taller in her seat. "He landed one of the most coveted positions of his graduating class. I would say his priorities are right where they need to be."

Tristan shrugged, unbuckled his seat belt, and got out of the car. "If it were me, there would be no way I'd let the woman I was in love with drive cross-country with a man I'd never met." He slammed the door behind him and moved in the direction of the restaurant.

"Where are you going?" she shouted through the rolled-down window.

"To eat," he said without turning around.

"But I have snacks!"

He shook his head, almost laughing. "You eat your snacks, Sam. I'm getting a burger." But before he opened the door to walk inside, he turned and retraced his steps almost reluctantly. He ducked down, looking at her through the passenger window. "Join me if you want," he said, tilting his head to the side. "Or don't. Your choice." He flashed her one of his first-class smiles, then stood up and walked inside, leaving her stomach filled with butterflies, and the sudden urge to call her boyfriend.

CHAPTER EIGHT

"GOOD AFTERNOON, Connor and Associates, how may I direct your call?"

Samantha shoved the last bits of jerky into her mouth and rolled down the bag. "Steven Mathers, please."

Tristan had been gone no longer than two minutes, but it was long enough for her to have a mini panic attack about her relationship. She was still seething over Tristan's comment about priorities. Possibly because the way he said it reminded her of Renee, or maybe it was the disappointment in his eyes when he said it, but it bothered the hell out of her. Tristan didn't know her. He didn't know how her and Steven's relationship functioned—yet he'd made a split second judgment about Steven's priorities.

"Hold please," the operator said, sending Samantha to elevator music while she tucked the bag of jerky back in her purse.

It wasn't until that moment with Tristan, that she realized she hadn't told Steven at all that she was leaving. Not because it was a secret. Because he was busy with work and she didn't want to bother him. But now that Tristan's words were in her head, she couldn't help but feel guilty.

What if he *was* upset she'd gone with Tristan? What if Tristan was right, and Steven didn't like the idea of her driving cross-country with a man he'd never met?

Though he had met him... A long time ago, but he had.

At first she was angry, but the more she thought about it, Tristan may be right. If the situation were reversed, and Steven was driving cross-country with a woman she'd never met, she wouldn't like it one bit. And she wasn't even the jealous type. Her stomached coiled deep inside and she worried her bottom lip.

Steven's voice came through the line, hurried and out of breath. "Steven Mathers," he answered, making her anxiety flair and her face to cringe with regret.

She'd caught him at a bad time, she was sure of it. "Hey, it's me." She whisper-replied.

"Sam." He lowered his voice and muffled the receiver. "Everything okay?"

"Yeah, I—"

"Can I call you later? I really shouldn't be on the phone."

She bit her bottom lip, determined to get the words out. She glanced through the window of the restaurant, where Tristan could be seen looking at a menu. "I'm calling to tell you I left for New York this morning."

"*What?*" he questioned, a little shocked.

"Yeah... You see, Renee's brother was leaving today, and she thought it would be a good idea for us to drive together."

"And this was so important you called me at work?"

She frowned. "You're not angry?"

He hesitated a moment, as though contemplating the question. "Are you a big girl, Samantha?"

She picked at her fingernail, then scrunched her shoulders

68

nervously. "I don't know? You're not jealous because I'm with another guy?"

"Should I be?"

She shook her head, looking down to her lap. "No."

"Honey, I trust you. You've never given me any reason not to. You make your decisions, and I make mine. That's what I love about us. I don't want to be one of those couples that can't make decisions without the other. I'm secure enough in my manhood to trust the woman I love."

Samantha closed her eyes, pulling in her first real breath in the last five minutes. "You're right." She sighed. "I don't know what I was thinking."

He chuckled. "I really have to get back to work now. Are we good?"

She nodded. "Yes, of course."

"Okay, be safe baby. I love you."

"I love you too."

SIX YEARS EARLIER

THE RIDE BACK TO THE MONTGOMERYS' was surprisingly uneventful. Samantha and Renee had been seated at the back of the van, where Samantha buried her face in a pillow and covered her head with the hood of her jacket. But Tristan had sat catty-corner in the captain's chair, reading. Which was something she'd never seen him do before.

Was this new for him, could it be some secret tactic to make her fall for him a little more, or had she simply never paid enough attention to notice? But she was paying attention now—so much so, she couldn't seem to look away. She watched him out of corner of her eye, each expression as he got lost in his story—and when he smiled, that wicked grin that made her heart skip a beat, she almost rolled out of her seat.

Last night's kiss had haunted her so much she'd barely slept —because she kept wondering if he'd been affected the same way. If he had any inclination about how many times she wished she would have followed him down to his bedroom. But mostly, she thought about Renee. About what she would say when she told her the truth.

As the hours passed by, Samantha began planning out each word she would use to explain what happened. The exact punctuation, down to the tone she would use as she told Renee about her first kiss. But when they pulled into the driveway of the two-story craftsman, she realized five hours wasn't nearly long enough time to prepare. She'd been practicing nearly every minute, yet nothing had come to her that was good enough. Nothing could justify the fact that she'd kissed her best friend's brother, really kissed him without holding back. The boy they'd hated together for as long as she could remember. The one thing that bound their friendship from the very start.

"Well, we made it!" Mr. Montgomery said, throwing the van in park. He looked to back seat, where he shoved Tristan's knee to make sure he was awake. "If we can get this ship unloaded in thirty minutes, I'll buy everyone pizza."

Tristan, who ate more than anyone she'd ever met, immediately grinned, then popped open the sliding door and climbed out of the van.

They'd driven straight from Big Bear to Los Angeles without stopping, and Samantha's legs were stiff and sore when she finally joined him. Tristan was already untying the straps on the roof when she stepped down to the driveway. He never once looked her way. Why that bothered her was baffling, especially considering she had told him to keep it a secret just that morning. But it still left her feeling forgotten.

Would she ever be comfortable here again? At the Montgomerys' home? Around the people who'd been like a second family since second grade? Renee came to stand by her side, a purple blanket wrapped around her shoulders, and leaned close to her ear. "Don't look now," she whispered, "but lover boy is waiting at the front steps."

Samantha whipped around, her heart jumping to her chest. Steven Mathers sat on the front stoop, his glossy brown hair neatly combed, looking like he'd just come back from Sunday school. She looked over to Tristan, who was untying the luggage with urgency.

"I thought you'd never get home," Steven shouted from the steps. He stood up, walked slowly toward the van, and stopped directly at her side. He grinned, then leaned over to whisper in her ear. "I missed you," he said, in that way that was comfortable and familiar. Like he thought she missed him too.

She didn't.

In all actuality, it was the complete opposite. "Hey," she whispered back. "I gotta go help unload the van. You want to wait inside?"

Steven nodded, but paused for a few moments before picking up a couple of sleeping bags and following Mrs. Montgomery into the house.

As soon as he was out of view, she turned toward the van again. She should've been relieved, but she still needed to talk to Renee, and she couldn't do that with Steven around.

Renee opened the back of the van, and Samantha immediately began helping with the luggage. She pulled a brown suitcase from the top of the stack, just as Renee elbowed her in the ribs.

"He's like a puppy," Renee whispered in her ear. "A perfectly groomed puppy wearing too much cologne. Can't he leave you alone for one stupid weekend?"

Samantha closed her eyes, then yanked another bag from the pile and set it on the pavement. Normally she would defend

Steven, but right now she agreed. He was like a puppy, a sad, loyal puppy, and she couldn't wait to get rid of him.

Renee took her small duffle from the back of the van, immediately gripping the door to steady herself. She looked over to Samantha and cringed. "Sorry, Sam, but I think I need to go sit down."

Samantha patted her on the back. "Go, I don't want you passing out on me."

Renee headed for the house, leaving her and Tristan to unpack the rest of the luggage alone. Samantha didn't mind though, because it gave her time to think about how to get rid of Steven. He really was a good guy, and she knew that someday he'd make a girl very happy. She just wasn't that girl. Tristan was right about that. She couldn't sacrifice her own happiness to supply someone else's.

She turned around to place another suitcase on the growing pile, just as a red car, filled with half a dozen former seniors pulled along the sidewalk of the house. Girls and guys, laughing and horsing around as they piled out of the car.

"T-Man!" one of them shouted to Tristan. "It's about time you got home! Where's the party?"

Tristan turned to lean against the van and lifted his chin. "What's up, Beef?"

They bumped shoulders, did some sort of hand shake thing as two girls wearing much too little clothing came to latch themselves to Tristan's sides.

She closed her eyes and turned away. She recognized them. Barely. They were cheerleaders from West Valley high. People she barely knew, and she liked it that way. But a sinking feeling grew in the bottom of her stomach, bubbling up until it began climbing her bitter throat.

Is this jealousy? Whatever it was, it was a feeling she'd never felt before, and one she was sure she shouldn't be feeling right now. *This was Tristan,* she reminded herself. He wasn't just a guy she got to know at the lake, but the lead quarterback of his varsity football team. The guy who had a friend named Beef, and who had more attention from women than she wanted to know about.

The realization left her questioning everything. Could she like a boy who had more friends than he knew what to do with? A guy who was never alone, not even for ten minutes?

She continued pulling sleeping bags and pillows from the back of the van, anxious to be done with the task so she could go inside, but it was difficult when the other side of her was hanging on every word they said.

The Tristan she'd met alone in the woods wasn't like this. He was honest and open, and so much deeper than the guy leaning against the van. She didn't know if she could take it. If she could stand by and watch girls wrap themselves in his arms. Because right now she felt insecure and vulnerable, and that wasn't a feeling she liked very much. She was a girl who prided herself on being reasonable, on being mature. But one kiss from Tristan Montgomery had her insides screaming "bitch" when a tall brunette stretched up on tiptoe to whisper in Tristan's ear.

"It's my birthday," she said rather loudly. "My parents bought a keg. Come over later?"

Tristan only laughed, but he did something interesting. He looked over at Samantha, their eyes locking for brief time and he shook his head. "I don't know, I'm pretty beat."

If she hadn't been looking for it, she would have missed it, but it was long enough for her heart to soar. For the message to be clear. He wasn't interested in keg girl. Whatever happened in the woods had meant as much to him as it had to her.

She took the last piece of luggage from the van feeling comforted, but very much needing to get away.

Mr. Montgomery was her saving grace. He came to stand by the van, and pulled down the back to slam it shut. He rested his hand on Samantha's head and ruffled her hair. "I got this kiddo. Why don't you run inside and find Renee?"

She only nodded, still too shaken by the shared glance to trust her voice. Without looking back, she turned toward the house and walked up to the steps, leaving Tristan and his party crowd reluctantly alone.

CHAPTER NINE

Six years earlier

As promised, Mr. Montgomery ordered pizza as soon as everyone was finished unloading the van—enough to feed a small army—or half of West Valley's senior class. But that was how it was at the Montgomery home. Sometimes it was over half the football team, more than twenty-five jocks and their girlfriends, filling the great-room and lounging on the sectional in the corner. Today, however, there were only ten, which filled the home with rowdy laughter that sounded like twice that.

Renee sat at the bar with Samantha and Steven, wrapped in a purple blanket she'd taken from the cabin. It was far too noisy for any of them to hold a conversation, so they sat in silence, trying to ignore Tristan, and his friends who seemed to monopolize the entire room.

Samantha didn't mind—because it took the attention away from her. Away from the guilt, the jealousy, and the desire she was sure could be seen on her face. Because her mind was preoccupied with something else. Two somethings, actually. One: she needed to figure out what to tell Renee. Because "I let your brother stick his tongue in my throat" didn't have the right ring to it. And two: she needed to apologize to Steven. Because that's what it would be. An apology.

She couldn't be the girl he wanted her to be. She couldn't like him the way he wanted her to, and she knew that fact would hurt him. She would say it as gently as she could, hoping with all hope they'd still have a friendship when it was over, but she was worried. It was all too much for a girl to take. Too much responsibility, too much stress. So much so that she thought she might have a nervous breakdown, right there in Mrs. Montgomery's kitchen.

She picked up another slice of pizza, hoping to dull her emotions with carbohydrates, but Steven's phone buzzed on the counter at that moment. He slid open the call, and held one finger to his ear as he excused himself to the front porch. Everyone was distracted, watching TV or playing pool, and Samantha knew it was the perfect opportunity to talk. She picked up her plate from the counter, then tossed it into the trashcan, intending to follow.

She found Steven sitting on the front sidewalk, still on the phone. Far enough from the house that the distance offered privacy from the rest of the party. Samantha sat down beside him, her feet stretched out to the road, waiting for him to finish his conversation.

"Okay, okay..." He held up one finger. "Yeah, I'll wait outside." He said goodbye, looked over at Samantha, and slid his cell back into his pocket. But he didn't say a word for a good moment. Just stared at her. As though they both waited for the other to speak. A moment passed, and he turned in her direction, resting his elbow on his thigh. "Sorry, that was my mom."

She nodded, though her throat tightened with anticipation of what to say next, because she had no idea where to begin. She'd never had a boyfriend before, but she imagined this felt much like breaking up. Ironic, considering they'd never even had a first date.

She worried her bottom lip, unable to pull the words from her tongue. But she finally turned to face him, her eyes intense.

"How long have you been here?" she asked, her hands in the warmth of her hoodie's pocket, pulling at bits of lint to calm her nerves. She closed her eyes, knowing she'd messed things up already. Feeling the tension rush in all around them. "I mean, before we got home?"

He shrugged a little, but his brows furrowed slightly as if sensing her discomfort. "About an hour. I walked here from Mr. Chavez's class—he wanted help setting up for the fall semester."

"Oh." She nodded, taking a deep breath before looking down to the asphalt. Not surprised, because this was such a typical Steven thing to do. He was the only kid she'd ever met who still went to school during summer. But she admired that about him. She admired a lot about him.

He turned to face her, swallowing hard before opening his mouth again. "Did you give any thought to my question?"

She looked straight into his eyes, knowing without a doubt he was referring to the proposition he'd given her before she'd left. About becoming his girlfriend junior year, about crossing the bridge from friends, to so much more than that. She looked down to the pavement, to the rocky texture that blurred through unshed tears. This was her chance to speak up, to say she was sorry if she hurt him, but that she couldn't do it. Because she was falling for someone else, someone who was unexpected, but the exact opposite of everything she ever thought she wanted. She chewed her inner cheek, unable to think properly. "About that—"

"Samantha," he interrupted, taking her hands in his and squeezing. "Before you say anything, know this—you don't like me as much as I like you. I know that. But you haven't really given me a chance."

"Steven, I—"

But before she could finish her sentence, he grabbed hold of her face and kissed her. Firm and hard—urgent…messy.

The exact opposite of Tristan.

She didn't know what to do, push him away, hurt him more than she already had to—or stay there. To bear the invasion to save his pride. His tongue pushed inside her mouth. Soft and velvety, but different. She waited for the butterflies to flutter. To grow in her belly and swarm to her lips until the feeling filled her entire body. The way they had when Tristan kissed her— the way they did when he even looked at her.

But they never came.

Tears pooled in her eyes and she squeezed them shut. Partly because it felt so wrong, but partly because she *wanted* it to feel so right. She prayed for her mind to go blank, to replace all the wild thoughts with something safer. With Steven. With the boy who did homework on the weekend. Who didn't have girls hanging on his arms every second of the day. But she couldn't.

Nothing came. No butterflies. No tingles. And eventually she pushed at Steven's chest, not hard, but hard enough to break away.

He scooted down the sidewalk, a good foot away, and looked down at his feet. A crease stretched across his entire brow, making him look older, upset, or almost angry. She pressed her hot lips together, still swollen and sore from their brief kiss.

"I've wanted to do that for a long time," he said, his voice low, but more emotional than she'd ever heard it.

She nodded, moisture threatening to seep through the corners of her eyes. Because she knew it was the truth. She knew that's what he wanted, what he'd always wanted. Which was the reason it was so hard to let him down.

"I'm sure it will get better with practice," he said, almost as though trying to convince himself.

She shook her head, knowing she had to speak up. "Steven—"

But before she could say the words, a bright blue hatchback pulled along the sidewalk.

Steven cleared his throat, quickly standing and dusting off the back of his jeans. "That's my mom," he said under his breath.

Mrs. Mathers waved from the driver's seat, smiling the same infectious smile as her son's. Steven looked down to sidewalk, where Samantha still sat on the ground.

He offered his hand, helping to pull her up beside him. But his dark brown eyes were searching hers, and seemed to have lost a little of their light.

She swallowed. "Steven, I don't think this is going to work—"

But one finger came to hush her, pushing her lips closed before she could say more. "You're confused, I can tell." He searched her eyes, as if trying to read her thoughts. "Don't answer now. Don't answer tomorrow. But when you get all this stuff sorted out in your head"—he cupped the side of her cheek—"call me. I'll be waiting for you."

She closed her eyes, overwhelmed by what was happening. He was right. She was confused, but it wasn't about Steven. Still, she could wait until tomorrow, wait until his mother wasn't around as a witness—because right now she had bigger demons to face.

When she finally stood alone on the curb, after Steven had driven off with his mom in her hatchback, Samantha shoved her hands deep into her pockets and headed for the house. She paused when she caught a glimpse of Tristan by the garage door, a two-liter soda in each hand as he walked into the house.

She held her breath, unable to move a muscle. *Had he seen them? Had he watched them kissing?* Her heart pinched with fear and she stopped at the front step. It had been the briefest of kisses, so much shorter than the one they'd shared in the woods. But if he'd been there for longer than a few minutes…

She bit her lower lip, not allowing herself to think like that, and walked back into the house.

When she entered the great room, her heart instantly eased. Tristan was laughing and joking with his friends, playing pool with Beef, and looked exactly like he had last time she saw him. Relaxed and confident, like he didn't have a care in the world, like he was the brightest star in the sky, and everyone had the privilege of dancing in his light.

She took a seat next to Renee, relieved but still breathless, and took another slice of pizza. The whole ordeal with Steven made her ravenous…and despite still having one conversation left to go, she took a bite of her pizza.

Renee leaned in close and whispered in her ear. "How'd it go?"

Samantha only lifted her shoulders and locked eyes on the television screen. A rerun of *I Love Lucy* caught her attention as she started chewing.

"Did you tell him?"

Samantha shook her head. "No—not yet."

Renee let out a heavy sigh, picked up her paper plate and jumped down from her barstool. "I can't take it anymore. They're too loud, and I have a headache. Are you staying the night?"

Samantha swallowed, knowing her time to procrastinate was coming to an end, and glanced over one shoulder to nod at her best friend. "I think so."

Renee tossed her plate into the metal trash can, adjusted

her blanket, and headed for the stairs "Okay. I'll pick out a movie. Hurry up, okay?"

"Okay."

She took another slice of pizza, adding more to her plate that already held too much. But she wasn't ready. How could she tell Renee about what happened? To tell her she'd kissed her brother, and that she wasn't even sure it would be the last time.

Tristan was still playing pool behind her. Joking with his friends, occasionally laughing, and already she craved his attention. For him to sit beside her, too close, like he had in the woods. She craved more than that though. She wanted to talk to him. To get to know him—the way others never took the time. But all that would have to come later. She swiveled in her chair, ready to jump to the ground and find Renee, but immediately stopped.

Tristan was standing straight across from her. His arms were braced on either side of the pool table, and the brunette who had told him about her keg was standing right in the middle. His lips were lifted in a flirtatious smile, and his hips were pressed against her body, pinning her in place as if staking a claim. He leaned forward until his lips touched the side of her ear.

They were too close. Much too close for it to be innocent, and no excuse Samantha could come up with would explain what he was doing. She'd seen it a thousand times. Tristan standing too close to other girls. Too flirtatious, too—much. Pizza began to climb up her throat, making her nose burn with heartache and humiliation.

She didn't understand it. How could he be one way with her, yet brazenly flirtatious with another woman while she sat less than ten feet away? A tear slipped down her cheek, but she quickly wiped it away, not allowing herself to cry over him.

She finally hopped down from the chair and tossed her

paper plate and the rest of her food in the trash. She felt dizzy, broken, and sick to her stomach—but she somehow made it to the staircase.

Before she allowed herself to climb, she turned around, and found Tristan watching her. His hands were still on either side of the brunette, his hips still pinning her in place. Samantha didn't look away. She needed to see it. To burn the image of him like this in her memory. Because she would never again fall for a guy like Tristan. Not even for a moment in the woods, not even when the timing was so perfect it seemed to come from a fairy tale.

Tristan looked down to the girl held in his arms and smiled. He whispered something in her ear, then picked up his cue stick and began playing pool again, leaving her dazed and smiling. She was the next girl to sit too close to Tristan Montgomery, but that was her problem.

Samantha finally made it to Renee's room, where she crawled into bed beside her best friend and nestled under the covers. The opening credits to *The Notebook* were playing on the large screen, and a box of tissues was front and center in the middle the queen sized bed.

Samantha let the top of her head fall to her best friend's shoulder, fighting back tears that still clogged the back of her throat. "I've decided I'm going to say yes to Steven."

Renee sat up, grabbed the remote, and paused the movie. She turned to Samantha and looked into her eyes, studying her in a way that was all knowing. "Are you sure?"

Samantha squared her shoulders and nodded, because she'd never been surer in her life. Steven was honest and stable, and would wait for her for all eternity. Until just a moment ago, she hadn't realized how important that was. "Yeah, I'm sure."

Renee bit her lower lip, then looked down to the bed. There was no hiding the fact she was disappointed, but when she looked up again, she grabbed Samantha's hands and squeezed them with her fingers. "Is that why you've been acting so weird all day? Because you've been afraid to tell me?"

Samantha looked down to the sheets, knowing that hadn't been the reason at all, but Renee tightened her grip on her hands, forcing her to look back up again.

"Never," Renee began. "Never be afraid to tell me anything again. You're my best friend, and if Steven is the boy who makes you happy, I'm ecstatic for you. Don't ever forget that, okay?"

Renee pulled Samantha into her arms, and the tears she'd been holding for too long landed on her best friend's shoulders.

"Are you okay?" Renee asked, "You're worrying me."

Samantha nodded, plucking a tissue from the box and wiping her nose before sitting back against the headboard. "I'm fine. I must be close to my period or something."

Renee searched her face for another second, as though trying to figure out what this all was about. "Do you still want to watch the movie?"

Samantha looked into her best friend's eyes and nodded, maybe a bit too vigorously. She sank down deep into the pillows. "I want that very much."

Renee un-paused the movie, nestling deep under the covers next to Samantha—but it felt different. There was a secret between them for the first time, one Samantha would never share. There was no reason to anymore. That night on the lake with Tristan, that kiss, was just one mistake, one stupid and vulnerable moment that had the potential to hurt forever. It would never happen again, of that she would make sure.

CHAPTER TEN

PRESENT DAY

IT ONLY TOOK two minutes to get out of the car and find Tristan in the back of the restaurant. He was unmistakable, already swarmed by female servers leaning against the booths beside him. Without saying a word, Samantha slid into the bench across from him and remained quiet. She waited there a moment, until all eyes were focused on her, then leaned across the table and whispered, "You're wrong, my boyfriend *trusts* me. That's why he doesn't care I'm with you."

Two servers raised their brows, as if making the assumption she intended, then took the carafe of coffee and headed for the back room.

Tristan only shrugged, as though slightly amused by her response. "Okay."

"Okay?"

"Yes," he confirmed, grinning.

"That's all you have to say for yourself?"

He laughed, not in a humorous way, but in a way that was

cocky and irritating. "I'm glad he trusts you, Samantha, that's great. But he's a fool."

She narrowed her eyes. "You wouldn't trust me?"

"Not as far as I could throw you."

"Why?" She'd never had anyone say that before, so blatantly and matter-of-factly. She would have screamed had no one else been around to hear.

He opened the menu, dismissing her, then changed his mind and looked up again. "You're only one bad decision away from climbing into my bed. You, and everyone else."

She choked. "You're full of yourself."

"I'm honest."

She grabbed his glass of water and downed it by half, even though what she really wanted to do was throw it in his face. "Maybe that's what you're used to," she said, around large gulps of water. "But that's not me."

He leaned back in his seat and smiled. The one that wrinkled his eyes at the corners, and made her stomach twist with nervousness. "It only takes one moment, Samantha. One twinge of doubt. One single disagreement for someone to cheat." He leaned forward again, bracing his forearms on the table. "He shouldn't trust you. You, or anyone. That's what I'm saying. It's nothing personal."

She leaned in, not intimidated. "You say my boyfriend shouldn't trust me, yet in the same breath say it's nothing personal? Who does that? Who says things like that, expecting someone to not take offense? It *is* personal Tristan. Very personal, and I take great offense to it."

He leaned back in his seat. "Sorry. I didn't mean to offend you."

But he didn't look sincere. Not sincere in the slightest, and she began to shake her head. She picked up the menu to cover her face, needing to get away from him in any way she could. Her blood was heating throughout her entire body. She was so angry she couldn't see straight—and that was something she didn't want him to see. For him to know how much his words had affected her.

This conversation was completely ironic, too. Because not so long ago, this man had taken her first kiss. Not only taken it, but ripped it out from under her like a magic trick. Then not even twenty-four hours later was shoving another girl in her face. Yes, he had made no promises, no verbal commitment that anything would come from it, but no words were needed after a kiss like that. No promise could replace what their bodies had told her.

"I feel bad for you," she said quietly, unable to resist.

"Why?" he answered, amused.

"Because you have no faith."

"It makes things easier."

"How so?" She lowered her menu, having expected him to disagree. But he didn't. He answered in such a nonchalant way that she needed to see him.

He was leaning back in his seat, his arms braced on either side of the booth. "Because—when you don't care, they can't hurt you." He set his napkin on the table, then stood and looked down to the hall. "Now if you'll excuse me, I need to make a phone call."

She watched him walk away, unable to form a response because bile had begun to climb up her throat. The way he said the words was so heartbreaking. As if he knew all too well what hurt felt like. As if he'd experienced it more than once.

He pulled open the back door, took his cell from his back pocket, and began talking. He was still in her line of vision, and she couldn't look away. His expression became angry and intense as he walked around the corner, and then she couldn't see him any longer.

She remembered what Renee said about him having a hard couple of years, and for the first time, she wondered what happened. What could have been so terrible to cause such a jaded view on life? Wondered if the person he was talking to now was the cause of it?

The server came back at that moment, pulling Samantha's attention as she set two plates on the table. Both the same order. A cheese burger and french fries.

"What's this?" Samantha asked, without looking up.

"A burger," the woman replied. "Is that not what you wanted? He said—"

"He ordered me food?" She looked up, slightly out of breath from shock.

"Yes," the server answered, confused.

"Why?" Samantha searched the server's stressed face, then took pity on her and shook her head. "You know what —" She placed her napkin on her lap and decided not to over think it. "It doesn't matter. Thank you, it looks delicious."

The woman nodded, still flustered, then turned to the nearby table and began clearing it.

Samantha had barely touched her fries when Tristan came back inside and immediately started eating. She glanced up at him, a weird feeling tightening in the bottom of her stomach. "Why did you order me food?" she couldn't stop herself from asking.

His eyes met hers, bright blue but distant. "Do you always ask so many questions?"

"Yes." She nodded. "How did you know I'd come inside?"

He lifted his burger to his mouth and took a bite. "Because," he began, "I could tell you were hungry."

She tilted her head to the side, clearly confused.

"Either that or—" But he shook his head, as though deciding not to answer.

"What?" she asked.

"Doesn't matter."

"No. You can't do that. You can't just say something like that and not finish."

He popped a fry into his mouth and grinned. "Why not?"

"Because it's like dangling a carrot in front of a starving person."

He paused with a fry halfway to his mouth, seeming amused. "And you're the starving person?" he asked. But he said it in a hushed tone. One that sent a shiver down her spine.

She swallowed hard, trying without success to recover, but then he pushed his plate to the side, and leaned forward in his seat, as though what he was going to say held great meaning. "What I was going to say was that you looked hungry. Either that, or you haven't been fucked well in a really long time."

Her breath caught in her throat, because she'd never been talked to like that in her life. She looked over her shoulder, to make sure no one had heard him. "My sex life is none of your business," she whispered back.

He leaned back in his seat and took a bite of burger. "You're absolutely right," he said then. "Absolutely."

"I can't believe you just said that."

"You told me to."

"I never thought you'd be so crude."

He shrugged. "I never promised to be a gentleman."

She paused briefly, a fry halfway to her mouth.

He met her eyes, too, as though something had sparked inside him, but then he looked away.

She recovered a second later, stuffing her mouth with a handful of fries to end the conversation. His words had struck a chord. One that was fresher than she thought it would be. Because once upon a time, he *had* promised to be a gentleman. And she had believed in him. For a moment too long.

THE REST of their meal had gone on without much conversation. They ate their food quietly, not even making eye contact until the server brought the bill. Samantha insisted on paying, she didn't have the money to spare; it was simply out of principle that she couldn't let Tristan pay. In the end, he'd slapped down a couple of twenties in the middle of the table and walked out of the restaurant, leaving her with a choice.

A choice to either take the money and pay with her card, hoping to sneak the twenties back into Tristan's wallet without notice. Or swallow down her long resentment for the man who'd taken her first kiss, and let him win. She chose the latter, because in the end, she knew she needed to pick her battles with Tristan. They had a long journey ahead of them, and she had an inkling this wouldn't be the last disagreement they shared.

Back in the Mustang, she climbed into the passenger seat and fetched her ear buds out of her bag. She'd loaded a dozen audiobooks onto her iPod before she'd left, and now she started one of them. One she'd been itching to listen to for months but never had the time. It was a story about a woman returning to her best friend's wedding. Which was ironic considering that was exactly what Samantha was doing. But it comforted her like any good story always had. Giving her the distraction she needed from the man who sat beside her.

Eventually, she took one of her pillows from the back seat and let herself fall asleep, only to wake sometime later, parked in a Motel 6 parking lot.

Tristan handed her a key, and they both went to their separate rooms, where Samantha sat now, the phone to her ear, listening to it ringing as she called her best friend.

"Sam! Thank God it's you, I'm so freaking stressed."

She laughed sleepily into the receiver, so happy to hear Renee's voice, and lay back on the bed. "Now that's a greeting. What's up? Why are you so stressed?"

Her friend let out an audible breath. "I should have never tried to pull off a wedding so close to a show. People are calling me left and right, and there are rehearsals and performances. I feel like I don't have any time to breathe."

Samantha frowned, hating the fact all this was happening so close to the wedding, but at the same time felt helpless. "Is there anything I can do?"

"Nothing. Well, except get here faster."

Samantha closed her eyes, because she wanted nothing more. "I'm working on it. Believe me."

"How's everything with Tristan…? Are you guys getting along?"

"Everything's fiiiine," Samantha said, drawing out the vowels to make the question sound needless. "Why do you ask?"

"I don't know. I talked to him earlier. He was weird. I thought maybe it had something to do with you."

Samantha pulled in a deep breath and picked at her fingernail. She wished she knew what he'd said, but asking that sort of question would only make her sound guilty. So she shook her head, stuffing down the frustration for Renee's benefit. She wouldn't add to her best friend's stress by complaining about Tristan. She didn't have to share what a cocky bastard he was. Not now, anyway. She would save that for later.

"Things are fine, Renee. Better than fine. We're making good time, and I'm mostly listening to audiobooks." Which was true. It was all the times in between that felt like hell.

"Are you sure?"

"Yes, I'm sure."

Renee took a deep breath, as though some huge weight was lifted from her chest. "Okay, good. Where are you guys? How much longer until you get here?"

Samantha's eyes fluttered with exhaustion, but a curve

pulled at her lips as she glanced around the room. "Motel 6. I have no idea where though. I fell asleep."

"Ahh… Well, go to sleep, Sam. It sounds like you need it."

Samantha nodded, agreeing completely. "When I get to NY, let's have a spa day. Just me and you: massages, facials, the works."

Renee sighed. "Sounds like heaven."

"It will be." Samantha let go of the phone, anchoring it in place between her face and the mattress, feeling herself start to doze again. "We should get off the phone and get some sleep. I'll call you tomorrow?"

"Sounds good."

"Night Ren."

"Night Sam."

CHAPTER ELEVEN

PRESENT DAY

BRIGHT, blinding light streamed into Samantha's motel room as she sat on the edge of the bed. It was just past nine in the morning, yet a chill lingered in the room, reminding her they were no longer in California. She wrapped her hoodie around her shoulders and zipped it shut. She was in a bad mood.

Not because of the cold, but because she'd been awake for hours, and they were no closer to their destination. Which left her listening, waiting for any indication he was awake. A floorboard creaking, the sound of running water to indicate a shower had started, but there was nothing. All morning, which left her patience incredibly thin.

She inched to the edge of the bed, trying to ease the stiffness in her neck that had gathered there during sleep. She was anxious to be on the road already, to get this trip over with, and be with Renee, but nothing at all seemed to be helping.

The last two months had been especially hard without her best friend. Yes, there were the daily phone calls, even Face-Time every now and then, but it wasn't the same. She longed for the days they stayed on the couch all day, buried in blankets and sharing a box of tissues as they watched the saddest movies they could find on Netflix.

But the moment Renee had gotten engaged, Samantha's life had changed forever. Because never again would she live under the same roof as Renee, or fight over the last scoop of ice cream in the freezer. It had all changed with one phone call, and she wasn't even given time to prepare.

Air. She needed air.

Having been dressed for over an hour she slipped on her comfortable brown sandals and pushed herself from the bed. Maybe she'd even check out the complimentary breakfast while she was at it.

She flung open the motel door, finding Tristan's Mustang right away, parked just below their joined rooms. Knowing the sight would only make her angry, she ignored it, and gazed out to the bright blue sky and the town she didn't recognize. In her twenty-three years, she'd only traveled out of California a handful of times. She'd always wanted to, but with family close, travel wasn't one of her parent's top priorities.

It was a shame—because there were so many places she wanted to go. So many sights she wanted to see, and now she wasn't sure she'd get the chance.

The wrought iron banister was chipped and worn, but she leaned against it anyway, taking in the empty road below, and the trees covered with tiny buds she was sure would be gorgeously green in a few weeks.

What was stopping her now? Why not travel now? To Paris, where she'd dreamt of going ever since she was little? To see the sculptures, the architecture, and culture that inspired her even to this day.

It didn't take long to come up with an answer: she had no one to go with.

Her best friend had moved across the country, and Steven

was too busy with his career to even consider as an option. The truth was, that at twenty-three, she was nearly tied down to a man she'd known since junior high; and she had only a handful of wild stories to carry with her into the future.

Pushing all the regrets away, she tucked her hands into her oversized hoodie and walked down to the first floor. In the back of her mind, she knew this was her last adventure. She tried to convince herself otherwise, to believe there would be other opportunities, but she knew the truth. Steven would be too busy with his internship for the next few years, and once she got started with her "real" career, there would be no time for her, either. Yes, this was her last hoorah, one she had planned to take with her boyfriend; instead, she was stuck here with Tristan.

She continued past the royal blue doors to the long corridor, taking in the white paint that had a yellow hue that showed its wear. They'd traveled only a day, yet reminders they weren't in California were everywhere. She loved it. She loved the age of the place. The fact it showed its wear without being hidden behind a million layers of paint.

In her hometown, the lowest priced home was over a half million. A three bedroom, two bath modest home. Women got Botox at thirty, and graffiti was covered the second after it was placed. All evidence of age or flaws were brushed under the rug and forgotten about. As if they didn't exist.

To Samantha, it was like erasing history. Laugh lines of happiness and joy or pain that shaped a person to who they were. Painting over this stuff was like sand blasting a Cathedral —criminal. But when she took in a lung full of crisp clean air, she let it all go on an exhale. The money, the perfectionism, the facade of a perfect life. And she took in the refreshing, exhilarating air she couldn't get in Los Angeles. Fresh, somewhat cool, and without even a trace of smog.

She continued into the main office, where the scent of

perfume and dust made her clear her throat. Glancing around the room, she looked for any sign of life, and locked eyes on a little old man sitting at the counter. He wore an oversized brown sweater and wool-lined slippers propped high on the wooden desk. He was fast asleep, peaceful, with deep wrinkles that formed crevices all over his face, and he didn't show any signs of waking up.

Not wanting to disturb him, she carried on down the hall where a propped up sign with red removable letters told her the breakfast menu: bagels, cream cheese, and fresh fruits.

Perfect.

She made it to the bar, where the factory cut pineapple and too ripe bananas were left on the counter. She wrinkled her nose, then moved to the end of the counter and pushed down two bagels into the shiny red toaster.

It was peaceful here. So quiet she could hear herself think. She filled a mug with steaming coffee, sat down at a nearby table, and picked up a discarded copy of the Salt Lake City gazette.

They'd made it to Utah. She smiled at their progress, and some of the tension from her shoulders eased away. Rocking back in her chair, she enjoyed the quiet, and then a moment later, ate her bagel in solitude, while reading the classifieds and snickering about an old woman who owned one-hundred-and-one cats. Attached was a photo, slightly underdeveloped and dark. All you could see was the little woman's white fluffy hair, surrounded by nothing but fur and eyes.

When she was done with her meal, Samantha wrapped up the last bagel in a white paper napkin and filled a brown card-board cup with coffee to bring to Tristan. It was nearly ten now, and if he wasn't awake by now, he would be very soon.

With the bagel tucked into the pocket of her hoodie, she tapped gently on the door to his hotel room.

There was still no movement, no running water, nothing to

indicate he was even awake. She tapped again, heat creeping up her neck, but she took a deep breath and immediately knocked louder. "Tristan, it's me. I brought you breakfast. Open up!"

Nothing.

She looked down to the parking lot, seeing his Mustang still parked below, and knew she was about to lose it. She headed for her own room, placed the breakfast on the nearby table, then rid of every last drop of patience, began pounding on Tristan's door.

"Wake up you lazy bastard! Wake up, or I swear to God I'll beat this door down with my fists."

A large boom sounded from inside the room, and Samantha smiled with satisfaction as she continued to pound. "That's right," she whispered. "Get up you lazy ass—"

But before she could finish her sentence, the door was yanked out from under her. She stumbled forward, barely able to catch her footing, and slammed face first into warm, solid, skin.

She froze, because the glimpse she caught on the way down wasn't one she ever thought she'd see. It was a very large, very bare, and very "Good morning" version of Tristan Montgomery.

"Please tell me you're not naked," she whispered, but it was mostly to herself, because she didn't really need him to answer. She squeezed her eyes shut, took one step backward, and turned around.

They both stood there, quiet and still, and she tried to recover her heart. The sight of Tristan in nothing more than his birthday suit left her feeling dizzy. She'd seen many naked men in her days, though until now, the only one she'd seen in person was Steven. Especially this close up.

"Well?" he finally asked, when she remained silent.

Well? Well… Tristan was much…larger than Steven. Much larger in every way imaginable.

She cleared her throat, knowing her voice would've cracked otherwise. "It's ten in the morning," she answered with more confidence than she felt.

"And?" But his voice was thick and husky, and she could swear he was having as difficult a time recovering as she was.

"It's time to go."

"Is it?"

"Yes," she said, hating how the tone of his voice sent a shiver down her spine. "And you should really put some clothes on. The people of Utah don't want to see…that."

He chuckled, but shifted slightly behind her. "Hate to break it to you sweetheart, but a lot of people want to see *that*."

She cringed, because she knew it was true. Like in high school, she knew women lined up to catch the barest glimpse of Tristan.

He moved quietly behind her, his steps so soft you'd never know they came from a man of his size. "You can turn around now."

She raked her teeth over her bottom lip, taking the very corner and chewing it before turning to face him. He still had no shirt on, his feet were bare, but he wore a pair of old gray sweats resting so low on his hips you could tell he wasn't wearing anything underneath.

"Aren't you freezing?" she asked, feeling a shiver run through her own body.

"No," he said, leaning against the doorway and crossing his feet at the ankles. A tiny grin teased at the corner of his mouth, and she knew he was having too much fun at her expense.

She turned toward the Mustang, not attempting to hide her irritation. "I brought you breakfast," she said quickly.

"That's nice of you."

"It's not nice. Just my way of getting your lazy ass out of bed."

He threw his head back with laughter. "Are you always this pleasant in the morning?"

Pressing her lips together, she wasn't about to let him pull her into another argument. "We need to go," she said, turning on her heels and opening the door to her room.

She walked inside, hoping the action would give him the hint to do the same. "I'll have your breakfast waiting for you in the car." But before she closed the door, she could swear she caught him smiling.

"My God." she whispered, resting her forehead against the wall, taking in all the air she'd forgotten to take over the last two minutes. "Three more days. Just three more days of Tristan Montgomery." She repeated the last words over and over, gathered up the rest of her belongings, and headed for the car.

CHAPTER TWELVE

PRESENT DAY

SAMANTHA THREW her oversized pillow to the back of the Mustang, as visions of Tristan standing in the doorway still clouded her mind. It had been over ten minutes, but she could still see each detail of his perfect body. She remembered all of it—his abs, his arms. Though they were larger now, and a scar ran across his right shoulder that hadn't been there before. For some reason that fact bothered her. She wasn't sure exactly why—maybe because she wasn't sure how he got it, but it left her with a weird feeling in her gut.

She'd spent most of her adolescence with the Montgomerys, which meant she also spent a lot of time with Tristan, whose life goal was to see how many hours he could spend of it shirtless. She'd become accustomed quickly, or as quickly one could with a half-naked Adonis lounging around by the pool—but a three-inch long scar was something she was sure she wouldn't have missed.

Climbing into the front seat of the Mustang, she told herself it shouldn't matter—but for some reason it did. What had happened? Was that why he'd left Texas U? Mostly, she wondered why Renee had never mentioned it.

She shook her head and lounged back in her seat, knowing she was telling herself lies. She knew the reason… Because she was an asshole, that's why. An asshole friend who'd kissed her best friend's brother, then never wanted to hear about him again. Whenever Renee would bring him up, Samantha would quickly turn the subject to something else. Renee was smart and caught on quickly—and stopped bringing him up altogether.

Feeling a little bit shitty, Samantha leaned forward once again and set Tristan's now cold coffee in the center console. The fact she'd been so shaken by him frustrated her. Yes, he was a beautiful man, and yes, he had been naked right there in front of her. But she was a twenty-three year old woman. And an erect penis was something she'd seen at least a thousand times… But this was Tristan. And for some reason, the sight of him made her feel like she was sixteen all over again.

She squeezed her eyes shut, determined to shed the memory from her thoughts and move on. This was natural, right? It was biological. Not a reaction to Tristan himself, but rather a man-woman sort of thing. She set the bagel on the dashboard, found her freshly charged iPod at the bottom of her bag, and began loading up her next audiobook. But when she looked up, she couldn't help but notice the stark black arrow pointing directly to the red E on the gas gauge. They were out of gas.

"Great. Just great." She pulled in a calming breath, grabbed the balled up molding clay from the bottom of her purse, and began needing it with her fingers. She kept it around for moments like this. When her blood was heated, and she needed a way to calm down. The smooth, hard texture immediately eased her mind, and she glanced across the street to look for a gas station. They were already behind schedule, and now they had yet another delay. Yes, it was only to get gas, but Goddammit, they were never going to get out of Utah. Then right on cue, Tristan appeared on the balcony. He was dressed simply, wearing weathered jeans, a plain t-shirt with a hoodie over the top—but now she knew what lay underneath, and for some reason that changed everything. It sent a wave of guilt through her chest, and left her with an overwhelming urge to call Steven.

Her fingers began to knead more quickly and she suddenly felt guilty—because she shouldn't be obsessing over a man like Tristan when she had Steven waiting for her at home.

But as Tristan came down the steps, she couldn't look away. He was rugged, and big, and he looked both dangerous and inviting at the same time.

He threw his backpack over his shoulder, took one step and stretched his arms overhead—which only added to her bad mood. Because he seemed calm, collected, rested, as if he had all the time in the world.

And looked just as sexy with clothes on as he did naked. Goddammit!

He walked down the rest of the way, his white t-shirt showing off how remarkably tan his skin was, and flung his backpack to the back seat with her pillow. The roughened up leather bag landing directly onto of the soft white cotton pillowcase, where the vast contrast in materials made her shiver. It was a much needed reminder of how different they were. About how right she was to walk away all those years ago. He was rough and ready Tristan Montgomery. She was Samantha Smiles, the girl who needed to pull her shit together and stop day dreaming!

Next she knew, the driver's side door flung open, and he climbed into the car beside her. He took a large gulp of coffee and fastened his seat belt before glancing over at her. "Ready to go?"

Samantha licked her lips, knowing right well that coffee was frigid. Yet he hadn't even winced at the temperature. He didn't complain at all, which she wasn't used to at all. Steven always complained about things like that. Always. Steven always wanted things perfect.

"We need gas," she stated all at once, turning in her seat to fasten her own seat belt. "I think there's a station just across the street."

He put the car in reverse, glancing in the rearview mirror before backing up. He grabbed his bagel from the dashboard, and ripped off a healthy chunk with his teeth before answering. "We don't need gas," he replied with a mouth full of bagel. He threw the car into gear, then pulled out to the open road. "I filled up yesterday."

She glanced over at him, as calmly as she could, faced with such arrogance, and tapped on the glass of the odometer with her fingernail. "See that red line there? Right next to the E? This says otherwise."

He laughed under his breath and took another bite. "It's broken."

She leaned way back in her seat, far enough to get a good look at him and squeezed the ball of clay in her palm. "You're lying."

His mouth only lifted slightly, but his eyes remained fixed on the road ahead. "I don't lie." But he said the words as fact, as though he was talking about so much more than gas. He leaned over in his seat, practically in her lap, so close she could smell the soap on his skin. He pulled out a small brown bag from the glove box and handed it over. "See for yourself."

She grabbed hold of the sack, slightly out of breath from the brief touch, but somehow pulled out the contents and laid them on her lap. There was a small, crumpled up white receipt, and a pack of winter-mint gum. That was it. But her eyes instantly closed as a rush of memory washed over her body…because she was suddenly reminded of their kiss. About his breath on her face, and the delicate scent of winter-mint gum that would forever give her chills.

"I filled up last night," he said. "While you were sleeping."

She looked down at the receipt, finding the faded black writing revealing his truth.

12.3 gallons, supreme unleaded, $32.87

She shoved the receipt back in the bag and set it down between them. "This does nothing to comfort me."

He only shrugged, but didn't explain further.

"You're telling me we're driving three thousand miles in a car that has a broken gas gauge?"

His shoulders lifted once, but he continued to focus straight ahead. "I've gotten us this far, haven't I?"

She turned in her seat, shoving the clay back in her bag, and taking out her iPod to load her next audio book. "That is such an asshole thing to say."

He almost choked on his coffee, which for some reason caused her lips to involuntary curve in a smile.

"You're right, I am an asshole."

His response was so unexpected, her grin instantly widened, but she tried to force it away. She wasn't sure what she found so amusing. Maybe it was the fact she'd called him an asshole and all he did was agree, or maybe it was because it felt good to do something crazy—like drive cross country in a car with no gas meter. She glanced over at him one last time, eyes narrowed, but really looking at him, and seeing to her dismay the boy she'd met all those years ago by the lake. "Well I'm glad we can finally agree on something."

He choked back a laugh, covered his mouth as if trying to hold it in, but he couldn't. A deep boisterous sound exploded out of him surprising them both. But he didn't seem to be laughing at her, or even so much the gas meter. She wasn't sure exactly what he was laughing at, but the sound was so genuine she found herself biting her lip to hold in a giggle of her own. He looked like a little kid. A giddy little boy who had had way too much sugar, and the sound was so contagious, soon she couldn't help but laugh too. Their laughter grew, one feeding off the other until they were both struggling to breathe. It was the gut gripping kind of laugher that made her stomach hurt, one she hadn't experienced in as long as she could remember. Laughing with Tristan made her feel free, like a twenty-three year old woman should feel… and that wasn't a bad feeling at all.

IT WAS HOURS LATER, after the "Welcome to Colorado" sign had come and gone, that Tristan glanced over at her. Her feet were curled under her bottom, her head resting on the pillow she'd wedged between her door and body, trying to find comfort. She froze. It wasn't the first time he'd done it either. Actually, he'd been doing it ever since they left the motel. Just looking, without saying a word, and it was driving her crazy. She'd already started her book three times because she couldn't concentrate. What was he looking at? Why was he paying her any attention at all? The questions kept coming, and finally she gave up.

Only yesterday, this arrangement had worked perfectly. She was able to listen to her audiobooks, and he the radio, as though they were in completely different worlds. But something had changed. Somewhere between her going to bed last night, and getting up this morning. She couldn't stop her mind from flicking back the motel, to her cheek pressed against his skin, and his completely nude body millimeters from her own.

"Soo…" he said, making her spine tingle all the way to her toes. "What have you been up to these past few years?"

She lowered her blanket, trying to pretend the fact that he

was trying to engage her in conversation didn't surprise the hell out of her. She removed the ear buds from her ears and paused her book. "School. Work. That kind of thing." She pushed her hair back behind her ears and sat up.

"Where to?"

She took a deep breath and shoved her iPod back in her bag, reluctantly thankful for something else to do. "I graduated from Laverne University last summer."

His brows rose. "And work?"

"I work at a bar." She cleared her throat, almost embarrassed by the answer. "And you?"

He took a good minute, and Samantha turned back around to see if he'd heard the question. "How about you?" she repeated, but her eyes drifted down to his shoulder, where she knew the scar lay just under his clothes.

"I run my own business," he finally stated.

"Doing?"

"Cleaning pools."

She pressed her lips together and looked up to see if he was joking. "You're a pool boy?"

He glanced over again, clearly not finding the humor in the question. "Yes."

"Oh," she whispered, but she was mentally kicking herself for being an ass. She couldn't help it! Not really. All she kept thinking about was that movie with David Duchovny as a pizza boy. Where the word "anchovies" indicated an order for sex.

She turned to study his profile, noticing he hadn't shaved since yesterday. "So you're a pool boy. What happened to football?" A lump formed in her stomach, but she had to ask the question. It had been bothering her all day. Killing her that she didn't already know the answer.

The Mustang lurched forward, and she gripped the bottom of her seat.

"I got hurt," he answered. It was curt and to the point, and so much different from the open demeanor he used when talking about anything else.

She took a quick breath, because the confirmation made her heart hurt a little. "Oh..." she said. She wanted to ask more. To ask how it happened, to ask if his injury still bothered him. Because she knew all too well what it felt like to have a dream yanked from under you like that. But she adjusted in her seat instead, deciding it was much too personal a question to ask. "How did you get into your line of work?"

His shoulders visibly relaxed, as if he'd been anticipating something different. He opened the pack of gum between them and slid a piece from its sleeve before folding it in half and popping it into his mouth. "A year ago I was hanging out at a bar." He cleared his throat, raising his brows an inch as though indicating he knew this wasn't a surprise to her. "Some lady was complaining about her husband and their disgusting green pool. It all started from there."

She smiled, the scent of winter-mint gum making her shiver. "Go on."

"Well, people started joking around. And someone mentioned she should get a pool boy—one who was good looking enough to make her husband jealous. Some guy mentioned my name." He fanned over his body sarcastically. "One thing led to another, and what started as a joke, quickly became my new career."

She raised her brows and turned to look out the window. "Oh."

"What?" he asked, obviously confused by her answer.

She bit her bottom lip, hating the fact that she showed everything on her face.

"You better tell me or I'll assume the worst," he muttered.

She squeezed her eyes shut, took a stick of gum and popped it into her mouth. "Fine. I just realized that's why you're so tan."

He laughed. Something she hadn't heard in a long time. But then he went sober, so much so she turned to see his expression. He wore the barest grin at the corner of his mouth, and he had a sultry look about him that made her heart skip a beat.

"Glad to hear you've been paying attention, Samantha."

She hit his chest, not hard, but in a way that was playful. "Oh stop it." She laughed. She adjusted in her seat, dragging her feet up to her lap to sit crisscross. "So you're saying there's no sex involved?"

His chest began to shake again, and he shot her a "What the hell are you talking about?" expression. "No, there's no sex. I don't know what kind of pool boy you have, but I hope you tip him well."

She immediately blushed, then started laughing too. "Haven't you seen that movie? About the pizza boy? And anchovies…"

Her words trailed off, and she shook her head feeling embarrassed. But he must have taken pity, because he immediately started talking again. "Actually," he said, cupping his hand over his face, trying to mask his laughter, "I don't even clean pools anymore. I have a crew under me, so only when they're sick do I go out on the field—which is why I'm able to be here with you. The tan is because I like to surf. Most of my job is paperwork, which surprisingly isn't sexy at all."

She played with the paper wrapper between her fingers, grinning at the fact he was trying to make her feel better, and glanced down to her lap. "You'd be surprised."

"By what?" He turned to look at her. "You think paperwork is sexy?"

"I don't know…" She lifted her shoulders. "A man with brains…it's not a bad thing."

He only grinned, as though some unspoken understanding had transpired between them. A small bud of tolerance had blossomed. It was tiny, and would likely blow away with a gentle breeze, but for that moment, she decided he wasn't as bad as she'd thought. Maybe she could do this. It was only for a few more days, after all.

Six years earlier

SAMANTHA LAY on Renee's bed, her head hanging over the side, causing her long blond hair to cascade to the floor. It was after school on the last day before fall break, and they'd both ditched, intending to find something better to do. But it was almost dinnertime, and they were still here, in Renee's upstairs room, doing nothing.

Renee stood in front of her closet mirrors, where she'd been practicing her turns for the last hour. She'd been chosen for the part of the Sugar Plum Fairy in the upcoming performance of the Nutcracker, and scouts were coming all the way from New York to watch her. She was nervous, but Samantha had no doubt she'd do great. Renee was the most graceful person Samantha had ever seen in her life. She was strong, athletic, and moved so easily it was as though it took no effort at all. Just like all the rest of the Montgomerys. Physically fit, totally beautiful, and kind... All except Tristan.

"Where's Steven?" Renee asked, pulling Samantha's attention back to the mirrors. Renee was standing up on her toes, going up and down in releve so quickly it almost made Samantha sick.

She pulled herself up to sit, then stretched her oversized sweater over her knees. "Palm Springs," she answered. "He's playing golf with his grandparents."

Renee prepped for another turn, then pushed off before answering. "Fun," she said sarcastically.

Samantha shrugged. "Yeah, well he's probably having more fun than we are at the moment." She paused to look in the mirror, pushed herself off the bed and grabbed her phone from the nightstand. She walked across the room googling the number for Vincenzo's before turning around. "I'm hungry. Do you want to order pizza—" But before she could finish the question, the sound of Mrs. Montgomery's scream caused the hair on the back of her neck to rise.

"What the heck?" Renee yelled. She flung open her bedroom door and ran down the stairs, Samantha on her heels, running down after her friend. Her stomach felt like cement, her heart hammering in her chest.

They stopped in their tracks at the entrance to the kitchen. Renee's mom was still screaming, though now it was mixed with laughter and squeals—because Tristan Montgomery held her in his arms and was spinning her in circles.

"Tristan Montgomery! You put me down right this instant! I mean it!" She hit him on the shoulder with her oven mitt, and he finally lowered her to the ground. His smile was so wide it was almost infectious. She quickly pulled him to her chest, throwing her arms around his neck and gripping him so hard you'd think he'd come back from the dead. "I wasn't expecting you until tomorrow," she whispered. Her voice thick with emotion. "I thought you had a game tonight?"

He grinned, then stepped backward and pointed to his walking boot. "I got an early ticket."

Mrs. Montgomery covered her mouth, pulling in a quick gasp before meeting his eyes again. "Tristan! What happened?"

He only shrugged, then hobbled over to lean against the counter. "It's football, Ma. These things happen."

It was odd being witness to this interaction. Because in all the time she'd spent with the Montgomerys, Samantha had never seen Mrs. M so emotional. She wasn't crying, but she looked as though she was trying hard not to. Tristan had been hurt like this so many times it was impossible to keep track of. From the look on Mrs. M's face. It was as though it had happened for the first time. Even from ten feet away, being there, watching this reunion between mother and son felt like an invasion of privacy. Witnessing a special bond that was only theirs to hold... But she couldn't make herself look away.

Mrs. Montgomery turned toward Renee and Samantha, who had gone unnoticed until this point, and pointed to Tristan's leg. "And *this* is why I've always preferred ballet."

They all laughed, except for Samantha, because she was still in shock. This was her first time seeing Tristan in months, and for some reason, he looked different. The sight of him caused an ache in her chest to burn so painfully it was as though it had never stopped. She told herself it was because she was still angry, but it was an anger she'd never felt before. It made her chest tight and her stomach clench as though she was going to throw up.

He turned to her, watching her as though he'd lost something in her face. Searching her eyes, without the barest apology. It was odd. She'd looked people in the eye before, but never once had she felt so naked. Because he seemed to look deeper than everyone else, everyone combined, and she turned away, sure everyone could read their history on her face. But Tristan carried on as though none of what she'd experienced affected him at all.

"Sis," he said, resting his back on the counter.

Renee grinned, then pushed off her spot in the doorway and walked toward him. "Can't you walk into a room like a normal person? Do you always have to cause such a scene?"

He grinned and came toward her, hobbling forward before pulling her into a hug. "Normal's overrated," he stated. He threw his arm over her shoulder and looked toward Samantha.

She tried to keep herself under control, taking deep breaths and smoothing her hair behind her ears. Renee told him about her upcoming performance. About the scouts, and New York, and her big role in *The Nutcracker*. There was actually a smile in her voice as she spoke to him, as though she had missed him as much as her mom did. And Tristan—he listened to all of it. Saying how proud he was, how he'd come back to watch her no matter what the cost.

He told them all about his injury, about it being one of the many trade-offs for being the quarterback of a team. But when the conversation dwindled, he leaned against the counter and glanced between Samantha and Renee. "Any parties tonight?" he asked.

It was the first he'd spoken to her since he'd gotten there, and for some reason she couldn't answer. Cotton had filled her throat, making it impossible to speak. Renee eyed her with an odd expression, then elbowed Tristan in the rips. "Like I want my big brother tagging along with me," she scoffed.

He only laughed, as if her elbow had gone unnoticed—but then he moved toward her, like a cat about to pounce. "Oh yeah?" he asked. "You don't want your big brother tagging along?" He took her head under his arm and started rubbing his knuckles back and forth against her skull. "What's the big secret, Nay? What are you doing that you don't want your brother seeing?"

"Tristan!" She screamed, punching in him the gut while laughing at the same time. They circled each other, gripped together in some sort of double headlock move, until Mrs. Montgomery finally had enough.

"Tristan, let her go!" she shouted.

But Samantha only stood there, watching her best friend play fight with her big brother—in a way she'd never seen before.

They both finally stopped, pulling quickly apart, though Tristan had to ruffle Renee's hair before letting her go. "Good to know you can defend yourself, sis." He laughed.

"Good to see college hasn't made you grow up."

He winked at her, grinning ear to ear. "Never."

Renee's mom leaned against the counter, watching her two almost grown children banter like politicians, but there were tears in her eyes. "You kids aren't going anywhere tonight!" she stated. "I just got you back, and we're going out to dinner to celebrate. Now go get ready!" she ordered. "Your dad's working late again; you kids aren't leaving me alone."

She turned to Samantha, her voice softening a bit more. "Call your parents, dear. See if you can join us."

Samantha only shook her head, tucked her hair behind her ear, and looked down to her feet. "No, I really couldn't—I don't want to intrude."

"Nonsense, dear." Mrs. Montgomery said, then picked up the phone and started dialing. "I'll call them. You go get ready."

Samantha swallowed, unable to look Tristan in the eyes as she passed him in the hall. She followed Renee up the stairs, her back straight as she started climbing. She told herself not to look back, even though she desperately wanted to. To see if he was watching her. To see if five months without seeing her was enough to erase their past. To erase the one night she thought about daily. And she didn't stop until she entered Renee's room and closed the door, realizing that for some reason, her heart hurt worse seeing him now than it had the night they came home from the lake.

CHAPTER THIRTEEN

PRESENT DAY

BY THE TIME they stopped at their next hotel, they'd been on the road for thirteen hours straight. She could hardly see, hardly walk, and Tristan looked much the same.

Like before, they went to their separate rooms right next door to one another, where Samantha sent a text to check in with Steven, then took a shower and laid out her things for the next morning.

She was about to climb into bed when a soft tap at her motel door made her heart lurch to her throat. She thought about ignoring it, but it came again, followed by Tristan's deep voice. "Samantha, it's me. Are you still awake?"

She hadn't turned out the lights yet, so pretending she was already asleep was out of the question. She climbed out of bed, straightened her large t-shirt over her breasts, and opened the door. "Did you need something?" she asked.

He was wearing the same gray sweats he had on that morning, though now he wore a tank top, cut low on the sides to reveal his arms. He was gripping his skull so hard it looked painful, as he tilted his head in apology. "Sorry to bother you, but I have one hell of a headache. I was wondering if you had any aspirin?"

He looked so pathetic, she immediately opened the door wider, gesturing for him to come inside. "Yeah, I think I do, let me go check."

He walked in and closed the door behind him, where she waved him toward the bed and told him to sit down.

"How long have you had it?" she asked, digging through her toiletry bag, looking for anything that would help.

"A few hours...though it keeps getting worse."

She paused holding a small bottle of lotion, realizing she'd been sitting beside him in the car and hadn't noticed. He'd been suffering silently and hadn't said anything. She found a small bottle of Motrin in the bottom of her makeup bag, filled a glass with water, and brought them over to him.

"Here, take this," she said, placing two pills in his hand and waiting for him to take the water.

He placed them on his tongue, threw his head back, and finished the whole glass. But he didn't move, only sat there, his eyes still closed as though he was in immense pain.

She sat down on the bed beside him, feeling helpless and not knowing what else to do.

He cupped his forehead as though willing it to stop pounding. "Sorry to bombard you like this. I'll leave in a second——"

"Stay as long as you need," she interrupted. Her voice nervous—even to her own ears, but he didn't seem to notice. He just sat there with his eyes closed, and eventually the crease in his forehead began to soften.

The sight of it made her relax. Why seeing him in pain bothered her so much she wasn't sure, but she was anxious for him to start feeling better. She glanced down at the quilted bedspread, finding a loose thread and began wrapping it around her finger. "Honestly, I'm surprised by how *not* tired I am," she muttered. Which was the truth. She'd been exhausted just the moment before, but now she had adrenaline pumping through her veins.

He grinned a little, the action softening his features and making her smile. He nodded then, tilting his head a little to the side. "Thank you."

"For what?" She asked.

"This."

He didn't elaborate, and she didn't ask him to. She looked up again, finding his eyes still closed, and a couple day's worth of stubble on his cheeks. Though now his hair was damp, and she knew he must have taken a shower. She couldn't pull her eyes away. They drifted over his perfect arms, to the scar on his right shoulder, where she could see it much better than she had the night before. The room was so quiet you could hear crickets chirping in the background, even the wind whistling softly outside. It was so relaxing she couldn't keep her mind from wandering—to the night Renee and her family had left on a sudden road trip to visit Tristan. It was three years ago, yet the scar was so pink it almost looked fresh.

When she looked up again, Tristan's eyes were on hers. She bit her inner cheek and turned in the opposite direction. "Sorry, I just don't remember you having that scar last time I saw you."

"That's okay," he said, and she turned once again to face him. His hand was now on his shoulder, cupping the scar in his palm.

"Does it still hurt?"

He shook his head, "Nah. Not really."

She pulled her leg up to the bed and began playing with the thread again. "How did it happen?" She was surprised she wanted to know so badly. Surprised that after all these years, she'd healed enough to care.

"Let's see…" He looked up to the ceiling, as if thinking about the memory. "It was the end of fall semester my junior year. We were on the road in Colorado and it was raining. I remember calling the play, lining up on the field, calling for the snap of the ball, and that's about it. The next thing I remember was waking up in the dark hospital room. My arm was in some kind of traction device, and I had tubes coming out of everywhere."

He glanced over at her and shrugged. "That was the last time I played for Texas U. I lost my scholarship, had to start over."

Her brow furrowed, and she glanced down to his shoulder again, but now her chest was tight, and she had to clear her throat to hold back tears. "How did you manage? Having something you loved ripped away from you like that?"

He met her eyes, almost as though the question shocked him. "It was easier for me than it was for my dad, let's put it that way."

She closed her eyes briefly, because his answer hit way too close to home. Tristan was the pride and joy of his father… just as she was for her parents, being the only child. Personal failures felt much less personal, and so much heavier because of letting them down. She swallowed back emotion but nodded.

They were both quite a good while, before he glanced down at her iPod that lay in the middle of the bed. He hesitated for only a moment before picking it up and turning toward her. "What are you listening to?"

It was the first time he'd shown any interest in her books, and she pulled in a deep sigh before answering. "Nothing you'd be interested in."

"Try me."

She plucked the iPod from his hand and placed it on the nightstand. "The Princess Bride."

A grin teased at his lips. "A fairy tale."

"And what's wrong with that?"

"Nothing, I like fairy tales."

She grinned. "Oh yeah, what's your favorite?"

He leaned back on his elbows and looked up the the ceiling. "Hmmm…I would have to say, Beauty and the Beast."

"Really?" She bit her lower lip and wrinkled her nose with disbelief.

"Yeah, it's relatable."

"Why, because you're the beauty?"

He frowned, shaking his head as he rose to his feet. He handed her the empty glass. "The opposite actually."

She tilted her head, but remained quiet.

He turned toward the door, before she could recover enough to respond, but glanced back over his shoulder, almost as an afterthought. "Thank you for the Motrin. I feel much better."

She stood up, realizing she didn't really want him to go. But she followed him to the door, where he quickly exited, but turned one last time around.

"See you in the morning, Samantha."

She nodded, leaning her head against the doorframe. "See ya."

It was past four in the afternoon when they stopped for gas in Chippewa, Nebraska. The weather was cold and foggy, but a small cafe was just across the road, promising the best split pea soup in town. Samantha climbed out of the Mustang, trying to shake the tingles from her legs where they'd fallen asleep, but it wasn't quite working. She found herself holding onto the side of the car to catch her balance.

Even though she still had enough snacks to keep a small football team satisfied for a weekend, she was excited for the excuse to get out of the car for a while. To warm her body from the inside out with a hot cup of soup.

Tristan got out of the car and stretched his arms above his head—which lifted his hoodie just enough to make his stomach visible. "I'll fill up," he yawned. "Why don't you go get us a table?"

Samantha raised her eyes, hoping he hadn't caught her staring. "Yeah, I was thinking the same thing." She grabbed hold of her bag from the front seat, then proceeded to limp-walk on pins and needles across the street.

They'd been on the road for over six hours. Six hours of talking about nothing—and about all the things that had been going on in their lives over the past few years. She never thought she'd have five words to say to Tristan after their night together, yet talking to him now came remarkably easy. He listened, which surprised her. Really listened, in a way that reminded her of Renee. She liked that. Liked how he made what she was saying important enough to pay attention to.

She pushed open the door to the cafe, where a large chalk-board told her to seat herself. A glance around the restaurant revealed a bar with classic red and chrome bar stools, and booths that had mini jukeboxes in the middle of each one.

Opting for a booth, she settled herself into the closest one that had a nice view of the street. A server pushed through the double doors a moment later and came over to say hello. Her hair was red, done up in a style that reminded Samantha of *I Love Lucy*, and her pink pinafore only added to the ensemble. She was young and pretty though, and had a sweetness about her that made Samantha smile.

"Howdy," the girl said, as she leaned against the booth. "Welcome to Peggy's Cafe. Best split pea soup in Chippewa."

Samantha smiled, knowing this was the only restaurant *in* Chippewa, but she kept that bit of info to herself. "Thank you. It's nice to be off the road and stretching my legs for a bit."

The server grinned, set two menus on the table and tilted her head. "I'm guessing you folks aren't from 'round here."

Samantha opened her menu, perplexed by the fact the server knew she wasn't alone and glanced over all the full color images of sandwiches, soups and salads. "California," she answered.

"Ooooh… I've been there once. To Malibu. I'd give my right tit just to go back for a weekend and get out of this cold." She sighed and took her tablet from the pocket. "Where y'all headed? You and that hot piece of somethin' you have 'cross the street."

Samantha glanced out the window, slightly shocked by the girl's choice of words, and found Tristan in the parking lot. He was the only person she could have been talking about, and Samantha nearly choked at the realization. "Are you talking about Tristan?" she asked, turning quickly around.

"Well I ain't talkin' 'bout Jesus, sweetheart. 'Course I'm talking about him, though I have to admit, I am right jealous."

"Oh. Well, no need to be jealous. He's not mine." She adjusted in her seat then glanced back at the menu. "We're only driving together."

"Bullshit." The server coughed, then sat quickly in the seat across from her. "I mean, I don't mean to pry—and my lady bits just tingled at the possibility of him being single, but no man looks at a woman like *that*, without somethin' goin' on."

Samantha followed the girl's line of vision, and found Tristan standing at the gas pump, filling the Mustang with fuel —and looking directly at her.

She turned away.

"See." The girl laughed. But her eyebrows rose as though she'd proven her point.

Samantha shook her head, resisting the urge to look again. "What kind of cheese do you use on your sandwiches?" she asked instead, hoping the change in subject wouldn't go unnoticed.

"Wisconsin cheddar," the server answered quickly, without skipping a beat. "So what's your story? If he's not yours, why are you driving alone together all the way from Cali?"

Samantha cleared her throat, tempted to call the manager and complain about this nosey server, but for some reason she felt the need to set her straight. "My best friend is getting married," she stated. "That hot piece of something is her brother."

The girl raised her brows in an all-knowing sort of way and laughed. "Well shoot! This trip gets juicier and juicer."

Samantha slapping the menu down to the table. "No. It's not like that. I have a boyfriend."

"Ho-le-shit!" the girl called. "And he let you drive cross country with *him?*"

Samantha frowned. "He trusts me."

The server scoffed. "Trust only takes you so far—"

Samantha had enough. She looked the server dead in the eye, taking a deep breath before speaking. "Can we have two coffees please? With cream?"

The girl must have taken the hint, because she cleared her throat, narrowing her eyes as she stood from the table. She straightened her pinafore, picked up her tablet from where she had laid it on the table, then scribbled down a few notes. "Anything else?" she asked begrudgingly.

"No," Samantha uttered. "That will be all."

But as soon as the server walked through the double doors to the back room, Samantha found herself looking for Tristan again through the window. He was still standing at the pump talking on the phone, his other hand in his pocket, and his eyes were locked right on her. He waved, sending goose bumps and tingles loose throughout her entire body. She glanced back at the menu again, realizing she hadn't felt this way in six years. Not since she was sixteen years old, and she sat too close to her best friend's brother.

God save her soul.

CHAPTER FOURTEEN

Familiar faces filled the downstairs great room in the Montgomerys' home. Just like they had nearly every other weekend before Tristan went off to college. It was like a reunion of sorts. The past year's senior football team, now mixed with new faces. Some from Samantha's class, and some the year ahead, all laughing, and flirting, and messing around.

Samantha sat at the bar with Renee and a boy from their biology class. But all she could think about was how Tristan had stared at her all throughout dinner. Not really stared, but she caught him looking a time or two. When she was buttering her roll, she caught him. And again, when she'd glanced up to look for the saltshaker. Honestly, it sent tiny butterflies loose all throughout her belly. But at the same time, it made her think about their kiss. The kiss she still hadn't told Renee about.

The kiss that had the potential to ruin their friendship.

She tried to push the thoughts away, but the more time she spent, the more it became impossible. In fact, she found herself watching him now. Witnessing the cocky grin as he passed one of his teammates and headed for the garage.

Her heart began to thud in her chest. Because now was her chance. To talk to him. To make sure everything was cool, so he would never say anything to Renee. As she swiveled in her chair, her heart felt like it was about to explode, but she stood up and pushed through the crowd of people as quickly as she could. She raked her teeth over her bottom lip, heading for the hall with sweaty hands. She wiped them over her jeans, then reached for the garage door. It came swinging toward her, nearly knocking her flat. She stumbled backward, almost knocking against the wall behind her, but Tristan caught her by the wrist. He yanked her forward, his other hand catching her at the waist to hold her steady—and his bright blue eyes bore into hers.

Her heart stopped beating.

Not because of the fear of a fall, or because they were alone for the first time since their kiss. It was because of the way he held her. His hand touching the sliver of skin between her shirt and jeans. His fingers wrapped around her wrist, so large in comparison to her own. It was almost as if they were dancing.

She licked her lips, knowing she should pull away, but she couldn't. By now, she was more experienced than she had been last summer. Having been kissed and touched more times than she could count...but it was different with Tristan. She couldn't help but notice that. Like a sort of electric current pulsing under her skin and making all her senses wake up. She didn't want it to end. She craved it. Like a drug so addictive it scared the crap out of her.

She opened her mouth to speak, to say what she came to say, but all the words were stuck at the back of her throat. It was as though her body was holding them captive, knowing that if it let them out, this moment would end. So she stood there, the silence almost like a bandage, clouding the memory of him pressing that girl against the table. Healing all the hurts she'd denied for so long.

Someone called her name from afar, and she looked up in time to see Steven round the corner from the living room.

"Oh hey," he said. But his expression instantly changed. From happy to surprised, then confused.

Samantha stepped away, tucking her hair behind her ear with nervous fingers. "I um—was just going to get a drink," she gestured a hand to Tristan, knocking into one of Mrs. Montgomery's vases on the table. She paused to take a breath, straightening the vase before it fell, thankful for the excuse to look at anything beside the two men in front of her.

"You remember Renee's brother?" Samantha asked, after too much silence. "He's visiting from college."

Steven held out his hand to Tristan, completely oblivious and composed—as though he hadn't been witness to their compromising position a moment earlier. "Steven Mathers," he said. "Samantha's boyfriend." They shook hands, then Steven looked down to Tristan's walking boot and frowned. "I think I remember you from West Valley. Quarterback, right?"

Tristan glanced over at Samantha, but only for a second. "Yeah, I think I remember you."

Steven nodded, backing away, and grabbed hold of Samantha's hand. Not hard, but in a way that showed possession. "You're visiting?" he asked, drawing out the last word with a note of suspicion.

"Yep. Just for the weekend."

Samantha searched for something to say, anything at all that would make things any less awkward, but she couldn't think of anything. Because all she could think about was how a brief touch from Tristan had sent heat through her whole body, but now, holding Steven's hand, all she felt was the slight perspiration that glued their hands together.

Steven carried on about his grandparents, and how everyone had fallen asleep while watching *Downton Abbey*. Tristan listened to every word. Laughing at the appropriate times, even nodding and commenting when appropriate, but he never looked at Samantha again.

She grew increasingly nervous, because she had found herself standing beside the only two men she'd ever kissed. But only one knew about the other, and she was determined to keep it that way. Finally, she glanced up and realized too late that she'd been blocking Tristan's exit.

She moved out of the way, stumbling over a lame apology as Tristan hobbled his way down the hall to join his friends. But before he left, he flashed Steven one of his genuine smiles. The one he gave to everyone, that made girls fall in love with him, and guys want to be his best friend.

That's when she realized she was just another victim. Another girl caught under the spell of Tristan Montgomery… and she was kidding herself for thinking anything they'd done together meant anything to him. Kidding herself to think whatever they'd done meant enough to tell Renee about.

Samantha went out to the garage, needing air. Steven followed closely behind her, where she found a grape flavored Fanta on the top shelf of the fridge and cracked it open. She took a long sip, contemplating how remarkably unaffected Tristan could be, when she was practically shaking.

She closed her eyes again as Steven wrapped his arms around her from behind. "You okay?"

She focused on the bubbles rushing down her throat from her soda and nodded her head. Because she didn't trust her voice to speak. Because after all these months of worry, she finally realized she didn't need to think about Tristan anymore. As far as she could tell, everything she felt that night in the woods was completely one sided. And he wasn't going to tell a soul.

Present day

Tristan came into the building, bringing the wind and his large, dominating presence with him. He was impossible to ignore, and Samantha found herself looking up, seeing the same face from all those years ago. He began to walk toward her, and for some reason the tiny wild horses ran hard across her chest again. Maybe because of their past, or maybe because of all the things the server had said that Samantha couldn't quite deny. But there was a part of her that knew it was more than that. More than words or glances. Because being around Tristan again had awakened something vulnerable inside her. Something she'd been repressing for a long time.

He grinned as he came closer, as though he'd missed her during their short separation. He unzipped his coat, letting it drop down his shoulders before draping it across the back of his seat and sliding into the booth.

"Anything sound good?" he asked, reaching out for a menu.

She cleared her throat, still slightly dazed as she nodded her head. "Well, it would be a shame not to try the soup."

Her voice was barely audible, but he smiled nonetheless. "You're probably right."

The server came forward, and set two mugs on the table while eyeing Samantha warily. She didn't say a word, but the way the girl watched her made Samantha nervous. As though she'd seen Samantha's reaction to him entering the room. As though she knew everything Samantha was feeling without her saying so.

"Are ya'll ready to order?" she asked, filling their mugs with piping hot coffee. "Or do you want me to give you another minute?"

Tristan shrugged, lowering his menu to look at Samantha. "I'm ready if you are."

She took a breath, turning toward the server before nodding her head. She could feel the walls of doubt closing in around her. Doubts about this trip, her relationship, her sanity.

"Can I have half a grilled cheese, and a cup of soup, please? Split pea," she confirmed, then she rose from her seat without saying another word and excused herself to the bathroom.

Alone in a stall, she fished her phone from the bottom of her bag and called Steven. She needed to hear his voice, to hear him say he missed her, he loved her, anything that would ground her back to the life that seemed to be slipping through her fingers by the second. Steven's phone rang a half dozen times, then finally rolled to voice mail, making her heart drop.

"Hey babe," she began, her throat constricting as she thought of words to say. "We're in Chippewa Nebraska. It's so cold I can see my breath." She paused, resting her head on the toilet roll and feeling almost sick. She began to laugh, not hard, but in a way that could easily shift to crying given the opportunity. "I think it may rain before we stop; isn't that crazy?" She pulled in a breath. "I already miss our sunshine. I miss you." But as the words crossed her lips, they didn't quite feel genuine. They didn't quite feel hers. "Call me."

She disconnected the call, lowering her head to set her ears between her knees. But all she could think about were the words Tristan used back at her apartment. "I don't remember much about you, either."

"Much." What did that even mean? The more she thought about it, the more impossible it became to ignore. He had to remember something. Maybe not their time in the woods, but something.

When she finally made it back to her seat, their food was already set on the table, and her brow was set with determination to get some answers. She slid into the booth, finding him relaxed and eating his meal, yet looking so perfect, Samantha had to force herself to look away. Her mind was clouded with confusion. So much so, she could hardly see straight. Because two days with Tristan had sent doubts about *everything* scorching through her veins.

She poured some creamer into her coffee, fetched a spoon from the table and began to stir. "What do you remember about me?" she whispered. She meant for the words to sound confident, like one of the random questions asked around a bonfire. Like the ones they asked each other in the car. But it came out unsure. Almost frightened. Not strong and steady like she'd intended them to.

His brows furrowed and he put down his burger. "What do you mean?"

"I don't know?" She shrugged. "I mean, Renee and I have been best friends for ten years. You can't possibly remember nothing…"

Her words trailed off, and he pushed himself back in his seat and tilted his head. "Hmm… I remember you always wore two braids." He paused. "Split right down the middle on either side." He took a sip of coffee and grinned. "I remember you played the flute."

She nodded and began organizing the sugar packets, listening. "That was me," she agreed. "Anything else?"

He only shrugged, narrowing his eyes slightly as he sat forward. "I remember…"

But the way he looked at her made her heart start beating faster. Made her grab her spoon and take her first bite of soup.

"That you and Renee were attached at the hip."

She took a breath, her lips curving downward. "Yeah," she agreed. "We sure were."

But then he did something that surprised her. He leaned forward and asked a question of his own.

"What do you remember about me?" His voice was low, almost suspicious. Which caused her heart to squeeze and run on overdrive.

She glanced down at the table, grabbed a cloth napkin, and unfolded it in her lap before looking up again. "I remember a lot," she said. "I remember you were popular. I remember you having friends by your side every second." She looked up into his waiting eyes. "You were the quarterback for the West Valley Panthers." She licked her lips, everything she wanted to say lingering at the tip of her tongue. "I remember…all the summers we spent up at your family's cabin. Especially the last one." She was proud of herself for saying it, but at the same time her chest filled with anxiety as she waited for him to speak.

He took another sip of coffee, his eyes intense as he watched her. As though trying to read her thoughts. She could feel it. The tension accumulating between them. So tight it was as though they were both caught in a vice.

He nodded slowly, a slight confirmation causing her nerves to ignite like fireworks inside her.

"The cabin," he said, rubbing the back of his neck with his hand. "I did some stupid stuff there."

Her heart pinched at his statement and she turned to look out the window again. "Yeah." But what she really wanted to do was cry. "We all did."

The server came then, breaking up their conversation to check on their meals. "Everything okay over here?" she asked, topping off their mugs with fresh coffee.

But when neither of them spoke, she left for the back room again, and Samantha turned to face him. It was as though all the anger and frustration she'd kept bottled inside came exploding out of her. "I remember a few more things," she began, her chin held as high as she could manage. "You were a player. A cheater, and someone who cared about nothing but himself."

He took a long sip of coffee, his expression hardening before her very eyes. It was like a Tristan she'd never seen before. A Tristan she never wanted to see again. He pulled out his wallet and placed a couple of twenties on the table before getting up to leave. "You're right. That's exactly who I am. Exactly."

She cringed, her heart aching because she knew she'd hurt him. She'd meant to, even though he'd done nothing but tell her the truth... Though now she felt like a complete bitch. "Tristan, wait!"

But he didn't listen. His large legs had already carried him halfway across the restaurant, far away from her and her tongue that had lashed out to hurt.

CHAPTER FIFTEEN

WHEN THEY FINALLY GOT BACK TO the Mustang, Samantha was in a foul mood. Partly because she hadn't slept in days, but also because she deeply regretted what she'd said. The server had meddled so much, all the memories she'd tried to forget about were rising to the surface. Memories she hadn't thought about for a long time. Memories she'd buried deep for good reason.

As soon as she buckled herself into her seat, she bent forward to fish her iPod out of her bag and start a new book. It was one she'd listened to at least a thousand times but always found comforting. Like a threadbare old t-shirt, or a bowl of homemade chicken noodle soup. *Harry Potter and the Sorcerer's Stone*—the story about the boy who lived.

She closed her eyes, listening to the voice that had lulled her to sleep on too many occasions to count, and tried to forget about the past. To forget about everything. To not worry about the what-ifs, or the reasons he didn't remember. But to focus on an epic tale about good vs. evil. About power, and temptation, and growing up.

Before long, a good four chapters into the story, something

changed. She felt the car slow, decreasing in speed at a steady rate that caused panic to lurch in her chest. She quickly opened her eyes, sure they hadn't been on the road long enough to justify stopping, and realized they were pulling off to the side of the road—on a pitch black two-lane highway—in the middle of nowhere. Samantha pulled the ear buds from her ears and straightened. "What are you doing?" she asked. "Don't tell me you're going to go to the bathroom out there."

But there was something different about the way they were moving, like something was wrong, and a sinking feeling settled in the bottom of her gut. "We ran out of gas, didn't we?"

The car rolled to a full stop, and Tristan, who still hadn't said a word, put it in park. "I filled up less than three hours ago."

Samantha shoved her iPod back in her purse and swallowed. A cold draft rushed over her face and neck as Tristan got out of the car. She quickly followed after him, wrapped in her red wool blanket. "I can't believe this! I told you this would happen. I knew we could run out of gas."

He lifted the hood and propped it open. "For the last time, we didn't run out of gas!" He pulled his cell from his pocket and flipped on the flashlight. "Something's wrong. It's just too dark to see what."

He turned around to sit against the car, then held his phone up in the air and moved it side to side looking for a signal. "Shit! There's no service."

Samantha closed her eyes, not allowing herself to panic. "What are we going to do?"

He zipped his jacket all the way up to his chin, closed the hood, then finally looked at her. "You're going to get back into the car. I'm going to go try to find help."

"Like hell I am! I'm coming with you."

"Sammie." He closed his eyes, his head lulling back to his shoulders. She knew what he was going to say. That it was too dangerous, that he was big and heroic, that he was going to take care of her like the male chauvinistic ass that he was, but instead, he surprised her by looking up again. She waited for him to speak, to tell her why she couldn't come, but he said nothing. His blue eyes reached hers, making her feet unstable. He finally shook his head, as though not sure what he was getting himself into, and turned on his heels. "Fine."

It took only a moment for her to recover, to realize she'd actually won the argument, and to hurry after him. How had she won so easily? Why did Tristan Montgomery keep surprising her at every turn? She wasn't sure of the answer; all she knew was that her teeth were already chattering and she had left her warm jacket back in the car. "Where are we? How close are we to the next town?"

"Iowa," he answered. But that was all he said. Because he didn't know how far they were to the next town. He didn't know anything at all.

Samantha took her phone from her pocket, and held it up to illuminate their path. "Has this ever happened to you before?" she asked.

"No."

"Are you sure we're not out of gas?"

"Yes."

"How do you know?"

Silence.

"Tristan, how do you know?" A chill ran up her spine, though it wasn't from the cold this time. It was because of him. He raked his fingers through his hair, giving away his stress, and that made her even more nervous. He was the guy who let everything roll off his shoulders. Who didn't give a shit. But now—

"Because I know my car," he finally said.

"Oh God," she whispered. Only to herself, but that didn't matter.

He stopped dead in his tracks. Turned around, and looked her dead in the eye. "Do you have a problem?"

She clenched her jaw, telling herself to be quiet, but she couldn't. "Yeah. Actually, I do." She lifted her chin, higher than she felt confident, and took a step toward him. "I'm supposed to be at my best friend's bachelorette party in two days. *Two*. And you're giving me the cold shoulder and saying things like, 'I know my car.' "

He laughed under his breath and pressed his thumb and forefinger into his eye sockets. "What do you want me to say, Samantha? What?"

"I don't know! I want you to give me a real fucking answer!"

He snapped! Picked up a rock, and threw it into the dark forest—so hard that the sound echoed through the secluded night. He took a breath, as though frustrated and out of control, as though he was trying to compose himself enough to face her.

He finally turned around, his jaw tight and clenched, but so much emotion was etched on his face that her eyes immediately went blurry with regret. It was as though a thick blanket smothered the Tristan she'd known all her life. His confidence, his smile, his easy nature. "It's my fault, is that what you want me to say? That it's my fucking fault?"

Tears rushed to her nose and throat. She couldn't bear to see him this way. "No," she said. "No, that isn't it at all."

He gripped his forehead and turned around again. "I should have never agreed to this. I should have said no."

She froze, her heart thumping. "Agreed to what?" she asked, standing still.

He turned around, squeezed his eyes shut as if not realizing the words had come from his mouth. "Nothing."

"No." She wrapped her arms around her belly, not letting it go. "What did you agree to, Tristan?"

He remained silent, giving her all the answer she needed. She looked down to her feet, tears stinging the backs of her eyes. "Renee talked you into this, didn't she? You don't want to be here any more than I do."

"Samantha—"

But she shook her head, stopping him.

"Look—I'm frustrated, too." He moved toward her. "But we're in this together."

Emotion quickly gathered in her chest, and she clenched her arms at her side. "I know."

"I didn't mean to scare you."

She nodded, her chin quivering.

But scared wasn't the feeling that was cutting her like a knife. It was something else. Something heartbreakingly difficult for her to admit to. Because hearing that he didn't want to be there sent a chill over her entire body.

He came closer still and draped his heavy jacket around her shoulders. "I'm sorry, Samantha." He tightened the jacket around her shivering body, fastening it at the bottom before zipping it up to her chin. But he didn't move away. He stayed there a second too long, his thumb by her chin, causing all the air to expel from her lungs.

She looked up to his throat, only inches from her lips. She wanted to kiss it, to wrap her arms around his large body and have him hold her. To hold him. It was so cold she could see her breath. So cold their breaths mingled together, and for some reason, she stepped closer.

She wasn't sure if it was his warmth that drew her in. The heat that radiated from his muscles and bones. Or if it was the pain in his eyes. It seemed to say a thousand words all on its own. That he was sorry, that he was scared, too. But it wasn't an average "I'm sorry." It was a sorry from a man who carried the world on his shoulders—who took the blame for everything, even when it wasn't his fault. Her mind screamed to move away. To not get too close to the man who had shattered her heart after only one night, to get away before it was too late, but she couldn't. She craved to be close to him, even though she knew it would bring nothing but pain to too many people.

He placed his hand on her hip, wrapping his fingers around her lower back and exerting pressure. As though he needed her just as much as she needed him. As though he'd given up on resisting her and the gravity that pulled them together.

She lifted her chin, knowing it was wrong, but knowing she couldn't stop it. Whatever was between them was stronger than her will. Stronger than her conscious. But as their lips touched for the briefest moment, a set of dull headlights began to shine in the distance. As though a higher being had rushed in to save her from herself.

Tristan turned around, clearing his throat as if he himself had been caught in the same spell. He took his phone out of his pocket and waved it overhead. "Hey!" he yelled. "Hey! Over here!"

A moment later, down the long flat road, came a beat up old van with a million stickers on the windows. The door opened, and a woman with a large pregnant belly hopped down to the road. She rested her hands on her lower back, exaggerating the ripe, swollen shape, and shined a bright flashlight over their faces, blinding them.

"Now what in the devil's name are you two doin' all the way out here?"

CHAPTER SIXTEEN

PRESENT DAY

THE WOMAN'S name was Patty. They learned that soon enough. After a short game of twenty questions that Samantha wasn't sure they won, and an interrogation of Tristan about how they ended up in this predicament, she agreed to take them back to her house where they could find warmth and sleep.

"It's a good thing I stumbled upon you two." She nodded. "I'm afraid the closest payphone is over a hundred miles away and we don't have a cell tower yet. They say it's coming, but I'm not holding my breath."

She waited for them to gather their things, while Samantha and Tristan thanked her profusely for her generosity. There were two sleeping toddlers snoring away in the back seat, though Patty looked to be no more than twenty-five. It was odd —seeing someone so close to her own age with a growing family. One the woman seemed proud and protective of.

Tristan took their bags from the trunk, while Samantha gathered her purse and tried to recover from their almost kiss.

She wished she knew what he was thinking. Wished she could rewind the last ten minutes and have more self-control.

Samantha approached the oversized van a moment later, where Tristan helped her into the front seat and handed her the seat belt.

"We'll be okay," he whispered in her ear. "I promise."

She knew he was talking about the car, about being stranded right before the wedding, although she couldn't help but wonder if he was talking about more. She took the seat belt from his hand, thankful for the darkness so he couldn't read all the insecurities on her face. Right now they were out there for everyone to see, and she couldn't put them away, because for the first time in six years, she began to question what she was doing with her life. With Steven. If she could feel so much for a man she hadn't seen in half a decade, how could she even think about a future with Steven?

Tristan moved away a moment later, allowing her the space to breathe. The Jackson Five's "ABC" was playing on the radio, and Samantha turned to look out the window. Tristan climbed into the back seat, putting their backpacks to the floor, and settling himself between the two car seats. He seemed oddly comfortable there, even though his broad shoulders hardly fit. But he was always like that. Always comfortable. Never complaining—so unlike Steven.

Steven. She couldn't help but cringe at the thought of him. He was honest, hardworking, and didn't deserve this. He was meeting her in NY on Friday, and this needed to stop. Whatever *this* was, whether curiosity, or an unfulfilled girlhood fantasy, it would end here. She wouldn't risk their relationship. She wouldn't risk her heart.

Closing her eyes, she tried to force all the emotions from her body. But the fact was, a simple touch from Tristan caused lightning bolts to shoot through her limbs. A simple touch from

Tristan made her ache for more. A touch from Tristan wasn't easily forgotten.

The road ahead became dark and twisty, making Samantha's stomach roll with nausea. Either that or from the speed at which Patty navigated the narrow path so easily. Patty's large belly was pressed against the steering wheel, and her eyes were focused on the path ahead, but neither stopped her from talking.

"Ya'll are lucky," she said to Samantha, glancing over from the corner of her eye. "Really lucky."

She clucked her tongue, then turned down the radio and continued to ramble. "I don't normally come out this way so late at night. It's only because Mr. Miller had a heart attack last week, and I had to check on the cattle. That's the only reason."

Samantha nodded her head, though Patty must have noticed her increased discomfort, because she quickly slowed the van.

"What brings you 'round these parts anyway?" she asked, almost as a distraction technique.

Samantha swallowed, hoping the action would calm her stomach. "My best friend is getting married," she answered. "We're on our way to New York."

"Yeah?" Patty grinned. "Are you the maid of honor?"

"Yes. Though I haven't seen the dress yet." She smiled.

"I bet you'd look beautiful," Patty said softly. Then she glanced in the rearview mirror to look at Tristan. "Don't you agree?"

He didn't hesitate a second. "Stunning."

Samantha looked down to her feet, realizing that, just like everyone else, Patty thought they were a couple. She didn't blame her, given the scene she'd pulled up upon. Samantha would have thought the same thing.

They continued talking. About everything and nothing. About the town. The people who lived there, and when they finally turned off a bend, Samantha's stomach had settled quite a bit. "I should have gone out hours ago," Patty confessed. "I'm ashamed to admit I got caught up in one of my shows again. The new season of *Felicity* was delivered this morning, and I plain lost track of myself." She glanced over again, seeming pleased by Samantha's condition, and gave her a nod of approval. "That happens a lot when Trevor's gone."

"Is Trevor your husband?" Samantha asked.

"Yes." Patty agreed, rubbing slow circles on the top of her belly. "He got me a seventy-two inch TV for Mother's Day. I told him it was a guilty conscience for leavin' so much, but really, it was the most thoughtful gift I've ever received." Her smile was sleepy, but her eyes were bright and filled with tears when she looked over again. "You're lucky to have a man to warm your bed at night."

They pulled into the driveway of a small white home, and Patty threw the van into park. "Well this is it," she said quietly. "Home, sweet home."

Samantha wanted to correct her about her and Tristan, but decided clarification would only bring more questions, so she remained silent. She glanced out the window of the van—to the horseshoe-shaped driveway lined with little lights to illuminate the cobblestone path. Patty popped open the door and unfastened her seat belt. "Well, I best get these little ones to bed."

She yawned before hopping down from the cab, then slid open the back door and began unfastening her babies, one at a time, as they slept peacefully in the back seat. She took one out, then the other, holding them on each side like huge sacks of flour. But Tristan stopped in front of her and held out his arms. She looked up, surprised by the offer of help. But then she nodded, hesitating for only a moment before handing over a child.

The small toddler nestled his blond head into the top of

Tristan's shoulder, wiping his nose back and forth a few times before falling back asleep. Samantha smiled watching them. Tristan was so big and strong, but seeing him with a baby curled up on his shoulder, he looked like he couldn't hurt a butterfly.

She took a deep breath of the cool country air, then gathered the rest of their belongings and followed in after them.

She'd never seen Tristan with a baby before, and for some reason the image rocked her. She knew she wanted children, but the sight of Tristan cradling a small child in his arms caused a physical reaction to stir low in her belly. One she'd been repressing for a long time. That sort of primal longing she'd always heard her mother talking about. That ache deep inside for a family of her own. She told herself she was being silly and her reaction was still the effects of the car ride, but she knew it was more than that. Because in all her childhood daydreams, all the games she played with Renee as a girl, she always imagined herself like Patty. With a round pregnant belly and a baby on each arm. It was only since Steven her dreams had changed. With his goals for his career and ideas of success, he wanted one. One child. Not three or four. He was realistic, always took her wild eccentric dreams and reminded her of reality. Starting a family in their late thirties was the goal. When he was sure to have good medical care, stability, and a home.

She walked in through the open door of Patty's home a moment later, finding it cozy and warm, and Tristan and Patty both standing in the living room by a wood burning stove. True to Patty's word, a seventy-two inch television sat front and center. It was odd seeing such an extravagant appliance in the middle of what was otherwise a modest dwelling, but after knowing Patty for no more than an hour, Samantha would have expected nothing less.

Patty put her keys on the kitchen counter, hitched her baby

high on her shoulder and looked over to Tristan. "There are pillows and blankets in the hallway closet. You all help yourselves. Given how cold it is tonight, I don't expect you two will mind a good cuddle."

The baby slipped a fraction of an inch as Patty yawned. But she hitched him back up again and continued down the hall. "I'm going to have to excuse myself from hostess duties tonight. These babies have downright tuckered me out." She then lifted her chin to Tristan, then turned slightly to indicate he should follow her.

"This here's the potty." She stopped again, pointing to a door to her right. "Take a shower if you like. Towels are in with the pillows." At the end of the hall, she took the sleeping toddler from Tristan's arms and closed the door behind her.

Tristan stood there a second, rolling his shoulders backward as though he'd been relieved from a large weight and emotion rushed to Samantha's face and throat.

She turned around, surprised by the panic that surged inside her. She wasn't sure what caused it, but right now she felt unsteady—being alone with Tristan, seeing a young mom so prideful and happy with her family. Her simple home. The last thing she needed was to be alone with Tristan. It was the last thing she needed.

There was only one couch.

She wrapped her arms around her belly at the realization and took a deep breath. The couch was large, but not big enough. She unzipped her jacket—Tristan's Jacket—feeling odd that she still wore it and draped it across one of the chairs. Somehow, he was slipping through all her walls, one by one, and she no idea how to bring them back up again.

She picked up her bag off the cushion and began fishing in the pocket for her cell phone. She needed to call Steven, to tell him where they were, that she was okay, but again, there were no bars. Tristan was right behind her, and she could feel him moving closer. "You don't happen to have a signal do you?" she asked.

He shook his head slowly, shoving his hands deep in his pockets.

She stuffed her cell back in her bag and zipped it shut. "Figures," she mumbled. She threw her bag on the couch and moved to the kitchen window "It's pretty here." Her voice was broken, but she needed to say something so the silence didn't kill her. It was agony. Torture. Because all she wanted was to know what he was thinking.

He nodded, then rested his hip on the counter beside her.

You have a boyfriend. He loves you. You love him.

She flipped around, bracing her hands on the counter, trying to hold herself steady, but it wasn't working. Her heart was pounding so hard her legs became weak—she didn't want to do this. "We should go to bed. We have a big day in the morning," she whispered. But he didn't move from his spot.

"Are we going to talk about it?" he asked, his voice gentle.

She pushed off the counter like a snake had just bitten her. "No. Let's not talk about it." She shook her head. "Let's forget about it." She wrapped her arms around her body, realizing she sounded ridiculous. But it was too late. "I'm not going to climb into bed with you, Tristan."

He smiled, having to cover his mouth to prevent a laugh. "I didn't say you were."

She rubbed both hands over her face and took a deep breath. "There's only one couch."

"I'll take the floor," he said softly.

They were both quiet for a moment, and she could feel tears threatening behind her eyelids. "I have a boyfriend."

"I know."

She turned toward the hallway. There was a sort of charge holding her back, keeping her from running, but this time her conscious won the battle. "I'm going to go take a shower," she whispered. "Do you need anything in there before I go?"

"No."

She nodded, wishing she could see his expression. To know what he was thinking… but she couldn't look back. If she did, she wasn't sure she could resist throwing herself into his arms.

"I'm sorry about what I said in the restaurant. It's not true." She forced her hands to her sides, took her large bag off the couch, and went to the bathroom. Pulling in a shuddery breath, she turned the faucet on in the shower, and let herself cry. What was happening to her? She wasn't sure, but something was changing. Or maybe her doubts about Steven had been there the whole time and she wouldn't allow herself to feel them. It was as though the wool had been ripped from her eyes, allowing her to see how bright the world was. How many shades of color she'd been missing. And it had taken Tristan to allow her to see them.

CHAPTER SEVENTEEN

NEXT MORNING, Patty drove them to meet the mechanic in the middle of the next town. It was smaller than she'd expected, though still quaint and lively for being so early in the morning. People were out on each corner, strolling from flower shop to antique stores too many to count—and bars—she counted at least three as they drove in from the main road.

Patty dropped them off at the corner, where she kept the car running so her babies wouldn't fret. "Tell Bob that I sent you," she said. "He's a good mechanic and won't send you a on goose chase if he knows you're with me." She then gave them each a brief hug, and hopped back into her van without lingering. "Look me up if you ever come back this way. I've downright enjoyed your company."

They both grinned, then grabbed the rest of their belongings from the back of her van before slapping it shut and sending her on her way.

The auto shop was old fashioned, with stacks of tires along the whole fence line. They entered through the back, where Tristan's Mustang was already on lifts in the middle of the garage. A man in denim coveralls was poking around in a tool chest, and looked up when they entered the building. As he walked toward them, he wiped his hands on what used to be a red rag. "I'm guessing this beauty is yours?" he said, around a mouthful of tobacco. "Haven't seen a '67 since I went to a car show in two-thousand." He reached his hand out to Tristan and gave it a firm shake. "My name's Bob."

"Tristan." Tristan replied, then glanced up to his car above their heads. "I'm hoping you know what's wrong with her?"

"Well," the man said, clearing his throat. "Thing is, there's some good news and some bad news." He looked to Samantha, nodding his head in hello. "Good news is, it's only a bad radiator cap." He turned back to Tristan. "Bad news is, the nearest I can get one is a two towns over." He spread his legs wide and shoved his hands into the back pockets of his coveralls. "I've already sent one of my guys to get it, but I'm afraid I won't have the car ready 'til morning."

Tristan ran a hand through his hair and cringed. "Shit. Are you sure? We're on our way to a wedding—"

Bob shook his head, cutting him off. "I'm afraid so. I wish there was more I could do. But truth is, y'all are lucky I found one even that close." He then looked at Samantha. "I can see you're disappointed ma'am, and it hurts my heart. But there's a great bed and breakfast just across the road. People come from all over to stay there. Tell them Bob sent you, and they'll give you a discount on your stay"

Samantha smiled, then turned to Tristan. "Well, I guess that settles it then. We're staying the night in Colton, Iowa." She was trying to make the best of the situation, to lower the pressure she could see stiffening Tristan's shoulders, but he wasn't really paying attention. He was looking at his cell phone, deep in thought, and there was an odd expression on his face.

He finally excused himself, holding up one finger before walking out of the garage.

Samantha looked down to the ground, to the oil-stained

floor, as a weird uncomfortable feeling grew in her stomach. She finally looked back up, thanked Bob for his recommendation of the B&B, then walked in the opposite direction from Tristan, wanting to give him privacy. She sat on the curb in front of the shop, kicked her legs out in front of her, and dug through her purse looking for her cell.

Three notifications waited on her phone. Two of which were from Steven. She punched in her pass code, and began playing the messages.

"Hey babe, I need to talk to you. Call me as soon as you can?"

"Samantha, I really have to talk to you. Call me when you get this, okay?"

Her brows furrowed, and she frowned. *What did he need to talk to her about?*

The last message was from Renee.

"Hey Sam! Are you and Tris killing each other, yet? This is taking forever, and I'm not even in the car! Call me when you can. Love you! Bye!"

Samantha closed her eyes, leaning back on the pavement to let the sun warm her face. "This is almost over. You'll see Steven in a couple of days, and everything will go back to normal."

She sat up again, straightening her back as she dialed Steven's number. It went straight to voice mail, and she began to leave a message.

"Hey babe," she began. "You're probably working, but I wanted to call while I had reception." She blew out a breath and looked back over her shoulder to the garage. "We ran into some car trouble, unfortunately. It seems we'll be delayed about a day." She paused for a moment, her eyes focused on nothingness. "Call me when you can." She hung up the phone without even saying goodbye.

When she looked up, Tristan was standing above her. His

sunglasses were covering his eyes, but the tension couldn't be hidden from his face. "I guess we should go get some rooms?"

She pushed herself from the pavement, but Tristan grabbed hold of her arm and pulled her up the rest of the way. His grip was firm and strong, yet sent goose bumps to cover the length of her body in a second. "Everything okay?" she asked, searching his face for answers.

He nodded, but immediately looked away. "Yeah. You?" he asked, meeting her eyes once again.

"Yeah," she whispered. He still looked upset, and all she wanted to do was yank the glasses off his nose and demand that he tell her what was wrong. Why he'd suddenly changed from the easy-going Tristan she'd always known him to be, to this. But in these few short days she'd become closer to him than she was comfortable with. Closer to him than was healthy. She needed to keep her distance, to keep her walls up and not let them fall. "I guess you're right. We should go get some rooms."

They both stepped off the curb separately, keeping distance between them as they walked toward the bed and breakfast.

True to the mechanic's word, the bed and breakfast was stunning. Samantha was sure it had once been an old Victorian home. Brick walls, a castle-like roofline, and shutters on every window. But there was a large pool in the center of the court-yard that was modern and sleek, and looked exhilarating. Lush foliage surrounded the property, offering privacy, yet the building sat in the center of town, not even a half block away from the public.

They followed the intricate stone path past the magnolia tree scattered with huge white blossoms, then to the gold sign that took them to the front office.

A pretty blond woman waited at the counter and looked up as soon as they entered the building. "Welcome to the Gumtree Mansion. How can I help you today?"

Tristan took his wallet from his back pocket and braced his forearm on the counter. "Two rooms please," he said, but his voice betrayed his exhaustion.

"Oh..." The woman's brows furrowed and she began clicking at her computer. "Let me see..." She clicked a few more times, her frown growing deeper and more intense. "That's what I thought." She looked up, glancing from Tristan to Samantha. "I'm afraid I only have one room for tonight."

Tristan looked over his shoulder to Samantha, where she violently shook her head. She couldn't stay the night with him. Not after their too close moment the night before. Not alone.

He turned back to the woman and put his wallet back in his pocket "That's okay, we'll go somewhere else."

He pushed off the counter to leave, but before they could exit the building, a high-pitched squeak caused him to turn around.

"Sir!" the young woman yelped. "We're the only hotel in town. Anything else is over a hundred miles away. "

Tristan closed his eyes, ran his hands through his hair and dropped to a squat. Like the whole world had become too heavy for him to bear.

Samantha's heart lurched in her throat and she stepped forward. "You know, one room will be fine." She turned toward Tristan, nodding. "It will be fine." She walked closer, wanting nothing more than to pull him to his feet. "I was being silly. It will be fine."

He rose to his feet, the crease in his forehead softening a bit, but he pulled out his wallet again and placed his card on the counter. Samantha shook her head, opening her purse to pay. "I'll get it," she muttered. But he ignored her and shoved the card farther on the counter toward the receptionist. "It's one room, Samantha."

She swallowed hard, because as silly as this was, she could see he needed this. To feel like he was in control. Like he was taking care of the situation. Like he was somehow fixing things. She nodded once, then turned around and allowed him to pay. When her cell began vibrating in her pocket, she walked toward the door to the courtyard. "Excuse me, I'll be right back."

She pushed through the glass doors and walked a good distance over to the magnolia tree by the pool "Hello?" she answered softly.

"Hey!" Steven said. "Finally. God, it's been hard to get ahold of you. I got your message. Are you okay? You need anything?"

Samantha let her back rest on the smooth bark, lolling her head back and taking in the peaceful yard around her. "We're fine. It's only the radiator cap. Can you believe it? I had no idea such a thing was so important."

Steven laughed in response. "Me either, honestly."

She nodded, set her bag on the ground, and turned to face the pool. It was completely empty, so peaceful.

"Other than that, are things going okay?"

She took a step forward, a tightness in her belly growing with each second. "Yeah. How are things with you? How's the new gig?"

There was a smile in his voice. "Busy…" He went on to tell her about his boss, about working until eight at night, and how he'd already lost five pounds. But then he cleared his throat, and she realized there was something he needed to say.

"I've actually been trying to get hold of you for a while now," he said. His voice lowering before he spoke again. "They're sending me to San Francisco this weekend. I won't be able to make it to the wedding."

Samantha's knees went weak, and she grabbed hold of the bench in front of her to hold herself steady. "What do you mean? Can't you get out of it?"

"Sam, I'm not going to tell them I can't go. It's a huge opportunity."

"But the wedding has been planned for months!"

"I know, but when your boss needs you for a favor, you do it. The fact he wanted me there is a big deal.

She closed her eyes, thinking about all the times Renee had warned her about this. About him always putting work and his dreams before her. "What about me? What about what I want, what I need?"

"Samantha, don't blow this out of proportion—"

"What? You're acting like I'm being ridiculous, but I told you about this six months ago."

"I know, but plans change. This is a really important step in my career, Sam. I'm sorry it means I'm going to have to let you down, but I'll make it up to you, I promise."

Before she could open her mouth to respond, he muffled the phone. "My boss is coming. We'll talk when you get home."

He was gone. Leaving her with tears rolling down her cheeks. Tears of rejection and anger. Of confusion, frustration, and embarrassment. She looked down to her phone and opened up a text:

SAMANTHA: No need to talk. We're over. I'm done.

SHE CLOSED HER EYES, her body trembling. She meant every word of it. With every fiber of her being. Every drop of blood, sweat, and tears she'd put into their relationship. She was done. She put her phone in her back pocket, then turned around to see Tristan watching. Standing in the path that led straight to her. His legs were braced apart, his hands stuffed deep in the pockets of his jeans. "You okay?"

He looked concerned, beautiful, and so completely

dangerous she didn't know what to do. She let out a sob, wiping over her face with her hand. "Yeah, I'm fine."

"Samantha…" He stepped closer.

But she shook her head, stopping him. "We broke up." She cried. "He's not coming."

He stepped closer still, ignoring her wishes.

She heaved out a heavy breath. "Aren't you going to say I told you so?"

"I'm so sorry," he said.

His response was the opposite of what she'd expected. He said it with emotion. As though his own heart was breaking to see her in pain. As though all he wanted to do was hold her. She looked down to her feet. So many emotions rolled around her chest, she could hardly breathe. It was as though every emotion, every disappointment over the last six months had come crashing to the surface—and her whole world was falling apart for him to witness. Her career, her friendship, her relationship. All ending, and she didn't want to hear he was sorry. She wanted to punch something. To scream, and yell, and hurt something the way she hurt inside.

"No!" She shouted, looking him in the eye. "Everything in my life is falling apart, and I don't want to hear any bullshit responses like I'm sorry."

He stepped toward her, holding out his arms, offering her comfort.

She stepped backward, emotion causing her own throat to choke her. "I should have never agreed to this. I should have just said no." She was throwing his words back in his face, wanting to push him away. He was scary, and he was Renee's brother, and she didn't know if she could resist him when he looked at her like that. She took another step backward, just as Tristan lunged to grab her—but it was too late.

"Samantha!" he shouted.

But she'd already hit the water, and was sinking to the

bottom of the pool. She let herself fall. Allowing the cool water to lift her hair and make her feel lighter than she had in months. There was a large splash above her, and soon Tristan's arms were wrapped around her waist, holding her body, forcing her back to the surface. She didn't want to go, she didn't want his arms around her, she didn't want any of it! She pushed at his arms, kicking her legs as hard as she could.

"Let me go!"

"Samantha, stop!"

"Let me go!"

But he didn't answer. He kept swimming with her over to the side of the pool until they both reached the shallow end. He put her down, her clothes and hair plastered to her face and body.

"Why wouldn't you let me go?" She sobbed.

"Because."

"Why?" she demanded.

"Because you can't swim!"

She suddenly stopped. Heaving as though all the oxygen had been expelled from her lungs. Because she could swim. She'd learned her junior year of high school. Right after the summer she'd spent with Tristan. "You remember." It wasn't a question, but a statement of fact. That was the only way his statement made any sense.

He was quiet a moment, but he grabbed her cheek as though trying to force her to look at him. "Samantha—"

"No!" she shouted again, pushing him away "You remember. Don't you?"

He only nodded, but his eyes never faltered.

"Everything?" she questioned.

"Yes."

She wiped over her face, over tears, and hurt, and anger. She brushed her hair back behind her ears and began walking toward the steps. "I'm going to our room to change. Then I'm going to get drunk. Don't wait up for me."

"Samantha—"

"Don't wait up." But before she stepped into the lobby to grab a key, she turned around and looked at him one last time. "And I know how to swim now, you asshole."

CHAPTER EIGHTEEN

IT WAS NEARLY DUSK when Tristan opened the back door of the bar and walked into the room. Samantha had already been drinking for hours, albeit slowly, because her heart wasn't quite in it. She sat at the long oak counter, passing her rum and coke back and forth between her fingers. The ice had melted long ago, causing a gradient separation between soda and water, where her eyes were focused now, tired, puffy, and empty.

He sat down next to her, two seats away, and braced his forearms on the counter to order a drink. "Whiskey and water, please," he said to the bartender, though he didn't even acknowledge she was there.

The bartender passed the drink along the bar a moment later, and Tristan picked it up. Samantha couldn't help but look up at him. He looked tired, maybe even more than herself. As if he'd raked his hands through his hair a hundred times, as if he'd walked a thousand miles, and right away she knew it was because of her. When she told him not to wait up, she'd meant it. She'd meant every word. But as the time went by, as her mind began to calm enough to process it all, she realized she'd been unfair.

What happened between them had happened when they were young. When she was a naive teenage girl, and he a boy too big for his britches. It was unfair to punish him for that now. To hold him captive for a crime he committed when he was eighteen.

Yet it surprised her how much the wound still stung. How learning that he still remembered was almost more painful than thinking he'd forgotten.

Tristan leaned back in his seat, still not acknowledging her, and began watching the Giants game on TV. She had no doubt he'd come to check on her, yet he hadn't even said hello.

"My phone died," she said as a way of breaking the ice. "It was in my pocket when I fell into the pool."

Tristan nodded, but still didn't look over. "I figured as much."

She smoothed her loose hair behind ears, then took a small sip of her drink. The alcohol loosened her insides, but her outside was still hard and tense. "How did you find me?" she asked, both curious and apprehensive.

He looked up, meeting her eyes for the first time since he got there. "This is the fifth bar I've been to."

She cringed, looking down toward her drink again. "I didn't mean to worry you."

He shrugged, his voice deep and hollow. "Well you did."

She placed her elbows on the bar and began rubbing slow circles at her temples with her fingers. "I shouldn't have yelled at you, and I'm sorry, but it seems my whole world is falling in around me. You were just at the wrong place at the wrong time."

He turned in his seat, just a little, and took another sip of whiskey. "Do you want to talk about it?"

At first she shook her head, but then she thought better of it and nodded. Maybe it was the alcohol, or the fact that she felt so utterly alone, but she needed someone to talk to. Someone to care about all that she'd been through.

"You know," she began. "Out of all the people I could imagine myself talking to about my problems with, it was never you." She laughed. "No offense."

He shrugged slightly before meeting her eyes. "None taken." But his brows furrowed, and he nodded his head, indicating she should begin.

She tore the corner of her cocktail napkin, not knowing at all where to start. To confess about how Renee moving away had rocked her off her axis. Or the fact that seeing him after all these years made her question every minute of her six year long relationship? She decided to start with something a little less intimidating.

"I had a gallery opening last month," she began. "One I've been planning for my entire life." She glanced up, finding his expression attentive, his eyes boring into hers. "It was a total flop. I sold nothing at all." She placed her feet on the rung of her stool, while trying to make sense of it all. "The thing is, people have been telling me my whole life that art wasn't something people succeeded at. That I would struggle. That I wouldn't make ends meet. But I was stubborn. So sure of myself until that moment—with my name in lights above my head, watching all those people pass by without stopping— That I realized how true it all was."

She took a large gulp of her drink, hoping to push down the emotion that seemed to be climbing up her throat inch by inch. "The sad part is it took me this long to discover I'm wasting my time. To realize I've wasted so many years of my life on a stupid dream."

His voice cut in, deep and firm, making her heart jump. "Does it make you happy?"

She looked at him, searching his light blue eyes as tears brimmed in her own. She'd never been asked that question before. Never by a single soul before him. "No. It makes me frustrated, and angry, and…"

He turned to face her, setting his booted feet firmly on the ground. "Forget about the money. Forget about the gallery opening. Does your art make you happy?"

She looked into his eyes, wiping at the corner of her nose with her cocktail napkin. "Yes. Yes, it makes me happy," she whispered.

"Then it's worth it."

She pulled in a shaky breath, her heart pounding in a way she hadn't felt in years. She didn't know what made him come find her, or what spurred his sudden interest in her happiness, but she couldn't help her own curiosity. "What makes you happy, Tristan?"

The corner of his mouth lifted and he looked down to his feet. "You wouldn't believe me if I told you."

Her chest heaved and she took another sip of her drink. "Try me."

He looked up then, his eyes crystal clear and sparkling despite the dim lights above the bar. "You do, Sammie Smiles." He reached out to wipe a tear that glistened on the bottom of her cheek. "Seeing you again has made me happier than I've been in a long time."

She didn't know what to say, but her heart was pounding so hard she knew she wouldn't be able to find words. Because she realized in that moment that he made her happy, too. This trip had been crazy, and emotional, and a complete disaster at times, but she'd never had more fun in her whole life. She planted her feet firmly on the rail of her barstool, trying with all her might to keep her world from spinning.

"I'm so sorry," she whispered, her chin quivering. "I'm sorry I said all those things. I didn't mean them. I didn't mean any of it."

His finger brushed over her lips, shushing her. He eased

himself off the barstool, took a couple of twenties out of his wallet, and tossed them in the direction of the bartender. "Let's go. Let's get out of here and get some sleep."

She swallowed, wishing desperately that the feeling suddenly rolling in her belly was caused from too much alcohol. But it wasn't. That feeling came from falling for a man— maybe for the first real time in her adult life. A feeling of wanting him so desperately her heart ached with it.

"I wanted to hate you," she whispered. "But I don't."

"I know."

She stumbled out of her chair, dragging her bag from the top of the bar, as she continued toward the door. "I don't hate you, Tristan Montgomery, and that scares the hell out of me." She continued walking, not bothering to look over her shoulder to make sure he was following. She knew he was. She felt him with every hair on her body, every drop of blood that surged to the surface of her skin.

"I don't hate you either, Samantha Elizabeth Smiles. I never have."

CHAPTER NINETEEN

THEY WALKED down the sidewalk back to their room. Their hands occasionally brushing, his body so close she could practically feel the heat radiating off his skin. It was then that she realized how much the four rum and cokes had affected her. She felt tingly and warm. All the way to her toes. All over her belly. But it was more than that which warmed her insides. It was Tristan. The way he walked, the sound of his voice, the way she felt from the simple brush of his fingers.

He guided her back to the B&B, past a donut shop, a movie theater, and a bunch of other shops she didn't remember. "Are you sure this is the right way?" she asked. "I don't remember any of this."

He only nodded, placing his hand on the small of her back to keep her moving forward. To be fair, when she'd left the room after changing, she wasn't exactly paying attention to the shops. She was fuming. Crying. Ridiculous. And for some reason, she trusted Tristan. She trusted him to take care of her. To keep her safe. To make sure she didn't fall. Honestly, she always had. For as many faults as Tristan had, he was someone who always looked out for his friends. That's why he had so many of them. He was someone who always looked out for his family—which now that she thought about it, was the reason he always bugged Renee so much. He was too protective. Too involved in her business. Just like a big brother should be.

Soon enough, down a sidewalk covered with too many pebbles, Tristan opened the door to their room. Once inside, her eyes set on the single king-sized bed set smack dab in the middle of the wall. Nerves tickled the back of her spine, and she walked quickly to their bags in the wardrobe closet. She fetched her PJ's from the front pocket of her backpack and carried them to the restroom to change. Neither said a word to the other as she moved around the room.

She set her bedclothes on the counter, bracing her arms on either side of the sink as she stared at her reflection. Her cheeks were pink and flushed, her lips red from crying too much, but she didn't hate what she saw. Her hair was down, a little wild from drying on its own. It framed her round face perfectly. She looked pretty. Sexy even—and she was single for the first time in her adult life. She looked to the door leading back to Tristan and frowned. Because behind that door was a single king-sized bed, and a man who sent shivers down her body and spine.

Not knowing what to do with this information, she quickly changed. It wasn't something she should even consider. Something she should think about at all. After brushing her teeth and splashing water on her face, she opened the door.

Tristan was sitting on the side of the bed, his long legs sprawled out in front of him, making him look large and confident. He looked into her eyes, down to her white t-shirt, then farther, to the sliver of blue that peeked out from the hem of her shirt. Perhaps it was the alcohol thinning her blood that made her do it, or the way he was looking at her, but she walked toward him, without a word, and stood between his legs.

He looked up at her, his voice deep with warning. "What are you doing?"

She shook her head, her hair hanging loose around her shoulders. "I don't know," she whispered. "I don't want to think anymore." Her heart was beating wildly, like a frightened bird, begging to be set free, but she couldn't make herself move away. She wanted him, wanted him so badly she couldn't think straight. She fell to her knees, to the patch of bed between his thighs, and he didn't move away. They were face-to-face for the first time in far too long, their hearts beating as one, and her body surged with sexual awareness.

She couldn't resist him any longer. She didn't have to. His scent was all too familiar, and she remembered it like it was yesterday. Masculine, earthy, raw. "I want you so bad it scares me," she whispered.

He let out a hard breath. "Samantha." There was a warning in his voice, low and soft, but he wrapped his arms around her waist, contradicting himself. He buried his nose in her hair. As though he knew this was a bad idea, knew it would lead to nothing but pain, yet he couldn't walk away any more than she could. He needed her just as much as she needed him. Like the sea needed the shore, like he needed oxygen to breath.

"How many drinks have you had?" he asked. His breath in her ear sent goose bumps down the length of her body.

She arched her back, allowing his five o'clock shadow to brush against her neck and her sensitive skin. "It doesn't matter," she whispered.

She pushed her fingers through his hair, gripping him, cupping his skull. She touched her lips to his throat, inhaling deeply.

A groan came from within him, deep and guttural. He shifted her to his lap and pulled her closer until her legs were spread and she was straddling his hips. The hard fabric of his waistband pressed against her sex, and the thin fabric of her shorts was doing nothing to dull her senses. The friction sent a surge of fire to grow in her belly. So strong she had to stop herself from calling out.

At first she froze, because she wasn't sure how far she wanted to take this. She'd broken up with Steven less than six hours ago. She and Tristan still had two days ahead of them on their trip, but her body quickly took over all thought. Her hips moved, almost involuntarily, as though she couldn't take any more deprivation. She'd denied herself too long, lied to herself too long, and her body was finally protesting.

She lowered her mouth to his neck, letting her tongue run along the sensitive skin of his throat. "You make me feel things, Tristan. Things I've never felt before with anyone."

He groaned again, grabbed hold of her face and kissed her. It wasn't soft, and it wasn't sweet. It was rough and textured and layered with want. Her hips moved against him again, circling, grinding, and rocking against him, back and forth. She could feel the tension building, could feel him hard beneath her.

His hands held her face steady while his tongue pushed into her mouth. It was a hungry kiss, a starving one. It was so urgent, raw, overwhelming, that she almost forgot to breathe.

The tension climbed inside her, excitement all-consuming, freeing her thoughts and senses. They were both completely clothed, yet she'd never been more aroused in her life.

As quickly as it all started, he lifted her from his body and tossed her onto the bed. He rose to his feet, as if he'd just been pricked by something sharp, and raked his hands through his hair. He stepped backward, shaking his head. "I'm sorry. I can't."

Every feeling of want collapsed inside of her, the heat in her belly quickly became frigid, like a bucket of ice had just been dumped over her head. She was mortified. Nauseated.

She rolled to the side of the bed and put her feet to the ground. Her stomach churned sickeningly.

"Samantha," he said, still out of breath.

But she didn't answer. She couldn't, because if she opened her mouth, she might cry.

"Are you okay?"

She closed her eyes, knowing full well she wasn't, but taking every last drop of willpower, she turned to face him. He looked tired. Tortured. Confused.

"Yes," she whispered. "I couldn't be better." She rose to her feet, walked to the bathroom, and flicked on the shower. She stripped off all her clothes and stepped under the water, so quickly it didn't even have a chance to warm up.

It was six years later, yet she'd let the same thing happen. Somehow he'd snuck under her walls, made her believe he'd changed, yet he couldn't have been more the same. He was the same Tristan who'd broken her heart all those years ago, and she was stupid enough to let him do it again.

She stayed in the shower longer than necessary. Washing every inch of skin he'd touched. Every bit of her he'd kissed. She then stayed longer—until all the water ran ice cold and her body was numb. She stepped back into the room, praying he'd gone to sleep, and found him lying in the corner of the room with a pillow. He didn't have any blankets, any comfort at all, but she didn't care. She climbed into the large bed alone, her hair still wet from her shower, and lay there, staring up at the ceiling, until she finally fell asleep.

———

SILENCE. That's what she gave him the next day. It was easy for her, being an only child. She was used to being alone, used to having no one to talk to, but she could tell it bothered him, and that was the goal. She was hurt, embarrassed, and she wanted him to know it. She wanted to push him away. To push him so far he would have no way of crawling back up to her heart again. Because he had fooled her once, and that was shame on him. But now he'd fooled her twice, and that was completely and utterly a shame on her.

Tristan received a message bright and early from Bob the next morning. The Mustang was ready. They stopped at a small cafe in town to pick up breakfast, then ate it in the car as soon as they were on the road. She could tell he was bothered, that he hadn't slept, but she wouldn't let herself care. She set herself up with a new audiobook, then zoned out for the long drive ahead.

At one point, they pulled off the road to get gas. Tristan unbuckled his seat belt and got out of the car to place the nozzle in the tank. "There's a cafe across the road," he said to her. "It looks pretty nice, if you're hungry?"

She adjusted in her seat and didn't answer.

"Samantha," he said again. "Are you hungry?"

She closed her eyes and continued listening to her book.

Before long, the headphones were ripped from her ears, and Tristan was standing beside her. There was hurt in his eyes. A hurt she knew she'd put there.

"Are you hungry, Samantha?"

She only shook her head, placed her headphones back on her head, and closed her eyes again. She expected him to go inside and eat without her, but he didn't. He got back on the road, where they carried on toward their destination with empty stomachs.

The hours passed slowly, more slowly than they had the whole trip, but eventually the sun began to creep its way down to the mountains. Tristan pulled off the road to the shoulder of the barren overgrown highway, and put the car in park. His arms were tense against the steering wheel, his eyes focused on the sun, which cast a golden hue to the whole sky. "Is this how it's going to be for the rest of the trip?"

She swallowed her saliva, her stomach rolling with sorrow, because the raw emotion in his voice caused her throat to instantly thicken. "Like what?"

"You not talking to me? Not looking at me." He turned in his seat to face her. He was a mess. There were bags under his eyes, deep dark circles, and a crease in his forehead she'd never noticed before. "Is this all because of last night?"

She turned in her seat toward the door and tried to open it. To get out of the car, because she could feel her eyes welling over, and she couldn't bear him seeing that again.

He leaned across the seat and pressed down the lock, not letting her go. "Answer me, Samantha."

She turned back to face him. Anger surged through her body and reddened her face. "Yes!" She yelled. "Yes, this is exactly how it will be."

"Why?"

"Because! If you don't want me, Tristan, then just tell me! If you don't want me, say it with words! Because I can handle words! But why let me embarrass myself like that? Why let me make myself a fool over you again?" Tears began to roll down her cheeks and she turned away.

He grabbed hold of her face, bringing her back, his thumbs brushing the tears from her lower lids. "You think I don't want you? You think that last night didn't almost kill me to push you away?"

She remained silent, but he kept talking. "I've never wanted anyone like I want you. I've never felt as out of control as I did last night. I may not be perfect, but I wasn't going to sleep with you while you were drunk."

Her chin began to quiver, and she opened her eyes. "I wasn't drunk."

"Yes, you were. You were stumbling all the way back to the room."

"There were pebbles."

"There were no pebbles," he whispered. The corners of his lips lifted in a hesitant smile.

Her cheeks flushed again and she closed her eyes, but he pulled her onto his lap, causing her to open them again.

His eyes met hers, intense but without apology. "I want you Samantha. I'm sure you can feel how much."

She swallowed. Hard and forcefully. Because yes, she could feel it.

He lifted her again and she spread her legs, straddling his hips like she had the night before. But he held her steady, not allowing her to move.

"What is it about you that I can't seem to get enough of? Why do I have dreams about you when I haven't seen you in six years?"

She shook her head, knowing she could have said the same words. There was something between them that drew them together. It was bigger than life. Bigger than anything she'd ever felt before.

He looked into her eyes, searching her face. Everything he was feeling lay out before her. "Do you want me, Samantha?" It was a question she thought she'd never hear, but one that sent every nerve in her body to stand at attention.

"You're my best friend's brother," she heard herself say, even though her body was screaming for her to give in already.

He pulled her closer, wrapping his arms around her body. "I know who I am. I know who you are. But none of that should have anything to do with your answer." He kissed her throat, causing her to loll her head back, allowing him better access.

It was wrong, so wrong to give in to this. To the Temptation of Tristan Montgomery, who was laying himself out there like a buffet of drugs to someone who had an addiction. "I want you, Tristan." It was soft, breathy, almost inaudible, but it was all that was needed.

His lips crashed against hers, and her arms wrapped around his neck. She was at complete surrender to whatever this was.

She moved her hips again, and this time he didn't stop her. He kissed her throat, her collarbone, then lifted her tank top over her head, leaving her bare to him. He cupped her breasts, taking each nipple into his mouth, and rolling it with his tongue.

Whatever this was, she couldn't stop it even if she wanted to. Their want for one another was like a magnetic pull, a gravity that only grew stronger with time.

She tugged at his shirt, not caring that they were on the side of the highway. She needed his skin against hers. She needed him now.

He pushed her back to her seat, and shifted his body above hers. He pulled off his shirt, his bronzed skin golden from the last bit of sun in the sky.

"You're beautiful," he whispered softly against her neck. He moved his hips, grinding into her, and the pads of her fingertips dug into his back. His touch felt so good, so achingly sweet, that she wanted to push him away and pull him closer all at the same time. Every movement with Tristan was like this, every kiss, every touch, felt like magic. A hundred times better than chocolate, a thousand times better than anything she'd ever touched, tasted, felt, in her entire life.

He rocked into her again, his lips exploring her jawline and throat. She reached for the button of his jeans, unable to take this torture any longer. Her movements were rushed, awkward, shaky, but she finally found him, then wrapped her hand around his girth, and he groaned.

The sound was almost guttural, mixed with all the relief

she felt simply by holding him in her hand. It was a sound of want, and she couldn't help but move her hand down his shaft to hear it again.

He found her waistband, his thumbs dipping inside right before he pulled them downward. She lifted her hips, allowing him to pull them all the way to her thighs, her legs, until he discarded them to the backseat where they belonged.

He didn't join her again right away. He just knelt there on his knees, looking at her, his eyes hungry, raking over her body, her breasts, her thighs. She didn't turn away. It was the second time she'd seen him naked, yet this time, she wouldn't allow herself to be embarrassed, to be scared. He was perfect. Sculpted. Muscular.

Then his fingers began to inch up her thighs. Slowly at first, softly, and she didn't look away. She wanted to see all of it. The way his cock twitched when he reached the apex of her thighs. The way his eyes fluttered when he discovered how wet she was. One finger dipped inside her core, deep and without apology, then the other. His fingers curled inside her, his thumb cradling her on the other side, adding the perfect amount of pressure. Her head lolled back, and she let out a moan.

His body joined her once again, solid, warm, heavy. She dropped her thighs open, completely surrendering to his every move, his every touch. The tension climbed inside her, strong, fast, to the rate it was almost scary. She didn't want to finish without him. She'd never felt this way before. With so much fire in her belly, so much delicious pressure inside every crevice.

She pushed his hands away, then grabbed his hips and pulled him closer. But he only looked at her and shook his head.

"I don't have any protection. I won't be able to stop." His voice was tight, guttural, almost strangled, but she didn't care.

"I'm on the pill." It was a simple invitation, but that was all that was needed.

His mouth slammed to hers again, his body anchoring her in place, until his hips found hers again. His whole back tensed. His hips, his stomach…but then he slowly sank inside her.

He was larger than she was used to, wider, but he stretched her in the most intoxicating way possible, and she welcomed the pressure. She lifted her hips, allowing him to sink even deeper inside, and then he began to move.

Slowly at first, in and out, rocking up and down like he was allowing her to get used to him. But little by little his speed quickened, his thrusts became harder, and she wrapped her legs around his back, squeezing them tighter, taking every move, every stroke, every achingly sweet, beautiful inch of him.

She felt herself building, but this time she didn't try to stop it. She called out his name, "Tristan!" Then let her head fall back to the seat and allowed her whole body to shatter around him. "Tristan," she said again, as his body collapsed on top of hers, and she felt his seed spill inside her belly.

His breath was heavy in her ear, his heartbeat pounding against her chest, and she wrapped her arms around his body.

"Are you okay?" he asked, not attempting to move away.

"Yes," she whispered. "Yes."

CHAPTER TWENTY

IT WAS ONLY LATER, when they stopped at a nearby gas station to clean themselves up, that Samantha started to think about Renee. About how sleeping with her best friend's brother would affect their relationship. About Tristan, about what happened between them might mean for their future.

She didn't even know if Tristan wanted a relationship, if he wanted to date her, or if he even wanted to see her again after this weekend. This was something she should have checked on before riding him like a wild pony, but in truth, she wasn't sure she wanted to know. She wasn't sure if she wanted a relationship, either. Single for the first time in six years, and not twenty-four hours later, she was sleeping with another man. Not *just* another man—with Tristan.

Her mother had a word for girls like her. It started with the letter S, and wasn't the most flattering. Sucking in a breath, she pulled a bottle of water from the fridge, then walked down the aisle looking for something to eat. She'd hardly touched her breakfast, skipped lunch, and after the best sex in her entire life, she was ravenous.

She was standing in the center of the aisle, contemplating

the selection on the mini-mart shelves, when Tristan came to stand behind her. He wrapped his arms around her waist, hugging her so hard it felt as though their bodies were melding together as one. She hesitated a moment, but the feeling was too wonderful, and eventually she couldn't resist anymore and let her body sink against him.

"What are you doing?" he asked.

She smiled at his question. It was whispered, soft, breathy in her ear, and made her whole body tingle from head to toe. "I'm trying to decide between salt and vinegar, or barbecue," she answered.

"Ahhh…" he began. "A tough choice."

She smiled. "It is. Because I like the way the vinegar feels against my tongue, but the barbecue is sweet and smoky."

He groaned. "Are you doing that on purpose?"

She laughed. "What?"

"Making your food sound so erotic."

She bit her lip, because that wasn't exactly what she was going for, but she would be lying if she said she didn't like his response.

He pushed away from her then and walked down the aisle to grab a soda out of the fridge. "Get them both, Samantha."

"Both?"

"Yes, because after your description"—he bit his lip, cocking one of his lopsided grins—"we'll need them both."

"We?" She laughed.

"Yes, *we*." He then winked at her, walked over to the counter, and paid for all their things.

WHEN THEY GOT BACK to the Mustang, the sun had completely disappeared from the horizon, leaving the night sky pitch black and covered with stars. She threw her bag to the back seat, just as Tristan's phone rang in his pocket. She opened the door, then glanced up to see his brows constrict. This wasn't the first time he'd received a phone call that seemed to bother him, and for some reason it made her stomach twist in knots.

He placed his soda in the front seat, held up his finger, indicating he'd be just a minute,-then walked to the back of the car and answered his phone. "Hello?"

She heard a woman's voice through the receiver, but he moved farther away from the car, and eventually she couldn't hear either of them any longer. She was sure he had friends, business associates…family that were women—who would call him for a variety of reasons. But it still made her chest tighten. He was fit, tall, and one hottest men she'd ever seen in her life… And she was just…her. It was hard not to feel self-conscious around him, to feel secure enough in herself to be wanted by the most popular guy in school.

God! She was making herself sick. She was acting like she was still in high school—only worse. Back then she seemed to have a good head on her shoulders. Now, she may as well be one of the groupies he had twisted around his little finger.

She settled into her seat, fastened her seat belt with clumsy fingers, and closed her eyes—she didn't like this. Didn't like this one bit. She opened her bottle of water and took a large mouthful, hoping to cleanse the bitter taste that had crept up her throat. What was she doing? Why was she acting like this? Why was she suddenly so insecure? But at the same time, how could she possibly believe this could work? He was Tristan, the brother of her best friend, the hottest guy at West Valley, and she felt like a sixteen-year-old girl again.

He topped off the gas a moment later and climbed into the seat beside her. His playful grin was back in place, but she sure didn't feel as confident as she had a moment before.

"What should we open first?" he asked. "Salt and vinegar, or barbecue?"

Her stomach rolled with all the unknowns, and she turned toward him. She wanted to ask who he was talking to, wanted to ask what he wanted…but she didn't do either. She looked down to the two bags between them and made a decision. There *wasn't* going to be a future for her and Tristan. This was a temporary relationship, a rebound from one place to another. She wouldn't allow it to be more than that. She wouldn't allow him to hurt her.

"Salt and vinegar," she said. The moment the decision was made, her mood instantly lightened. She looked up again and handed him the bag.

"Good choice," he said with a wicked grin. He then ripped open the bag with his teeth, causing a few chips to fall to his chest and scatter across his lap.

She plucked one from his chest and popped it into her mouth. "Mmm… That's good"

He grinned back at her and pulled back out to the road. "If you keep making noises like that, we're never going to make it to the wedding."

She licked her lips, then took another long drink of water to wash it down. She liked it this way. Playful, sexy, fun…and easy.

CHAPTER TWENTY-ONE

THEY TRAVELED A COUPLE MORE HOURS, snacking on chips and all the other things Samantha had stowed away in her bag for the trip, but eventually Tristan turned off the highway, just outside of Pennsylvania. Her brows furrowed, and she rolled up the bag of barbecue, knowing they still had a good two hundred miles yet before their destination. "Don't tell me we need gas again?" she asked.

He shook his head, his brow slightly furrowing. "Nah, I thought we'd stop for the night. I'm getting tired." He said it quietly, but there was something under the surface that made her stomach constrict. Because it wasn't true. By now she knew him well enough. Knew when he was tired and when he wasn't. She also knew when something was bothering him. She could feel it in her bones. If they drove a few more hours, they would be there. At the wedding, which was the point of this whole crazy trip. But she kept her mouth shut...because she knew exactly what this was. This was their last night together. Their last hoorah, their last roll in the hay.

A few minutes later, Tristan turned into the parking lot of the Grand Belleview hotel, confirming it. It wasn't the first motel they had passed, but this place was gorgeous. Ten stories high, all windows, with red carpets that led up to the entrance.

Tristan put the car in park, took his wallet from the center console, and pulled in a breath. Suddenly this felt like so much more than their last night. This felt like goodbye. Like she was stepping onto a plane with a one-way ticket. Tomorrow they'd be at the wedding, and all this would stop. If for no other reason, than for Renee. Because she didn't deserve this drama before her wedding. Because up until this point, as far as Renee knew, they were two people who couldn't stand each other. But at the same time, if this ride went on for much longer, Samantha wasn't sure she'd be able to jump off. She turned toward the window, pulling in a deep breath to give herself strength. "It went by pretty quickly, considering."

He leaned back in his seat, stretching his arms overhead. "Yeah, it did."

She nodded at his reflection, squeezing the door handle, knowing she was about to cry. She hated goodbyes, even when she knew they weren't forever.

She got out of the car, gathered her backpack to keep herself busy, then turned around to find him right behind her. He didn't say anything, just took the bag from her shoulder and began walking toward the hotel.

There was a large fountain in the foyer, with large purple and blue lights that moved like currents. It reminded her of an aquatic version of the solar system. With a thousand playful lights dancing on the surface like stars.

Tristan headed straight for the counter, but she touched his arm, making him turn around to face her. "I haven't talked to Ren in a couple of days—" she said softly. "Do you mind if I borrow your phone?"

He didn't even wait for her to finish before typing in the password and placing it in her hand. He held her fingers, loosely, but all encompassing, and his eyes met hers. As though asking what she was thinking. But then he smiled, a soft tender smile that made her whole body melt. "Tell her I said 'hi.' "

He let go then, setting a million butterflies loose in her stomach, before turning again to the counter.

When she moved toward the fountain again, she took a deep breath to clear her head. He was so perfect. So utterly amazing that she almost hated the fact she had to walk away. She began dialing Renee's number but she only got four numbers in before the contact pulled up. "Li'l sis."

She smiled at the name, but an unpleasant taste crept up her throat at the same time. She was Renee's maid of honor. The girl Renee should trust most in this world, yet here she was, sleeping with her friend's brother. Samantha pressed her forehead into her palm and sent through the call before she had time to think about it. With one step in front of the other she paced the floor, trying to decide what to do about the situation. On one hand, it was no one's business at all whom she slept with. Including her best friend. On the other, she'd always made it Renee's business to know all there was about her, and the last time she kept a secret it almost killed her.

"Hello," Renee answered, nearly making Samantha's heart seize in her chest. "I can't answer the phone right now. I'm getting married and stuff. Leave a message and I *might* call you back."

Samantha laughed at the message, as blood rushed back up to her face. She waited for the beep before filling her lungs with air. "Hey Ren, it's me…" She took a step forward, knowing a confession like this wasn't one that should be left in a message. She then sat on a bench and squeezed her eyes shut. "Long story short, but my phone is dead. We'll be in New York tomorrow afternoon. I'll tell you all the gory details then." She looked over at Tristan, unable to prevent her eyes from raking over his entire body. "If you need me, call Tristan, okay?" She cleared her throat, averting her eyes once again to the floor. "Bye."

She hung up the phone feeling somewhat relieved and turned around to head back to the reception desk, but a text notification popped up on the phone, stopping her.

"I CAN'T IMAGINE my life without you."

SHE LOOKED AWAY the second she saw it, before she could even see who it was from, but it was too late. She'd seen it, she'd read it, and her heart shattered into a million pieces.

Tristan stood across the foyer, his large form leaning against the counter. He was talking to the woman at the reception desk, his wallet out, deep in conversation. It was an invasion of privacy, but she didn't care anymore. She walked farther into the seating area and looked down to the phone again. It was locked.

She took a deep breath. "Good riddance." But she wasn't quite sure she felt it. Because something had wrapped itself around her heart, squeezing it harder with each passing second. Whoever was texting Tristan had nothing to do with her. Whoever it was, who thought they couldn't live without him, was none of her concern.

She gripped his phone tighter, then dropped her hands to her sides and walked toward the counter. The woman there was giving him directions to their room, but Samantha barely heard any of it. This was a temporary relationship, a rebound, and she wouldn't allow herself to get hurt.

He slung his backpack over one shoulder, then walked the short distance to the elevator. He pressed the call button, then turned around to look over his shoulder. "Everything Good?"

he asked, tilting his head as though wondering why she wasn't following.

She only nodded and stepped toward him. The elevator doors opened then, and she didn't stop until she was securely inside, leaning against the banister, where she was steady enough to hand him back his phone. "Thank you," she whispered.

His brows furrowed as he took it from her fingers. "Everything okay?"

She looked up, her stomach so twisted she thought she might be sick. "She didn't answer," she whispered. But a vice tightened around her heart and she couldn't remain quiet. "I don't think we should say anything to her. About this." She waved her hand around the elevator, but the meaning was clear. She didn't want to tell Renee about them. About whatever this was. Whatever had happened between them.

"Okay," he agreed. But it was a little too quickly. A little too soon...

Her brows furrowed, because for some reason his easy agreement hurt. She said it wouldn't, had told herself a thousand different ways that this time she could stop it, but... "She's the bride," she explained. "And I don't want any attention going anywhere else."

He nodded.

"I'll tell her later. I mean, if it comes up. When she gets back from Cabo."

He nodded again. "Sounds good."

The doors opened, but neither of them exited. He looked at her, a frown making his handsome features somehow more heartbreaking. "Are you okay?" he asked. "You're acting funny."

She was like a deer caught in headlights, unsure which direction to turn. Because if she went right, her future was waiting.

Without a career, without a relationship, without a best friend. But if she turned left, if she asked him about the message, she might find things she never wanted to know. Things that would cut deep, would alter all they shared together, and leave her broken at a time she needed to be strong. Instead, she walked toward him, right into the fire, and wrapped her arms around his body. His heat was scorching, his body solid and strong, and even if it killed her later, she would allow herself to hold him just a little bit longer.

He wrapped his arms around her waist, so tight it was almost crushing. "Are you okay, Samantha?" he asked her once again.

"I'm perfect," she whispered, though she knew it was a lie. But she was good at faking happiness. So good she'd fooled even herself for six years.

He grinned at her, apprehensively, but still sexy as hell, then lifted her in his arms and walked out of the elevator to the door of their room. He entered the card in the slot, not allowing her to slip. "Good."

He kissed her lips and pushed it open. It was a kiss of good-byes, of last chances, and not wanting to let go. He kicked the door closed, carried her to the bed in the middle of the room, laid her in the center, and knelt beside her. His eyes were only on her, as though she was someone to be worshipped. As though he was admiring a fine painting he'd spent a lifetime trying to see. He began unbuttoning her top, pushing it roughly over her shoulders before climbing on top of her to straddle her hips.

She was pinned beneath him, unable to move if she wanted to, but she didn't care. He unfastened the clasp of her bra, pulling the cups to each side.

"You're beautiful," he whispered. He then lay between her open thighs, and she wrapped her arms around his back, desperately. He rocked into her. She could feel him hard beneath his jeans, could feel his heart racing, but when she moved her hands to free him, he took both of them and held them above her head.

His mouth covered her nipple, causing her head to press back into the mattress. Because when he touched her, all thoughts were irrelevant. There was nothing else. No weddings, no secrets. No months or weeks. No days or nights. Just this one. She wanted this to last forever. For his lips to kiss her a thousand times, for him to keep telling her she was beautiful.

His mouth moved down her belly, and his hands unfastened her shorts. She lifted her hips, allowing him to slide them down her thighs, until she lay there completely naked, shaking with desire.

He knelt between her thighs again, and pulled his shirt over his head. Then he grabbed her by the hips and yanked her body toward him. His fingers ran down the tops of her thighs, all the way to her knees before climbing up again.

She pulled in a long breath, completely fascinated by his skilled fingers. He inched closer to the apex of her thighs, until one finger slipped between the slick folds.

"Fuck," he whispered. Two fingers plunged inside her, making her arch her back against the sheer pressure. "You're so wet." His eyes were on hers, hungry, starving, and watching her every move. He curled his fingers inside her, pressing up toward her belly. To a place she'd never been touched before. She trembled at the sensation, her body climbing higher toward climax in just a second. His thumb began to move in slow circles at her nub, his fingers rocking her, coaxing her.

She began to pant. She wanted him so bad she couldn't even think. She wanted him so bad it was hard to breathe.

His fingers plunged inside her. Again and again, curling, rubbing, stretching her. His head then dipped down, and suddenly his mouth joined his fingers.

She couldn't handle any more. She couldn't take one more

second of this sweet, sexy, titillating torture. She closed her eyes, clenching the sheets in her fists. His mouth was warm and soft, his breath cool, his groans heavy.

He began to kiss her. Really kiss her. His tongue plunging in and out, his whiskers abrasive against her inner thighs. Every inch of her body screamed for release. All her senses were stimulated at once. She felt her body involuntarily tighten, tense, and she knew she was about to release. She grabbed hold of his hair and tried to pull him higher so she could take him with her. He wouldn't budge. He only pinned her hands to her sides as he counted his slow torture.

He kissed her, sucked her, ravaged her, until she was a quivering mound beneath him.

"Tristan," she begged, even though she didn't exactly know what she was asking for. "Tristan." His fingers kept plunging, his thumb stroking, but he lifted his head slightly, his eyes hungry on hers. "Let go, Samantha. Don't fight this."

She shook her head, her pulse beating a thousand beats. "Tristan," she called out again.

"I got you," he demanded.

Her body instantly shuddered, giving in to his will. Her head fell back to the pillow, and her core clenched and pulsed all around his fingers. Her whole frame melted into the mattress, like butter under the sun. His body settled upon hers, heavy and solid, and she kissed his head, holding him firm to her breast.

"Where did you learn to do that?" she asked, but then thought better of the question. "Never mind, I don't want to know."

He laughed on top of her, kissed her nipple, her collarbone, up to her lips where she could taste herself on his tongue.

She was his. Wherever he wanted to go, whatever he wanted to do, she was at his mercy. She was his, and she was a fool to ever think otherwise.

His phone began to vibrate in his pocket between them, causing reality to crash down upon them all at once. He closed his eyes, cringing as the phone buzzed yet again. He rolled off her to the side of the bed. "I'm sorry," he said, forcing himself to sit on the edge of the bed. "I need to get this."

She pushed herself from the mattress and nodded. She couldn't see his face, but the tension in his back told her all she needed to know. It was the same person from earlier. Possibly the same person who couldn't live without him.

She got off the bed, took his shirt from the floor, and dragged it over her head.

"Hello," she heard him say, just as she closed the bathroom door behind her.

She looked at herself in the mirror. To her long blond hair that framed her now flushed cheeks. To Tristan's too large t-shirt that covered her trembling body. To her eyes that pleaded with her, telling her not to admit that she was lost. But she was. Somewhere along the way she had fallen, sometimes kicking and screaming, but there was no denying it any longer. She had fallen in love with Tristan Montgomery.

It was a bitter realization, and one she was reluctant to make, but she was fooling herself to think this could be only a fling. This was real, heavy, and bigger than anything she'd ever felt before. And it would shatter her soul before it was over.

Still hearing his voice through the door, she pulled the t-shirt over her head, and then turned on the water to mute out the sound. To not listen to the man she was falling in love with talking to another woman.

The water was hard and warm when she stepped into the shower. She let the stream beat down on her, hoping the feeling would offer some sort of distraction. The water warmed her, comforted her, but could never wash away the kisses he ferociously left behind.

The door to the bathroom opened a moment later, and

soon Tristan was standing behind her. His body pressed against hers, his arms wrapping around her waist, pulling her closer again. She told herself not to ask, to enjoy the rest of the evening, and the body that was only hers on loan, but she couldn't. She needed to know, she needed answers.

Turning to face him, she rested her hands on his bare chest and looked up into his eyes. She couldn't let herself fall and not try to stop it when she knew all that waited for her was thorns. "Who was that?" she asked.

He looked into her eyes, pleading for her not to ask the question.

"Who was that?" she asked again. She asked for the sixteen-year-old girl who was too insecure to call him out on his behavior. For the girl who wasn't strong enough to resist a six-year long relationship, even though she knew it wasn't what she wanted.

He cleared his throat and looked over her head to grab a bottle of soap. "It was my mom."

She ripped the curtain open, not able to bear his lies, and got out of the shower. She yanked a towel from the rack and wrapped it around her body. "Don't lie to me."

Her world was crashing in all around her, the walls, the ceiling. He followed after her, grabbed hold of her arms, and forced her to look up at him. "I don't lie."

That was the second time he'd said that to her, and her legs began to shake beneath her. "Is that who can't live without you?" The words were angry, unbelieving, and held all the insecurities that were overflowing from her very core.

She was outing herself. Making him completely aware of what she'd done, and the expression on his face shifted in an instant. He ripped a towel from the wall, wrapped it around his waist, and went to the bedroom. "Exactly."

She closed her eyes, not able to open them until the bathroom door closed behind him, leaving her alone, wrapped in guilt, hurt, and trembling like a leaf.

She opened the door again and followed after him, not sure if it was the look on his face or the sound of his voice that made her believe him, but she did. He was sitting on the edge of the bed, his head in his hands, and his back hunched over as though he was in pain.

Her chin began to tremble, but she walked toward him, pressing his head into her belly. "I'm sorry," she whispered. "I don't know what makes me become so insecure around you. I'm so sorry. It's none of my business—"

He looked up then, cutting her off and making her throat instantly tighten. "My father's having an affair. Renee doesn't have a clue, so that's why I didn't want you to know. I didn't want to put you in a position to have to lie to her, but please don't tell her." His voice was hoarse and shredded, as if he was confessing something that brought him great misery.

She pulled in a breath, trying to get hold of her emotions, because she couldn't bear seeing him like this. Suddenly she understood him. Understood the man who behaved as though he held the world on his shoulders. Because he did. His family's world. His sister's world. The people he loved.

She dropped to her knees in front of him and pulled him to her chest. He grabbed hold of her, wrapping his thick arms around her, hugging her, burying his head in her hair like he was desperate to be close to her.

"It was on a Thursday, right after I got off work. I saw him with my own eyes." He quieted for a moment, as though trying to pull himself together. "The bastard actually tried to tell me it was nothing."

She gripped him tighter and kissed the top of his head, urging him to continue.

"He's having an affair with a thirty-year old woman who

was supposed to be his secretary. He's been lying to us for a long time. Mom and Dad have stopped talking, so I'm trying to juggle all communication. They're going to try and play nice for Renee, until the wedding is over, but Mom's a fucking mess." The words rushed out of him, as though he'd been carrying the burden for far too long. "I've never seen her like this." His voice shredding and she pushed his hair repeatedly back from his face.

Her heart was breaking. Not only for him, but for all of them. Because the Montgomerys were solid. Always together. Always strong. "Renee doesn't know any of this?" she asked quietly.

"No."

She swallowed hard, knowing this wasn't a good idea. "She's going to know the second she sees them. She'll sense it."

He only shook his head, gripping the base of his skull between thumb and forefinger. "That's what I keep telling Mom, but she's stubborn. She thinks they'll be fine. I'm just waiting for everything to fall apart."

He then looked to her face, searching her eyes. For what she wasn't sure, but the vulnerability she witnessed made her want to give him everything. A moment later he stood, lifting her up from the floor and into his arms. He sat with her again in the chair beside the bed, gently rocking her. "Don't ever lie to me, Samantha," he whispered. "Promise me."

There was something so heartbreaking about him. So sad. Because she could almost see the little boy who lived inside him. The boy who was sorrowful to learn that his father wasn't the man he'd always idolized. That he'd cheated on Tristan's mother. Cheated on their family. "I promise," Samantha whispered back.

There were tears in her eyes, threatening to spill over. He grabbed her face, his fingers wrapping around her neck. He looked like he wanted to say something. To do something, but he wasn't sure what. She searched his eyes, silently asking him what he needed, because in that moment, she would do anything.

He finally settled his mouth upon hers, hard, rough, and crushing, as though he needed her body to pull him back from his grief. From the sadness inside that was too hard for him to bear. She kissed him, giving him everything she had. All her hope, all her strength, all her love.

He made love to her again, this time with his whole body. He kissed every inch of her, spilled his seed inside her belly, until his entire weight collapsed on top of her. Heavy, strong, beautiful. She wrapped her arms around him and took all of it. Because something between them had shifted. He'd shared a part of himself that he'd never shared with anyone else. He'd shared his secret, his burden, and she grabbed hold of it knowing she'd never let it go.

They fell asleep a moment later, tangled in each other's arms. Exhausted. Wasted. And everything between them forever altered.

CHAPTER TWENTY-TWO

IT WAS STILL DARK when she opened her eyes again. The bed was cold beside her, and she instantly knew something was wrong. Her eyes adjusted to the dim light, and she found Tristan sitting on the edge of the bed, looking off into the distance. She instinctively reached out to him, and he turned around.

He looked tired, thoughtful. "Did I wake you?" he whispered.

She pushed herself up on her elbows, yawning "What time is it?"

"Four in the morning," he replied. "Go back to sleep."

But there was something in his voice that frightened her. Something soft, uncertain, that told her what he said wasn't at all what he wanted. "Is something wrong?" she asked softly, sitting forward to gently rub his back.

"Nah," he whispered. He hesitated, only a second, but it was long enough. It was as though he had made up his mind about something. He turned around to face her, laying his knee up on the mattress to get comfortable. His face was partially covered by shadow, and he cleared his throat before he began.

"I'm going to ask you a question," he said seriously, "and I want you to be completely honest with me."

Her breath caught in her throat and she froze, because she didn't have the faintest idea what had brought this on. What had made him wake so late at night and look so heavy. She nodded though, because the tone of his voice told her it was important. Because the tone of his voice told her that how she answered meant a whole lot to him.

"How have I ever made you look like a fool?" he asked then. He wasn't angry, and he wasn't emotional, but there was something in his voice that was somewhere in between.

She pulled in a breath, then looked down to her hands and shook her head. "I don't know what you're talking about."

He turned completely around, his face now illuminated by the moonlight coming in from the window. "You said it in the car. On the side of the road. You said not to make you look like a fool again. What did you mean?"

She hesitated, but he grabbed hold of her hands, forcing her to look up at him before letting go. "If we're going to do this, I don't want anything between us."

Her throat was so tight she could barely swallow, but she knew he was right. She had to talk to him, to get everything out in the open. Because if their past wasn't put out there, they had no shot at a future.

She met his eyes, forcing herself to look at him even though it terrified her. "After the cabin," she said, playing with the edge of the sheet between her fingers, suddenly feeling all the emotions of a broken sixteen-year-old girl come crashing to her shoulders. "I saw you with a girl at the pool table. I thought you saw me, but—"

He suddenly closed his eyes, then made a noise, deep in the back of his throat, cutting her off. His head fell back to his shoulders, and he made a sound that could have been a laugh, or a cough. "That," he whispered. "That." But this time it was with a hint of amusement. He was quiet a moment, then he lifted his head to look at her, his blue eyes brilliant even in the faint light of night, as he stared straight into her soul. "I'm a jealous man, Samantha," he finally stated, as though that simple sentence was all that was needed.

She reached for his face, trying to understand what he meant, but he continued.

"I wanted to make you jealous too."

She shook her head, not comprehending why he would do that, but then she replayed the night over in her head and she remembered. She covered her mouth with a hand and her throat went dry. "You saw Steven kiss me, didn't you?" He didn't respond, but the look in his eye told her that was exactly what happened. "Oh, my God."

"Samantha…" But he said it in a way that dismissed their past. He said it in a way that said it didn't matter.

But it did. "When he kissed me, I was shocked, but I let it happen. Partially because I was young and didn't know how to push him away. He was my friend. One of my best friends, and I didn't want to hurt him. And partially because I wanted to know if kissing him felt even half as good as it felt kissing you. It didn't. It never did——"

He grabbed hold of her face, his eyes penetrating hers, his lips millimeters away. "If he didn't kiss you like I did, if you didn't feel with him the way you did with me, why were you still with him when I came back to visit? Why were you still with him six years later?"

Tears rolled down her cheeks, because he was asking the hard questions. Asking the questions she'd asked a thousand times but never let herself answer.

"I don't know…"

He shook his head, as though saying her answer wasn't good enough.

"Because…" she continued. "He was my friend! And I

didn't want to hurt him. He was my friend, everything was easy, comfortable, and I didn't want our relationship to fail. To fail at one more damned thing..." Her words trailed off, and she looked up at him through tear-laced lashes. "It wasn't until you came back into my life that I realized all I was missing..."

He cupped the side of her face, sending her pulse racing.

"I never thought I could have more. That there *was* more. Because I'm so scared, Tristan, so scared out of my mind of failing, that I haven't let myself live." The words came choking out of her, as if they were clawing up her throat, needing her to confess them. Ragged, with torn up edges, coming from deep within her soul.

Her chin began to quiver, and he pulled her into his lap, hugging her so hard it almost crushed her. He held her so tightly, it was as if there was no end to him or beginning of her. "You deserve *everything*."

It wasn't until he said those words that she realized that's what it was. That she'd convinced herself that her relationship with Steven was enough. That what she had with him was love. That she'd convinced herself she wasn't capable of more. Wasn't worthy of more.

Tristan's voice was harsh, almost jagged, as he whispered forcefully in her ear. "You deserve everything. Do you hear me?"

She nodded, crying in his arms, sobbing so hard, because for some reason, for the first time in her life, she believed it. She deserved a deep-seated love. The soul crushing kind she always dreamed about. And she deserved friendship at the same time, because she was worthy of all of it. He climbed with her back into bed a while later, where he held her in his arms, stroking her back softly with his fingertips. Eventually she fell asleep, for the first time in her adult life, feeling whole.

CHAPTER TWENTY-THREE

THE NEXT AFTERNOON, Samantha turned toward the window of the Mustang, letting the warm breeze blow over her hair and face. Last night had been an emotional roller coaster. Between finding out about Renee's parents, and Tristan holding her in bed all night, her body, mind, and soul were completely spent.

Feelings she didn't even know existed were ripped off her, like layers shed from an onion—things she'd buried so deep she didn't even know they existed. Yet somehow, Tristan knew they were there—and somehow, she didn't want to hide them from him any longer.

It was an odd feeling, because in the past any shortcoming would be brushed under the table. She didn't like others to see her flaws, her failures, her fears—yet it didn't seem as scary sharing them with Tristan. Maybe because he wasn't one to strive for perfection. Or maybe because the way he looked at her made her feel like all her imperfections were what he liked most about her.

They'd enjoyed the morning lounging in bed, making love, and eating breakfast brought to them on silver platters:

pancakes, fruit, and lots of sticky syrup that she thoroughly enjoyed licking from his fingers.

Even though they didn't talk about it, the wedding was looming over them, pushing them forward, rushing them through their time together, and by 10:00 a.m. they were packed up, back in the car, and ready for the last leg of their journey.

She looked over at him now, to his handsome face and his hands braced on either side of the steering wheel. His aviator glasses were shading his face, his lips serious, set in a straight line, but he was beautiful. And not just because of his outside. He was beautiful on the inside too.

Last night he'd laid himself out there, letting her see the little boy who lived inside him, hurt and broken by his father who he'd always idolized. Then about his jealous heart, that prevented them from being together all those years ago. But somehow, that was all over now. They'd overcome it.

"We finally made it," she said softly, though she didn't mean it just about the trip. It was said about so much more.

He glanced over at her, cracking one of his panty dropping smiles, and tilted his head down toward the GPS. "We should be there in an hour. Are you ready?"

She grinned. "That depends."

"On what?" he asked flirtatiously.

"On what you're asking I'm ready for." She raised her brows. "Because if you're asking if I'm ready to try on my bridesmaids dress, the answer is no. I sent the measurements three months ago, and I think I've eaten more burgers and fries in the last four days than I have in the past year."

"Well that's a shame," he said, with a serious frown. "Because burgers and fries are one of God's greatest gifts."

Her grin widened. "But if you're asking if I'm ready to see Renee and get out of this car, then the answer is a big fat one hundred percent yes." She leaned forward in her seat, fetched the last stick of gum from her purse and split it in half. "How about you?" she asked, placing one half in his mouth, and the other in hers.

He nodded in thanks, but shrugged.

"You're worried about your parents aren't you?" she asked quietly.

He shrugged again, then sped up to move around the car ahead of them. "Do you still not want to tell Renee?"

She bit her bottom lip and turned toward the window, knowing full well what he was asking her, and raked her upper teeth over the skin. "I think it's best, don't you?"

He was quiet for a moment, forcing her to look back over again, but he didn't answer.

"Last I spoke to Renee," she began, "I was still with Steven. How can I tell her only days later that I…" But she trailed off, because what she really wanted to say was something she wasn't quite ready to. That after last night, she could feel herself falling for him, so hard and fast it scared the crap out of her.

He took his glasses from his face and placed them on the dashboard. "I understand."

She pulled her legs up in her seat and got up on her knees to face him. "I don't think you do. Because if we say something now, this thing between us would be out there for everyone to judge. It won't be just ours anymore. It will be your mother's, your father's, Renee's. It's probably selfish of me, but I don't want to share this. I don't want to share *us*. I want you to myself. I also want Renee to have her wedding, and I want no one to talk about the girl who just broke out of a six year long relationship and is already falling for another man."

He remained quiet for a good five seconds, his lip lifting in a smile as he turned to look at her. "You're falling for me?"

The way he said it, with a shy hesitation, made her breath

catch in her throat. It was innocent, and sincere, and so utterly sexy. She laughed a little, tears blurring her vision. "Hard."

He reached out, grabbed the back of her neck, and pulled her toward him. "Good." He gave her a quick kiss, then let her go.

She settled down in the seat and burrowed into his shoulder. In less than an hour they would be at the hotel. In less than an hour, she couldn't sit this close to him anymore. He wrapped his arm around her, and she moved as close as she possibly could. Until then, she would enjoy this. Until then, she would take all of him she could get.

AT JUST BEFORE one in the afternoon, they pulled off the freeway to the supermarket right outside the city. Tristan hopped out of the car in a hurry, then held up a finger, letting her know to stay where she was. She frowned, wondering what he was up to, because by now she knew the car well enough to know they weren't in need of gas, and her eyebrows pinched together as she watched him walk through the double doors. He was gone longer than she expected, so long that she plugged in one of her audiobooks to pass the time. But eventually he came out carrying a brown paper sack and a bottle of soda. He opened the car door and handed her the bag as he climbed into the Mustang, then turned to face her and fasten his seat belt.

Her brows instantly furrowed and she looked at him suspiciously. "What is this?"

He gestured for her to open it, and she pulled out a long narrow box from inside. She glanced up, wrinkling her nose with amusement. "A cell phone?"

He grinned back at her and snatched the box from her hand. "If we're going to pretend nothing is happening, I'm going to need some way to get hold of you." He took the phone out of the box and began reading the instructions for set up.

"True," she said, biting her lip as she watched him do his thing.

He handed the phone back to her a short time later, satisfied with his handiwork as he lifted his chin. "There. Call me. Then I'll have your number in my phone."

She glanced down to the cell, instantly grinning at the name in the title bar. "Wild Stallion?" she asked, barely able to contain her laughter.

He only grinned. "It's a code name," he said shyly. But then he lifted his eyebrows and grinned wider. "I bet you can't guess what yours is?"

She giggled, amused by the fact that he'd given her a code name. "Oh God. What?"

"Mona."

CHAPTER TWENTY-FOUR

SAMANTHA'S STOMACH dropped as they rolled into the parking lot of the Hobart Garden Hotel. This was it, what the whole trip had been leading up to, but now that she was here, she wasn't quite sure she was ready for it. She looked over at Tristan, thankful they'd be so busy during the wedding that she wouldn't have time to miss him—but she feared that wasn't true, and squeezed his hand as they came closer toward the valet stand.

Renee had explained to Samantha how much money was being spent on the wedding, but there was nothing that could have prepared her for this. The hotel was a hundred stories high, like a wall of windows looking over the big city. Pristine, beautiful, and made her instantly self-conscious about the way she was dressed. She tugged at the tattered edge of her denim shorts and waited in the car for the valet to retrieve her from her seat.

"Madame," he said respectfully, offering his arm for her to hold onto.

She pulled down the hem of her tank top, then retrieved her backpack from the back seat before accepting his help.

"Thank you," she said, then stepped up to the curb, not knowing what else to do.

The valet turned to Tristan, offering a red ticket in exchange for his keys. "Should I send your bags ahead, sir?" the man asked, but Tristan only shook his head, set his glasses on the bridge his nose, and threw his backpack high on his shoulder.

"That won't be necessary, but thank you."

Samantha busied herself braiding her hair as she followed Tristan to the elevator. "Do you know where we're supposed to go?" she asked, looking around to the masses of people, all dressed in business suits and dresses.

He shrugged and smiled down at her. "I haven't the faintest idea." He reached for her hand, but she immediately retreated.

"Wild Stallion, remember?"

He cracked a smile, but ignored her warning and stepped toward her anyway. "You can call me that whenever you want to, baby." He then tugged on one of her braids and pressed the call button for the elevator.

They stepped out to the lobby a short time later, where a bus boy with a hopper full of matching luggage passed in a hurry. Samantha looked around for the reception desk, wondering if that was where they should try first. "Maybe we can call Renee—"

But before she could finish her thought, a squeal came from the other side of the elevators and traveled all the way down the hall. Not two seconds later, a flurry of light brown hair and skinny legs launched themselves to the top of Tristan's back.

"It's about time!" Renee shouted.

Samantha covered her mouth, watching Tristan almost tumble forward before catching his balance and reaching up over his head to flip his sister over his shoulders. She was in a headlock before she could even blink.

"Woah, woah, woah!" protested a very tall, very lean man who came to stand beside them. "That's my future bride you have there."

Samantha instantly grinned. She'd seen pictures of the handsome ballet dancer, but there were people who were more attractive in person, and Renee's fiancée was one of them. He had a sort of James Dean quality about him. Inky dark hair that was both perfectly combed but messy at the same time, and his eyelashes were so thick it almost looked like a chore to hold his eyes open.

Renee glanced up, head twisted around Tristan's death grip, and giggled. "Phin, you remember my brother Tristan."

Tristan let go of Renee, almost dropping her, then draped his arm over her shoulder, anchoring her arms at her waist. "Sisters," he said, holding a hand out to shake. "Can't live with 'em, can't live without 'em."

Phin only laughed, and shook Tristan's hand. "It's good to see you again," he said, then he turned toward Samantha and took the backpack from her shoulder. "And you must be Samantha. Renee has been talking about you for months."

Samantha glanced over at her friend, a lump forming in her throat as she held out a hand to Phin—but he immediately yanked her forward and into a two-armed hug. "It's good to meet you, finally."

Emotion hit her like a sack of onions—without warning, tears stung her eyes and she blinked them quickly away. After all this time, after all these months, she was finally meeting the man her best friend would marry. No, she wasn't just meeting him, she was pressed into his chest barely able to breathe. Renee was as close as she had to as a sister, and until this moment Samantha wasn't sure she liked Phin. He was a strange man who had swept in like Batman, capturing her best friend—with no plans to ever let her go.

But she did like him.

He was warm, protective, and he made Renee smile like Samantha had never seen before.

She finally closed her eyes, accepting the man who would be as close to a brother as she'd ever have, and hugged him back "The feeling's mutual," she said softly.

They all parted, realizing they were making a spectacle of themselves in the middle of the hotel lobby, and Renee came up to take hold of her hand. "I thought you'd never get here," she whispered, her head resting on the top of Samantha's shoulder in the familiar way she'd missed.

All of a sudden, it was like the last six months disappeared. Like it always did. Because Renee owned a piece of her heart. Reunions weren't awkward or uncomfortable; they were like finding an old pair of slippers after a long summer. They were worn, comfortable, and perfectly molded to your feet. She and Renee fit together, and she immediately felt at home.

The group continued talking and moving toward the reception desk, and for the first time since Renee had moved out, Samantha realized she wasn't losing her best friend. She would still miss her like crazy, would still have to adjust to not seeing her face every day, but you could never lose a person who held a part of your soul. Renee wouldn't be able to get rid of her even if she tried.

They began talking about the trip, about how different the city was compared to Los Angeles, and Renee stopped. She turned around to look at Tristan and tilted her head. "That reminds me. What happened with the car?" she asked, eyeing him up and down suspiciously. It was a normal question—one that should have been expected after being almost two days late to his sister's wedding, but he adjusted his stance and looked at Samantha. "Radiator cap. Of all things."

Renee's brows furrowed and she looked to Samantha. "And it delayed you for that long?"

Samantha nodded, taking hold of Renee's hand and

squeezing. "That's what happens when you break down in the middle of Colton, Iowa," she answered. It wasn't a lie, but for some reason it felt like one.

They continued walking, catching up on wedding stuff, while Phin escorted them to the reception desk to check into their rooms. Tristan and Phin took the task of checking in the car, while Renee rambled on about this weekend's itinerary.

"I was beginning to think you wouldn't make it," Renee said, playing with the ends of Samantha's hair.

"I wouldn't have missed it for the world—"

Renee interrupted, cracking a grin. "No, I mean the party."

Samantha narrowed her eyes. "I thought I missed—"

"No." Renee shook her head. "Phin and I decided to do them together, bachelorette and bachelor all in one." She got quiet suddenly, then rested her head on Samantha's shoulder again. "We only get to see you guys for a few days, and splitting up didn't make any sense." She turned around to look at her fiancé, causing her face to instantly soften. "I want you to get to know him, Sam. Really know him, and I'm worried we're going to run out of time."

Samantha frowned then, and shook her head. "There's plenty of time…" But she was saying it for her best friend's benefit, because the moment she thought about the days she had left, a hard knot formed in the bottom of her stomach and made her feel ill.

A buzzing noise began vibrating in Renee's pocket and she broke away to pull her phone from her pocket. She looked down at the screen then turned toward Samantha. "Betty, my seamstress, she's waiting for you in my room. I know you're probably tired, but do you mind if we run over there? I'll have the guys bring your key when they're done." She turned to Phin and Tristan, grabbing hold of each one of their shoulders and lifting up on her toes. "I'm taking Sam. Bring her key to my room when you're done. Okay? Okay!" Before waiting for an answer, she turned back to Samantha and took hold of her arm again. "I'm a mess. Can you tell?"

They walked arm in arm to the elevator, where Renee told her all about the events leading up to the wedding. About the caterer canceling last minute, about how her future mother-in-law was freaking out. But somehow it all had resolved itself in the end, because some big famous baker was coming into town and agreed to take the job.

They continued on to Renee's room on the fifth floor, all the way to the end of the long hall. The suite was almost the size of the apartment they'd shared back in LA, although there were twice as many clothes thrown about it.

"Betty!" Renee exclaimed, as she walked into the room.

A woman who looked to be about the age of Samantha's grandmother turned in her overstuffed seat. She set the pair of pants she was stitching to the arm of the chair and patted her salt-and-pepper bun.

"*This,*" Renee began, "is my best friend, Samantha." It was said in a way that said "Finally!" And she pushed Samantha toward the woman like a sacrifice to her maker.

"Ooooh…" the woman said, with a thick Italian accent. "She more beautiful than you say." She walked toward Samantha and circled her a couple of times before looking up. She then took one of Samantha's thick blond braids in her palm, and flipped it over. "After we sew, we cut."

"No, no," Samantha protested, shaking her head. "No cut."

Renee only laughed, pushing her forward again. "She means trim, and yes! I bet you haven't had one in two years."

Before she could even argue, Betty fetched a garment bag from the back of the door and thrust it into Samantha's arms. "Put on," she ordered.

Not wanting to argue with the tiny woman, she nodded,

then turned to Renee with her eyes open wide open and did what she was told.

———

JUST AS SAMANTHA FEARED, the dress was too tight. Much too tight. Getting into the thing was like trying to fit a hamburger patty into a hot dog bun. Bits of flesh were sticking out all over the place, but mostly in the top region. Betty circled her in the middle of the room, while Samantha desperately regretted all those pancakes she'd eaten on their trip.

"Okay!" Betty exclaimed. She took hold of each side panel and yanked them together. "One… Two…"

Samantha sucked in her stomach and blew out a breath.

"Three!"

The panels slammed shut behind her, and Renee, who was standing on a chair above her, tugged at the zipper. She made a few grunting noises as she tugged and stretched, while Betty shoved and stuffed Samantha with jabbing fingers. Then all of a sudden, as if the Gods had come out to show their mercy, the zipper flew up. Samantha pulled in a gasping breath, stumbling forward and steadying herself with a nearby chair, before she glanced up at Renee.

A full-length mirror was right in front of her, and her shoulders relaxed when she saw her reflection. It wasn't half bad. Which honesty surprised the hell out of her. The fabric was a blush color, not pink or peach, but a color somewhere in between. It flattered her skin tone perfectly. There was a silky skirt that draped to the floor, somehow making her look a little taller, but the only thing she didn't like was the A-framed bodice that pushed her breasts nearly up to her chin. And even that—aside from being completely public inappropriate, made her look gorgeous.

Betty circled a couple of times around the chair, scratching her chin and tugging at bits of the fabric as she went. "Hmmm…" she mumbled, before sticking a few pins in the hem. She came to stand right in front of Samantha. Her tongue tsked off the roof of her mouth as though deciding what to do. Then, as if not having any impulse control whatsoever, she lifted Samantha's breasts in her hands and started bouncing them.

The door to Renee's hotel room burst open at that moment, and Tristan and Phin walked in, carrying her bags. They both stopped dead in their tracks.

"And vhat do we going to do with these?" Betty asked thickly, still bouncing Samantha's breasts up and down.

Renee, who was still standing on the chair, must have been so shocked by what was happening she didn't move it all.

Betty looked at Renee, still standing up on the chair, and Renee looked at Phin who was standing by the door with Tristan.

But Tristan looked right at Samantha. Her face flushed with embarrassment and she instantly started to giggle. Renee started giggling too, which caused Betty to throw her hands in the air in frustration.

"Vhat?" she questioned sharply.

The whole room erupted in fits of laughter, doubling over. Except Betty, who stuck hands on her hips and stormed into the restroom.

Blood rushed to Samantha's face and neck as they came to, because there was no mistaking the look on Tristan's face. It was inappropriate, sexy as hell, and she couldn't breathe.

He covered his mouth with his hand, wiping over his chin, then down his throat, but his eyes never left hers. "I could really go for a burger and fries about now," he said to Phin. "How about you?"

Phin cleared his throat a moment later and looked to the floor. "Sounds good to me, brother." They placed Samantha's bags by the front door, her keycard on the entryway table, and turned toward the exit. Renee stepped down from her chair, waiting for the guys to close the door behind them, then stood right in front of Samantha and looked down at her breasts. "She's right you know. Vhat in fuck are we going to do with these?"

CHAPTER TWENTY-FIVE

AFTER A FEW POKES, much finagling, and a few prayers, Betty finally found a solution to the dress problem. She let out an inch or so on each side, took the pieces of fabric she'd cut from the hem and sewed them in under the arm panels...where no one was the wiser, but allowed Samantha the room to breathe.

Samantha put the dress back on the hanger, thankful to be back in her t-shirt and shorts, and zipped it up in the garment bag to hand back to Betty. She opened the bathroom door to Renee's room, anxious to find out what was next, and found her lying on the bed talking to someone on the phone. She hung the dress back on the clothes rack, trying to be quiet, then busied herself looking at all the wedding things strewn all over the chairs and tables.

There were small boxes which had various treats inside. Miniature cupcakes, chocolates, and other beautiful confections. Bottles of champagne with Renee's and Phin's names on the side, among all sorts of other favors.

For the first time, Samantha realized all she'd missed.

In a matter of days her best friend was getting married... She knew it was coming. Knew it would happen whether she was ready for it or not, but seeing these things thrown all over the room made her realize her life would go on, even though Renee wasn't there. There would be parties and babies that neither of them would be around for. And that was heartbreaking.

Samantha walked along the long table, looking at all the beautiful details she knew her friend had agonized over. Some she remembered, from photos she'd sent through text over the past months, but some were totally unfamiliar, because life couldn't be captured digitally. She stopped at the name cards lined up in a row. With burnt edges that made them look rustic and antique. Tristan's name was on the very top.

She picked it up, running her finger along the gold script lettering, realizing she missed him already. Five days ago she'd barely given him a second thought, but somehow on this short trip, she'd gotten accustomed to talking to him whenever she wanted. To him being there, listening, always paying attention, always watching her.

She placed the card back on the table, already craving his company, but at the same time, glad he wasn't around. Because there was no way she could hide how she felt about him, especially from Renee. She took a deep breath, hoping she'd be able to keep her feelings under wraps, and turned around to see Renee watching her.

Renee had finally hung up the phone and was rising from the bed when she spoke. "It's funny," she began. "It was so important for me to do all this stuff in the beginning, but now I'm sick of it. I can't wait to be married so I can give it away and never see it again." She laughed.

She came to a stop beside Samantha, who laced her arm through Renee's arm and rested her head on her shoulder. It was their signature position, and one that brought her comfort now.

"I'm sorry I missed so much, Nay. I'm sorry it's taken me so long to get here." *And I'm sorry I'm keeping secrets from you, but it's better this way.*

Renee shook her head. "Don't be silly."

Samantha straightened, having to clear her throat that was thick with emotion. "I always thought we'd do all this stuff together. I thought—" But she stopped herself, because she didn't want to make this into a big Samantha pity party. "You did a good job. I couldn't have done better, and that's saying something."

Her best friend grinned, then bit her lip and tugged her toward the door. "Come on, it's time."

"For what?" Samantha asked, suddenly feeling uneasy.

"To cut," she whispered in her ear, mimicking Betty's accent.

Samantha laughed, letting her head fall back to her shoulders, but allowing her best friend to pull her toward the door. There was no sense in arguing. Renee was going to win anyway. Just like she always did.

CHAPTER TWENTY-SIX

THE SALON WAS in the hotel lobby, just past the elevators on the right hand side. There were a half dozen white salon chairs all facing full-length mirrors, and surprisingly, only one was taken. They were seated right away, given a menu of complimentary appetizers and beverages, and soon Renee was whisked away to another room for a facial, leaving Samantha on her own to look through style magazines.

She should *not* have been trusted with style magazines. The last time she'd picked out her own hair, she'd ended up with minuscule bangs and a perm. She rocked forward in her seat, looking through the other reading material, when a buzzing noise sounded from her purse. She instantly grinned, knowing full well who it was, and fetched her bag from the hanger on the wall.

A text.

WILD STALLION: Are you alone?

SHE GRINNED WICKEDLY, then looked around to make sure no one was watching. Only the petite brunette sat in the corner with foils in her hair.

MONA: Sort of. I'm in the salon waiting for my haircut. Where are you?
    Wild Stallion: Sitting in my room, thinking of you.

HER STOMACH TIGHTENED and she crossed her legs.

MONA: I don't like being away from you. This is harder than I thought.
    Wild Stallion: You're telling me.

SHE BURST into laughter but quickly covered her mouth.

MONA: That's not what I meant and you know it.
    Wild Stallion: Did you hear about the party?

SHE GRINNED.

MONA: Yes
    Wild Stallion: I'll see you there.
    Mona: See you.

SHE TUCKED her phone back in her bag, just as Renee came back into the room wearing a green mask with slices of cucumbers on her lids. An esthetician was guiding her through the Salon, and finally plopped Renee down in the seat beside Samantha, and proceeded to attach a headrest to the back of her chair.

"I didn't want to wait back there all alone," Renee said. "I missed you too much."

Samantha laughed and hung her bag back on the wall. "Good, because I was just about to pick out my own haircut, and we all know how well that turns out."

Renee cracked a tiny grin. "Those itty bitty bangs you had in eighth grade," she stated. "But don't worry, I've already called ahead and told them exactly what to do."

Samantha grinned. "Thank you."

They sat in silence for a few minutes, as the esthetician reclined Renee back in her chair, positioning her feet up on a stool so she could massage them. When the esthetician began to knead, Renee visibly relaxed and almost melted.

"So," she began sleepily. "When does Steven arrive? I was worried for a minute he might get here before you and I'd have to entertain him on my own."

It was meant as a joke, one she'd made regularly when they lived together, but the whole energy in the room instantly shifted. Samantha cleared her throat, knowing her friend had no idea what had happened, and grabbed a copy of the Wall Street Journal from the shelf. "We broke up," she said softly, hoping the nonchalance in her voice carried to her best friend, but as soon as the words exited her lips, Renee removed the cucumbers from her eyes.

"What?" Renee whispered. "When?"

Samantha closed the magazine and turned to face her. "On the trip. Two days ago." She took a breath, trying to calm her nerves. "You were right. He put everything above me and I was sick of it. When he called to tell me he couldn't make it to the wedding, that was the end for me."

Renee frowned, sending bits of green mask to fall to her shoulders. "I'm so sorry, Sam."

She shrugged. "Don't be. I should have done it a long time ago…like you said."

A tear slipped down Renee's cheek, leaving a streak of flesh visible through the thin mask.

Samantha sat forward and grabbed hold of Renee's hands. "I thought you'd be happy. I thought—"

"I'm pissed, Sam. So angry he's treated you like this again."

Samantha nodded, her chin slightly quivering, because it was obvious how much Renee loved her, how ferociously she cared about her.

"This trip has taught me a lot about myself." She began. "One being that Steven and I were never meant for each other. I don't think even as kids, but especially not now."

Renee nodded, as though she'd known this fact a long time. "How did you do it? What did you say?"

Samantha winced. "I did it by text. I know it wasn't ideal, but he was always too busy to talk. I knew he'd at least check his messages."

Renee raised her eyebrows. "How did he respond?"

"I don't know. My phone got wet. I have no idea."

Renee laughed, then turned in her seat and looked at Samantha through the mirror. "Serves him right. Though honestly, I'm surprised he let you go that easily. I'm surprised he hasn't tried calling me to get to you."

Samantha sighed. "I guess he's resigned to it being over. He's focused on his career, and I'm honestly relieved about that. It will make things easier when I get home." She nodded for emphasis, then turned in her seat to continue reading. But a large burly man came to stand behind her at that moment.

"You must be Samantha," he said in a deep, husky voice.

She nodded, then glanced over at Renee with eyes as wide as saucers.

Renee giggled. "Tom, this is my best friend Sam. She just broke up with her boyfriend, and needs the hottest haircut within your ability."

Tom smiled, instantly transforming his face into something reminiscent of a teddy bear. "You got it, Nay," he said. Tom lowered Samantha's seat, indicating she should follow him, and gestured for her to sit down at the shampoo bowl.

"Lie back," Tom said. He then guided her neck down into sink, where he began delicately removing her braids. He then wet her scalp, sending the perfect temperature water over her head, and proceeded to wash her hair—with the strongest, most skilled fingers she'd ever felt in her life. Almost.

———

SAMANTHA'S HOTEL room turned out to be a mere two doors down from Renee's. *Two.*

Convenient for borrowing deodorant, but not so convenient if she wanted to sneak a certain someone into her room in the middle of the day. It wasn't that she wasn't having fun either, because spending time with her best friend was exactly where she wanted to be. She craved their interaction, their easy friendship that allowed them to speak freely, or be perfectly silent without any awkwardness at all.

At one point during their appointment, Renee was telling her about her and Phin's first date, and Samantha thought she might cry, she was laughing so hard. Or at another time, when Renee told her again the story of how he proposed, Samantha thought she might cry, but this time because it was utter sweetness.

And then, they had a long talk about Steven, and about

how Samantha feared she'd stayed with him for so long for all the wrong reasons. Because she was scared of hurting people, of saying no. Scared of rejections, and of failure. In the end, they had a big ol' cry fest about how much they missed each other, and made promises to visit each other whenever they could, no matter where they lived or how difficult life became.

But now, she was alone in her room, which left plenty of time to think about Tristan. She wasn't sure if it was the fact he'd become the forbidden fruit, or if it was something else, but all her hormones were bursting. Having him at her will for two days had ruined her for life. Already, all she could think about was kissing him, touching him, and him touching her. She dangled her feet off the side of the bed and let out a deep sigh.

She'd tried to take a nap as Renee was doing, but every time she closed her eyes, memories of Tristan's lovemaking played through her mind, making her feel...anything but rested.

Deciding to give up on sleep, she fetched her purse from the top of her dresser, and carried her toiletries and makeup to the bathroom. She arranged everything on the countertops meticulously, then hitched her leg up on a chair and began shaving her legs, taking ten times as long as she normally would for such a tedious task. But still, hours remained until she needed to be ready for the party. She turned around to rest her bottom on the counter and looked at the tub.

It had been years since she'd soaked in a bath. Years since she'd had one available. She pushed herself to stand from the pristine white counter and walked over to run her fingers along the cool porcelain edge. Her apartment back in LA didn't have a bathtub, and the idea of soaking her muscles sounded heavenly. She turned on the faucet and let the tub fill halfway with water before adding a scoop of bath crystals that were graciously provided on a silver bath tray.

Fragrant lavender and lemon filled the bathroom, and on impulse, she fetched her bag off the counter and pulled out her phone to send a message to Tristan.

MONA: Are you alone?

IT WAS A SIMPLE MESSAGE, well meaning and straight to the point... And not five seconds later, her phone rang and she slid open the call.

"Where are you?" he asked with a husky flirtation.

She sat on the edge of the bathtub, smiling as she tested the temperature with her fingers. "My room."

"That's a shame, you should be in mine."

She grinned, letting her bath robe slip down her shoulders then fall softly to the floor. "I'm about to get in the bath," she said. Tingles traveled down her body simply from the admission. She felt naughty, sexy, and she wished she could see his face.

"Where's your room?" he asked then. "I'll be there in two minutes."

She only smiled and put one foot in the water. "You can't. Renee's room is just across the hall. It's too risky."

He groaned. "I like risks."

She laughed and lowered her body farther. "Well I don't, and I'm the only one who knows my room number."

He was quiet a moment, and she could almost see him smiling. "Touché, little one."

She grinned and leaned back, resting her neck in the built-in pillow. "Little one?" she asked, her nose wrinkling at the pet name.

"It's only fact."

She nodded, letting her body relax. "So what did you do

today? Anything for the wedding?"

"Eh, this and that. Mostly hung out with Phin and his family. And thought about you in that dress."

She grinned. "Did you like it?"

"I did."

"Good," she said, leaning forward to turn off the water. The bath was completely full at this point, so she tightened the handles, then leaned back in her spot. The water must have made a splashing sound, because the line became incredibly quiet.

"Are you *in* the bathtub, Samantha?" There was a thread of humor in his voice, but she could hear it going deeper too.

She wrinkled her nose, then bit her finger as a rush of embarrassment warmed her cheeks. "Yes," she whispered.

He made an obvious clearing of his throat and spoke again. "Are you naked?"

She laughed, because what kind of question was that? "Of course I'm naked. What kind of baths do you take?"

He laughed then, and she could almost see him throwing his head back. "No no no... We're not talking about me, we're talking about you."

"Okay then. Yes. I'm very much naked." She was grinning ear-to-ear, feeling giddy and silly all at the same time.

"Are there bubbles?"

She laughed "Yes." She bit her lip. "Why do you ask?"

"Because I'm trying to visualize you, and every detail helps."

"Oh yeah? How am I looking?"

"Hot. Really hot."

She bit her lip, loving the playful tone of his voice. She leaned her head back, realizing she loved talking to him so much. She loved—everything about him. She sunk a little deeper in the water and whisked up a pile of bubbles with her fingers. "And where are you, Mr. Montgomery?"

"In bed," he stated. There was a seductive tone to his voice, but he didn't elaborate. Which left her mind running with possibilities. With naughty thoughts of what he could be doing there.

The line went silent again, and soon she sat forward wanting to ask where he went. But before the words crossed her lips, his rich sexy baritone came through the receiver again. "Grab the soap, Samantha."

She smiled, shocked by the request, and glanced toward the small box of soap sitting on the side of the tub before leaning back again. "I'm not grabbing the soap," she said firmly, but she couldn't quite contain her grin.

"Why? Do you not like soap?"

"No." She laughed. "I just know what you want me to do and I'm not about to do it."

"And what's that?"

"I'm not having phone sex with you, Tristan," she whispered, grinning ear to ear.

"I didn't ask you for phone sex. I asked you to grab the soap."

"Why do I feel 'soap' is the code word for phone sex?"

He laughed. "Because you're a prude?"

Her mouth fell open in shock. "I'm not a prude, I—"

But before she could finish her sentence, he cut her off. "Then grab the soap, Samantha."

She narrowed her eyes, because there was no denying the blatant "I dare you" in his request. She bit her bottom lip again, begrudgingly leaning forward to grab the little box. "Fine. You win."

"Good," he said in a cocky voice. "I like winning."

She smiled again, and slid the soap from its silver housing. "Well I like cocky men, so I guess we're both winners."

He laughed again, but only for a second, because the mood had suddenly changed to something more serious. She slipped the soap under the water, getting it good and wet before she spoke again. "Now that I have the soap, sir, what do you want me to do with it?"

He groaned, and she sunk deeper still, letting her head loll back until the tops of her breasts were all that could be seen above the water. But she could feel herself getting aroused, even though he hadn't touched her at all. Even though he hadn't even looked at her.

"Rub it between your fingers, Samantha. Squeeze it, until a thick white foam builds between your hands."

She did as he said, manipulating the soap and building the suds between her fingers, until they were slick.

He paused for a second, and she could hear his breath getting heavier. "Now place your hands at the top your knees. At the very top, where you have that one little freckle on the left side. Do you see it?"

She glanced down, placing her hands on the spot he spoke about—but she was choking up inside, because she was sure he was the only person in the world who knew about it. "Okay," she whispered. "It's there." How in two days had he memorized her so well? How in a matter of days could she love him this much?

"Now slide your hands down, slowly," he whispered. "Imagine my hands with yours, sliding the slick soap all the way down your thighs, until our fingers tangle in the hair between them, until we feel how wet you are." He paused for a long moment, and she could hear him breathing. "Are you wet, Samantha?"

Her body shuddered, and her stomach constricted as she touched herself. "Oh God, Tristan."

"Answer me."

She nodded. "Yes."

A loud knock sounded at the door, and she almost dropped

the phone. She sat up, letting the soap drop to the bottom of the tub and grabbed her robe off the floor.

"I gotta go!" she said quickly. "Someone's here." She slid the phone across the bathroom floor, quickly rose out of the water, and stepped out of the tub. "Just a minute!" Then she pulled a fluffy white towel from the rack and wrapped it around her head.

She was still tying the belt at her waist when she got to the door and stretched up on tiptoe to look out the peephole.

A bellhop stood in the middle of the hall. There was a hopper full of luggage behind him, and she mentally cursed him for interrupting them.

"What the hell does he want?" she whispered, but opened the door anyway and smiled. "Hi there. I think there must be a misunderstanding, because all my luggage is already here."

He glanced at his tablet, checking the room number, then back up to Samantha. "Are you Miss Smiles?" he asked, his brows rising as he waited for her response.

"Well yes, but—"

He then lowered a dolly from the hopper, and soon her bubble wrapped creation was positioned right in front of her door. "Is this not yours, Miss Smiles?"

She covered her mouth, shocked she'd been able to forget such a thing. "Yes, that's mine," she clarified. "I—forgot." She scratched the back of her head, and glanced around her hotel room, looking for a place to put it. "Would it be okay for you to put it in the bedroom? I don't want my friend seeing it when she comes over."

He nodded quickly, then disappeared to the bedroom a moment before Renee appeared at the door.

"What's going on?" Renee said, grabbing hold of a strand of Samantha's still dripping hair that had escaped from her towel. "You ruined your hair."

Samantha closed the door behind them, and stepped into the room. "It's not ruined. I took a bath."

Renee shrugged, just as the bellhop came back from the bedroom with the empty dolly. She raised her brows suggestively, then hung her garment bag up on the back of the bathroom door. "Sowing your oats already?"

The bellhop turned bright red, but came to stand in front of Samantha anyway. "Ma'am," he began. "Is there anything else you'll be needing this evening?"

Samantha shook her head, not knowing if she should tip him or not, but after Renee's comment, she fetched a twenty off her dresser and curled it up in his hand. "Thank you," she said. "I really appreciate it." She then escorted him to the hall, locked the door, and turned around, seeing her best friend lounging on the couch with her feet up.

"What are you doing here, anyway?" she asked Renee. "I thought you were taking a nap?"

Renee shrugged. "I couldn't sleep. Plus, I thought it would be more fun to get ready together." She rose to her feet and unzipped the garment bag before turning around. "I brought you something to wear."

Samantha laughed. "I brought my own clothes, you know."

Renee bit her bottom lip, "But your clothes are boring. Besides, I brought you something special. Something hot." She pulled a wooden hanger from the bag, and Samantha gazed at the small piece of black fabric that hung by straps as thin as spaghetti.

She raised her brows before looking at her best friend again. Because it barely looked large enough to fit Renee, and Samantha was much more voluptuous. "That's not going to fit me."

Renee pulled a pair of five-inch heels out of the bag. "Don't be silly." She then took Samantha's hand and began pulling her toward the bathroom. "Now, let's get your hair blown out and get you ready."

"Shouldn't I be the one getting you ready? Tonight is about

you, Ren, not me."

Renee positioned Samantha in front of the mirror and shook her head at their reflection. "You're single for the first time in six years, and there happens to be some really hot groomsmen."

"Ren—" she tried to protest, but Renee only pushed her down in the chair and pulled the towel from her head "You're going to let loose tonight, Samantha. That's all I want. And yes, I'm using my bride status to get you to conform to my will. Get over it."

Samantha was barely able to control her giggles as Renee began to work her magic.

For all the creativity Samantha had with clay, Renee had just as much when it came to beauty. She brushed, curled, and teased Samantha's hair until it hung in large, glossy waves down her back. Then she worked on Samantha's makeup, giving her skin a dewy, flawless finish, with smoky eyes and a pouty, nude lip that made her almost giddy.

"There," Renee said to her reflection. "Now you can go get dressed."

Samantha stood up from the chair, and Renee immediately took her place and began doing her own makeup.

The romper still hung on the back of the door, and she took it from its hanger before turning back to Renee. "I don't know, Ren. I don't think I can wear a bra with this."

Renee barely glanced up from applying her mascara. "You don't. There are pasties in the bag, just put those on."

Samantha wiped over her face, thinking Renee was crazy, but then she started to imagine what Tristan would think if he saw her like this. What he would say, or not say—and that was all it took for her to grab the romper and head out of the room. Immediately, she went to her bedroom, fetched a minuscule black thong and put it on with the pasties. She'd never worn such a thing in her life, but she'd be lying if she said she didn't feel sexy.

After stepping into the romper, she pulled the thin straps over her shoulders, and just like Renee said, it fit her perfectly, though there was barely enough fabric to cover her ass. She bent over, testing it out as she watched herself in the mirror. Luckily the bottom was shorts, because there was no way she'd be able to bend over otherwise.

She stepped into the five-inch heels and did a spin in front of the mirror to check all angles. Her back was almost bare, all the way down to the top of her panty line. The only thing covering it was the thin straps that crossed in the back in an X, and left no question about what was underneath...or what wasn't.

The front was actually the most conservative of the piece. The fabric extended all the way up to her neck, draping sensually over her breasts. She had to admit, it was sexy as hell.

She found Renee leaning against the doorjamb watching her. Her nose wrinkled like a raisin as she grinned from ear to ear. "You look hot," Renee said, pushing off the wall to stand beside Samantha. She wore a dress equally as short as Samantha's but made of a white lace. The color was a gorgeous contrast against her golden skin, and together they crossed the whole spectrum of sexual beasts. Day vs. Night. Light vs. Dark. Angel vs. Devil.

Renee handed her a couple of gold bangles and a pair of earrings. "Put these on. We should get going in a few minutes."

Samantha did as she was told, but before they left for the party, she excused herself once again to the bathroom. There on the floor, under a fallen towel, she found her cell phone.

WILD STALLION: Have you ever heard the term 'Blue balls'?"

CHAPTER TWENTY-SEVEN

THE ROOFTOP WAS ALREADY DECORATED when they got there. It was like a scene fitting of a James Bond movie. All elegance, class, and lights. Ten or so cocktail tables surrounded by dark wooden stools were arranged around the dance floor. Twinkling lights were strung along the rooftop, creating a canopy above them, and giving the illusion of stars.

Samantha and Renee walked down the steps to the dance floor, where Phin stood waiting. He had on a tailored suit, with a white dress shirt open at the throat, and looked sexy as hell. He raked his eyes up and down his future bride, and Samantha quickly turned around, wanting to give them some sense of privacy.

They would have perfect babies. Beautiful, strong, elegant babies.

The rooftop was already packed with people, maybe forty or so, all dressed to the nines. She immediately scanned the space looking for Tristan, but he was nowhere to be seen. She took her phone out of her purse and sent him a text.

Mona: Where are you?

She waited a few seconds for a reply that never came, then tucked the phone back into her bag and began walking toward the bar. Soft music played through the loudspeakers, and people were laughing and mingling all around her. She sat down at one of the oak seats at the bar and signaled for the bartender. She felt slightly naked, having never worn something quite so revealing out in public. But she held her head high, and tried not to imagine what everyone else was thinking.

"What can I get you?" the bartender asked, bracing his arms on the counter in front of her.

She cleared her throat and resisted the urge to cross her arms at her chest. "A martini, please. Extra olives."

He nodded, and she quickly turned around to look over the patio. There was a dark haired man sitting just two seats over, and she decided it wouldn't hurt to introduce herself.

She hooked her heeled shoe on the rung of the barstool and crossed her legs. "Hi," she began. "I'm Samantha. The maid of honor." After all, she'd be spending the next few days with these people. She might as well get to know them.

He grinned slightly, pushing his glasses up the bridge of his nose before nodding. "Devon Montgomery," he stated. "The bride's cousin. We've met before."

She bit her bottom lip, narrowing her eyes to get a better look. His eyes were dark, and he was very handsome, but he looked nothing like his blond haired cousin. "Devon? Oh my gosh, I haven't seen you...in, well... Since that summer you threw dirt in my ear."

He scrunched up his nose and took a large gulp of his drink. "I was hoping you'd forgotten about that."

She laughed. "I have a memory like an elephant. You're pretty much screwed."

He bit his lower lip and looked down to his feet. "I was afraid of that."

She ginned at him, then lifted her shoulders in a "Sorry to tell ya" motion, as the bartender set her drink down before her. Devon was older—maybe by five or six years, but the last time she'd seen him he was a scrawny teenager. One both she and Renee had a crush on.

"You look…" He eyed her up and down. "All grown up, Samantha."

She took a long sip of her Martini and smiled. "Do you live around here?" she asked, taking the cocktail stick and scraping an olive off with her teeth.

He nodded. "Manhattan, and you?"

"No." She shook her head. "I'm still in LA, though I'm not sure why at the moment. This city is beautiful."

He laughed heartily, sounding exactly how she remembered him. Robust and sincere… and possibly a little bit nerdy if that was possible.

She turned in her seat to take another drink, as another man came to fill the seat between them—but she barely noticed. Because Tristan appeared on the rooftop at that exact moment.

His eyes locked on hers right away. Possessive, brilliant blue, and caused a physical reaction to form in her belly. He raked his eyes up and down her figure, then began walking down the steps toward her. He looked as though he wanted to ravish her, though she didn't blame him. She wanted to ravage him as well. Because for every inch Tristan Montgomery lacked in polish, he made up for in pure sex appeal. He wore tight faded jeans, a tight white V-neck t-shirt, and a black blazer that somehow made his shoulders look even broader.

"Where in LA do you live?" the man who'd joined them said to her.

She turned in her seat to give him her attention. "Sherman Oaks." She swallowed. "Are you familiar?"

"No." He shook his head. "I was just trying to steal your attention away from whoever stole it." He grinned. "I'm Mark, by the way. One of the groomsmen."

She glanced down to the bar, knowing she was blushing, and downed the rest of her martini. "Samantha," she replied.

"Ahhhh… The maid of honor. Renee has told me about you." He held out his hand, and leaned back against the bar.

Suddenly, Samantha realized Mark was the one of the men Renee was trying to set her up with. She could see why. He was built, good looking, and had a voice like shredded sandpaper. Husky, sexy… She shook his hand.

"You're the artist, right?" he asked then, cutting off her train of thought.

She nodded, catching a glimpse of Tristan out of the corner of her eye. He already had at least three girls around him. One a ballerina that danced in Renee's company, a brunette who looked harmless enough, and a redheaded hussy.

"I'm a sculptor. How about you?"

"Firefighter."

Devon leaned forward again, butting into her new conversation. "I think I remember hearing about that. What type of sculptures do you do?"

She cleared her throat, slightly thrown from watching Tristan… But then she turned around, and a sense of calmness overtook her. "Modern—yet recognizable." She grinned. That was one of the quotes written about her work at the gallery opening. Modern—yet recognizable. She loved it. Because that's always what she strived to be.

"I like that," Mark stated. "Do you happen to have any images of your work?"

Her brows furrowed, and she opened her clutch to pull out her phone, but quickly remembered. "No, actually—normally

I do, but my phone got wet…" But her words trailed away as she saw Tristan watching her again. "All I have with me is the piece in my room that I made for Renee—it's their wedding gift."

Mark took a sip of his beer, almost studying her. "I'd love to see that, later."

She raised her eyebrows, aware he was asking to come to her room, and she shook her head. But just then the DJ's voice sounded through the speakers, saving her from giving any sort of reply. He was calling everyone to the dance floor, beckoning them, with his arms above his head, to come closer. Samantha immediately rose from her seat, excusing herself from the two men, and weaved her way through the crowd.

The DJ was standing in the middle of the dance floor and waited until most everyone had moved closer. "Good evening, ladies and gentleman. As you all may know, we're here to celebrate the last single days of both Phin and Renee. Untraditionally, they have decided to join their parties together, and share their last night with all of you. Every one of you is special to them, and they want you to get to know one another. So look around, say hello, and find a new best friend. To help you get started, we have a game! I have a couple of assistants walking around handing out pen and paper. Take one. Walk around the room and get to know one another. You'll need to gather both first and last names, plus the answer to one simple question: how do they know the bride or groom? Easy, right? Though if you'd noticed, there are no clipboards provided. Get creative. Backs—or fronts, make a perfectly acceptable surface."

A roar erupted from the crowd, and a guy across the stage ripped his shirt off and pointed to his chest.

The DJ laughed and patted him on the back. "To sweeten the pot, the person with the most *correct* information at the end of the night will win a prize. A two week, all-expenses paid trip to Europe, graciously donated by the groom's parents."

Everyone began cheering and hollering and moving around the floor.

"The clock is ticking, ladies and gentleman. You have one hour to get to know each other. Have fun."

Samantha glanced around all the people, hating her best friend as one of the DJ's assistants tapped her on the shoulder. The woman handed her a pen and paper, entered her information into a tablet, then smiled and nodded thanks before leaving to pass on to others. "Good luck."

Samantha clutched the paper in her hand, scanning the room, hoping to spot Tristan, but found Mark standing right behind her instead.

He grinned and narrowed his eyes. "We have to stop meeting like this." He teased. He then took his pen and paper, stepped around the table and placed it upon her back. "May I?"

She nodded, feeling a bit wobbly after only two sips of her Martini. "Go ahead."

"Samantha. Is that with two M's or just one?"

She laughed. "Just one."

"Last name?"

"Smiles."

"And how do you know the bride?"

She located Tristan just across the dance floor and cleared her throat. "We grew up together," she said, suddenly feeling winded, because he was talking to a tall blond, who had her paper flat against his chest.

"Can you be more specific please?" Mark grinned.

"Hartford Grove Elementary, playground, second grade."

His pen hit her back again, then he turned around and offered her his own. "Your turn."

She cleared her throat, trying to concentrate, but Tristan was laughing at something the blond was saying, and that irritated her.

"Last name?" She asked Mark.

"Wahlberg."

"And how do you know the bride and groom," she said, completely distracted.

"We all met on the set of Boogie Nights."

But before she could finish writing, Mark slipped out from under her paper and stood in front of her. "Okay, so who is he? Or she…? I'm open-minded like that."

Samantha blinked a few times, unsure what he was talking about. "Excuse me?"

He raised one eyebrow. "I'm not Mark Wahlberg. But I'm flattered you believed me."

Her eyes widened and she looked down to her paper. "Sorry, I—"

But he took the pen from her hand and began filling out his information. "Look, I told Renee it was too soon." He scribbled some words on the paper, handed it back to her, then draped his arm over her shoulder to turn her toward the dance floor. "Is he here? The guy who's captured your heart?"

She shook her head, feeling heat creep up her cheeks. "No. And I don't know what you're talking about."

He smiled, then patted her on the backside. "Must be my imagination." Soon he was lost in the crowd, gathering more names, and she began making her way back toward the bar. If she was going to get through this night, she was going to need more alcohol.

She introduced herself to as many people as she could along the way, collecting information until she saw Tristan heading for the bar as well.

She made a beeline, arrived first, and swiftly turned to order another drink. A hand settled low on her back a second later, and she pulled in a shaky breath, knowing it was Tristan. She turned around, finding him standing right behind her. He was clean shaven, smelled like heaven, and her heart picked up speed simply from being close to him again.

"You better leave," she whispered, "or someone's going to get suspicious."

He leaned in close, so close she could feel his breath against her neck. "We just spent four days driving cross country together. If we don't talk, people will get suspicious."

Her pulse quickened for the second time, and she couldn't help the smile that teased at her mouth. "You're right." But the alcohol had hit her harder than she thought, and she stumbled forward, requiring Tristan's hand to catch her at her hip.

She looked up into his eyes, feeling his fingers press into her skin. "I don't like watching girls hang on your every word. It annoys me."

He laughed, but glanced her over from head to toe before settling his eyes on her lips. "I don't like watching you parade around half naked when I can't touch you."

She laughed wholeheartedly and resisted the urge to pull him against her. "You noticed."

His eyes heated, and he looked her up and down again. "I'm pretty sure everyone in this dammed place noticed you."

She grinned again, moving around him to place her paper on his back. "Name please?"

His muscles tightened, and he reached around to grip her upper thigh to yank her forward. "You should know it. You were screaming it last night," he whispered.

She bit her bottom lip. "And how do you know the bride?"

"What bride?"

She turned around to offer him her back, and instantly felt his fingers trail down the column of her spine. "What do you say we get out of here?"

She pulled in a breath, wanting nothing more, but turned around to take his paper and place it on the bar.

He frowned. "I guess that's a no?"

She took another sip of her martini and filled out the paper. "Later," she promised.

He leaned in close to her ear, his perfectly shaved cheek like silk against her skin. "Later."

And then he was gone.

THE GAME PASSED by in a rush. By the end of it, the agenda had been completed. Everyone was laughing and talking, and much looser than before. Samantha stood at a cocktail table by the dance floor, deliberately selecting the spot because she had a perfect view of Tristan. He was still surrounded by women, but for some reason she didn't mind as much now. He was hers, and she knew he'd come to her the moment she curved her finger.

Mark came to stand beside her then, holding a beer in one hand, and martini in the other. "You look thirsty," he stated, placing her drink in the middle of the table. "Are you still trying to pretend not to care about that blond dude over in the corner?"

She pulled in a breath, shaking her head, and turned to face him "I don't know whatever you mean—"

But he winked at her, interrupting her words. He took a swig of his beer. "Samantha, your secret's safe with me. But I find it hilarious you think no one notices."

She bit her lip and glanced over at Mark. "Is it that obvious?"

He took another swig of beer before answering. "Yeah…it kinda is. Though don't worry, most people are too drunk to notice—plus, they're not as perceptive as I am." He then stepped closer, hunching down to whisper in her ear. "But my question is this, if he could have you, why is he making out with that brunette over there?"

Samantha whipped around, her eyes finding Tristan immediately, standing in the same spot she'd left him, with a blond woman by his side. But his eyes were narrowed and focused on Samantha.

She hit Mark's arm and shook her head. "You're trying to make him jealous."

Mark laughed. "Or make him realize what he's missing. There are two sides to every coin."

"True," she agreed, as a deep voice broke through the music again.

Phin was up on the stage this time, his arm around Renee, and the microphone in his hand. "Now that you've had a chance to get to know one another, we have another game."

The crowd erupted with laughter, and he held his finger to his mouth to shush them. "As I'm sure you're aware, Renee and I met at the Hamilton Ballet. We've since moved in other directions, but the company will forever have a special place in our hearts."

Mumbles began coursing through the crowd, and Phin motioned with his hands for them to settle down. "We're going to play a game," he said again. "One we learned not too long ago in an improv class and we'd like you to join us. There are only two rules." He grinned. "One, you have to have a partner; and Two, never stop touching."

He took Renee in his arms and started swaying. "It can be only fingers." He turned her out, letting her travel until only the tips of their fingers connected. "Or the whole body." He yanked her forward again, slamming her body against his, her thigh between his legs. "When the song changes, so does the person you're dancing with. Fair enough?"

Renee grinned and took the microphone. "Couples will be eliminated as we go, so be creative and don't let that happen." She raised her eyebrows. "There's a prize at the end, but you'll have to wait to find out what it is. Have fun everyone!"

CHAPTER TWENTY-EIGHT

IT DIDN'T TAKE LONG before everyone was grabbing a partner and heading for the dance floor. There were different couples, some conservative, some not, yet it didn't take long before the scene that unfolded in front of them looked like it could have come out of a Vegas nightclub. Deciding she didn't really care about prizes, Samantha turned to leave, but then she felt a hand rest on her lower back.

Mark stood just behind her, his lips close to her ear as he spoke to her. "What do you say—want to make him jealous?"

She laughed, because this was a horrible idea. She wasn't a dancer, and she wasn't about to start now.

But then Devon came to stand beside her and draped his arm around her shoulder. "Who are we making jealous?" he asked, his eyes narrowing as he looked over the dance floor.

Her eyes shifted downward, then she looked over at Mark. He caught her eye and winked to let her know it would be okay, then handed her a shot glass filled with some sort of brown liquid.

"Drink," he said to Samantha. Then he turned to Devon and lifted his chin. "It seems," Mark began, taking her glass that was now empty, "that Samantha has an admirer—but he's too much of a pussy to come over here and get her. So we'll have to draw him out."

Devon choked on his bottle of Corona and glanced around the dance floor. "Who?"

Mark waved him off. "Doesn't matter, Devon. What matters is that we make Samantha look like the most delicious morsel in the room." He took Samantha's arm, handed Devin her clutch, and bowed to her. "May I have this dance?"

She shook her head. "I don't think this is a good idea." But then she saw Tristan already out there, dancing with the redheaded hussy she'd seen him with earlier. The ginger turned to face him, her legs long and elegant as she walked around him, trailing her finger along his body.

Mark pushed her toward the dance floor, then pulled her around and gripped her fingers firmly in one hand. "Change your mind?"

Her lips curled in a playful grin and she nodded. "Do your worst."

As though her invitation flipped on a switch, Mark grinned and starting dancing like a Latin lover. He lifted her up at the arms—just high enough where her breasts almost hit his chin. He grinned. "Good girl." Then he gripped the backs of her thighs, adding enough pressure to urge them to spread. Her eyes widened, but he lifted again, causing her legs to straddle his waist. "Lean back," he whispered.

She did as he said, and he used her body to form a soft sweeping motion across the floor, causing her long hair to dust the ground. The people around them squealed with approval, and he pulled her up again. "I think we got his attention." But then he placed her on her feet again and whipped her out in a turn.

Tristan was right there watching her, staring at Mark before raking his eyes over Samantha. But he wasn't angry like she feared; he was actually grinning. She bit her lip, her stomach tightening with deliciousness, because the look on his face told her he knew exactly what game she was playing, and she was pretty sure she'd just started a war.

Tristan placed his hand on the small of the redhead's back and lifted her thigh to hook it on the top of his hip.

Mark turned her back in to his chest, and soon her body was pressed against his again.

"Looks like we have a challenger," he said, placing both of her hands around his neck and gripping her hips to move them to the rhythm. She took his lead, moving when he told her to, letting her body sway with each beat, each pulse, and soon they were dancing as one. Hips together, hands laced.

The music changed a second later, and the DJ's voice sounded from the loud speakers. "Now switch!"

Samantha spun around, looking for her next partner, and right there behind her was Devon. He grabbed hold of her hand and spun her into his chest. "I don't know who this other guy is, but I still owe you for the dirt incident." He grinned.

She giggled, partly because she was having so much fun, but partly because the alcohol was starting to affect her beyond her own control. She took hold of Devon's hand and turned herself around again. Wiggling her bottom against Devon's thighs, she glanced over at Tristan.

He had the blond he'd been talking to earlier, but he was barely paying her any attention. His eyes were focused on Samantha, eating her up with every move. She grinned again, then turned around and hooked her leg up to the top of Devon's hip. He caught it with his hand, lifting her up to drag her foot along the floor. She had no idea how she'd gotten so lucky, but her two dance partners could have easily been finalists on Dancing with the Stars.

Soon the music changed again, she was spun out into the

crowd, and her hand was yanked back behind her. She was pulled into a dark alcove over by the stairwell.

Tristan's head was close to her neck, his voice low and textured. "If we don't leave soon, there's going to be a fight," he promised.

She tilted her head back, allowing him better access to her throat. "Oh yeah?" she whispered. "With who?"

He laughed, because although he was partly serious, this was a game and they both knew it. "Whoever touches you next." He pulled back a little, just enough to look at her eyes. She palmed the side of his face, her legs already shaking. Because it wasn't a look of playfulness and lust that stared back at her. It was one of passion, of a need so great it ripped her heart right out of her chest—it was one of admiration, and she wanted to be looked at like that for all eternity.

She pulled in a deep breath, not wanting this dance to end. "Take me to your room," she whispered.

"As you wish."

Tristan left the party ahead of her, placing a keycard in her palm before walking away. After gathering her bag and belongings from the cocktail table, she nodded to Mark, letting him know they'd won, and began making her way to the elevator. She thought about making up an excuse for Renee, but her best friend was wrapped in her fiancé's arms, and Samantha knew she wouldn't be missed. She slipped out of the party without anyone noticing and pressed the button for the tenth floor.

Tristan's room was at the end of the hall, and she opened the door without even knocking. An ache was already coursing low in her belly, and her pulse quickened as she looked into the pitch-black room.

"Tristan?" she whispered, taking two steps into the dark room before his arms wrapped around her belly.

"Grrrrr…" He growled low in her ear, lifting her off her feet and making her feel lighter than air.

Her body instinctively tensed, but she melted against him, because she didn't have a choice… When it came to Tristan, she was like water—fluid, movable, completely translucent.

He whipped her around, grabbed hold of her ass and lifted her higher. He forced her legs apart and positioned them on either side of his waist. "You've had a little bit to drink," he said, walking with her over to the bed.

She grinned, taking his face between her hands so she could look at him better. "I've had a lot to drink. What are you going to do about it?"

He only stared at her as though there was something he wanted to say, but then he placed her to her feet and turned her to face the wall. "How do we get this off you?"

She giggled, pulling the straps down her shoulders in one motion. She turned to face him, the romper only hanging at her hips, the pasties in the shape of roses the only things covering her breasts.

His eyes raked over them, taking in every inch, every curve, and he dipped down, until he lifted her in his arms and cradled her against his chest. She could feel his heart pounding, see him visibly struggling to breathe. He laid her down on the middle of the mattress, and followed right behind her until he was nestled between her thighs.

"I missed you," he said, his voice hoarse and barely audible. Only his lips and eyes transferred the message. But it was clear. She was his. No one else's. And he was going to make sure she never wanted her legs wrapped around another man again.

THE NEXT MORNING she awoke with an ache between her thighs and her head nestled by Tristan's throat. He was still sleeping, and she gazed up at him, remembering every delicious detail of their lovemaking. The room was cast in the golden glow of morning, and although he had morning stubble on his face, he still looked incredibly vulnerable. Almost like a little boy.

Her heart pinched, and she rolled to the side of the bed. For some reason whenever she looked at him she thought about bigger things, deeper things. Like forevers, like children, and mixed DNA. But last night had been magical. More than arms and limbs and passion. It was about needing one another, trusting and cherishing. She'd never experienced anything like it before in her life.

She took a deep breath and pushed off the side of the bed. Because even though she wanted to spend all morning doing it all over again, that wasn't a possibility. She stretched her arms overhead and pulled in a deep breath. This morning was another story and she needed to get back to her room before anyone noticed.

She picked up her bag off the floor, took one last glance at the man who consumed her body, mind and soul, then walked to the bathroom. Deciding there were two hours yet before she had to worry about anyone trying to find her, she turned on the shower and stepped in before it had a chance to warm. After washing her hair, she combed out all the tangles as best she could with her fingers, then wrapped herself in a towel and headed back to the bedroom. The moment she opened the door, she immediately froze. Her face drained of all color as Renee stared back at her.

Her best friend's face was puffy and streaked with tears, yet she didn't say a word. She just stood there, silently blinking as Samantha tried to come up with an excuse as to why she was coming out of Tristan's bathroom. But there was none.

Because whatever this was, it was out in the open now. There was no hiding it, no wishing it away, no backing up and hoping for a do-over.

Renee had found her in her brother's room, and the expression on her face was one of complete betrayal. Renee closed her eyes, shutting everyone out as she tightened her fists at her sides. Samantha could only look at her, her friend's veins visibly pulsing at every pressure point.

Renee parted her lips, and mouthed the word. "Why?"

Samantha covered her lips, shaking her head as she took a step forward.

But Renee only retreated, gasping in gulps of air that sounded like sobs. "How could you do this?" she asked. "How could you do this?"

Then she ran from the room, leaving the door open, and Samantha fell to her knees in the middle of the doorway. She looked over at Tristan, who was sitting on the side of the bed, his body only covered by the sweats she was sure he'd put on to answer the door.

"Why was she here?" she whispered. "Did Mark tell—"

But he shook his head, cutting her off before she could finish. "Mom showed up this morning... Dad wasn't with her."

Tears stung behind Samantha's eyes and capped her hand over her mouth. "No. No no no." Because after finding her mother... "She came here," she whispered, choking on the words. "And she found us."

It wasn't a question; it was a fact. Because her friend who thought about everyone else before she thought about herself, had just found out that her father had been cheating on her mother. And when she'd come to talk to her brother about it, found her best friend practically naked in his room.

"I should go after her," Samantha whispered. "Explain."

Tristan only pushed his hand through his hair and shook his head. "Give her a minute."

Her throat was so tight she could barely breathe, but she nodded her head. He was right. Renee would need time after something like this. She would need time, and Samantha needed to be strong enough to give it to her. "We shouldn't have been so reckless. I shouldn't have—"

But Tristan rose to his feet. He stopped in front of her, pulled her to stand, and wrapped his arms around her body. She pressed her face into his chest and held onto him. She swallowed hard, fighting back tears that threatened to choke her "You were right. I should have told her."

But he remained silent. Not saying he told her so, not yelling like she knew she would have done, had the roles been reversed.

"My mom is down in the lobby," he said after a pause. "She's a mess." His eyes met hers again, and she could see the wounded boy she met all those days ago when he told her about his father. The boy who was protective, hurt, and so vulnerable. "Will you be okay without me?"

Samantha almost sobbed, but stepped away, already feeling guilty for keeping him this long. "Go. I'll catch up with you at the rehearsal."

He traced the rim of her lips with his finger, then leaned in close. His mouth hovered over hers, but didn't kiss. "It will be okay," he finally whispered, but they were words not meant for her. They were words meant for himself.

She grabbed hold of his neck, and kissed him with all her strength. As though wanting to heal all his wounds, wanting to take away his pain—but she knew she couldn't. This was something she couldn't take away, and she could only love him through it.

He took her hands from behind his neck as he broke their kiss, then paused for a minute before he walked into the bathroom to shower. She waited for the shower to run, then gathered the rest of her things and slipped out to the hall in the romper she'd worn the night before.

"Do not disturb" signs graced almost every door as she made her way back to her room. Trays with silver domes were left outside almost every door, waiting to be picked up—and although the same blue sign hung on her best friend's door, she couldn't keep herself from knocking. Her fingers rested on the hard surface, waiting for the answer, but one never came. She dropped her forehead down to the surface, feeling a knot form in her stomach. Because she needed her friend to know the truth. She needed her to know that Tristan wasn't just a fling to her. He was the man she'd been waiting for her entire life.

And she was falling in love with him.

THE REST of the afternoon went by without a word from either Tristan or Renee. She knew they were busy, but having not talked to anyone left her with a million butterflies swarming inside her stomach and chest. She opened the door to the ballroom, where everyone was already waiting inside, standing around, chatting, and sitting in chairs that tomorrow would be filled with the audience. Because in less than twenty-four hours, her best friend would be a bride.

Samantha glanced around the room, finding Mark, Devon, and the rest of the wedding party flanking the side of the wooden arbor. She walked toward them, wanting to take her place at the head of the bridal party, but noticed they all had weird looks on their faces.

She turned around and found Tristan in the corner of the room, his ear to his phone, not looking happy. She swallowed apprehensively, noticing Mrs. Montgomery sitting in one of the seats, crying. Renee was by her side, and she instantly realized Mr. Montgomery still wasn't there.

The wedding coordinator was standing at the top of the stairs by the arbor, and immediately urged Samantha forward. The woman positioned Samantha at the top of the line and adjusted her shoulders out toward the audience before looking over at Mark and Devon. "What's going on?" the woman mouthed, but they both shook their heads as though not knowing at all what to say.

Samantha's heart pinched in her chest, both tense and breaking at the same time. How could Mr. Montgomery not be here? How could he leave his family like this? His daughter?

The door to the ballroom opened, and everyone turned around, hopeful sighs released from their lips.

Samantha glanced up, saying a silent prayer that it was Mr. Montgomery, only to find Steven standing in the doorway. He made a face as though apologizing for interrupting, then walked into the room, wearing the pinstriped blue suit she'd picked out with him before he had interviewed with Connor and Associates.

The walls seemed to close in around her all at once, and she looked over at Tristan. He was still deep in conversation and hadn't noticed Steven yet.

Steven continued toward her, seemingly clueless about the tension in the room as he walked up the steps. "Surprise!" he whispered, leaning over to give her a kiss on the cheek.

Samantha stepped backward, almost crashing into one of the other bridesmaids. "What are you doing here?" she whispered, but all the blood had left her body, and she thought she might faint. She glanced around the room to Mark, Renee, and Tristan, and discovered all their eyes were on her.

Steven moved in closer, narrowing his gaze just bit as he looked into her eyes "I left work for you. I thought you'd be happy."

She shook her head, her throat so tight it was almost suffocating. "Didn't you get my text?"

His eyes narrowed and he adjusted his stance. "What text?" he whispered back.

Tristan swore under his breath, but before she could turn around, he was already walking out of the room. Her heart constricted with pain and guilt, but she turned back to Steven.

Everyone was watching. Renee's family, friends, Phin. But there was so much confusion in Steven's eyes, so much hurt and pain that Samantha knew she was causing. She blinked a couple of times, trying to make sense of what he was telling her. Her mind flashed back to the moment he told her he wasn't coming. To her sending the text. She had sent it right there in front of Tristan—and then she had fallen into the pool.

She covered her mouth, realizing what must've happened. The text didn't go through before her phone had died. Steven had no idea she'd broken up with him.

Tears gathered behind her eyes, burning her nose and throat. Steven may not be perfect, and not be the most considerate at times, but he'd been one of her best friends for most of her life.

"Can I talk to you privately?" she whispered, barely able to keep her voice from quivering to get out the words.

She walked down the steps, hearing whispers of disapproval as she exited the ballroom, but she had to do this. He had to be told what was going on. She found a private alcove in the garden ten yards away, where she sat down on a bench and waited for Steven to join her.

He sat down a moment later, an element of confusion causing the corners of his eyes to wrinkle. She swallowed, seeing all over again the twelve-year-old boy who had opened the door for her every day of sixth grade. But now his face was pale where normally golden, his eyes lifeless where normally smiling. She took his hands between hers and closed her eyes.

"Steven——" She choked. Because she knew she was about to hurt him. She knew she was about to hurt him so much.

He got down to his knees in front of her, causing her stomach to clench and her eyes to open. "What is it, Sam? What happened?"

She shook her head, her lashes heavy with tears. "I broke up with you, Steven. I broke up with you three days ago."

"I don't understand. Sam——"

"I sent you a text. I thought you knew. But I dropped my phone in the water, and the message must have not gone through. I thought——"

He pulled in a breath, and licked his lips as he searched her face. "Because of the job? Is that why?"

"No." She cut him off, needing to stop any further speculation. "This isn't working, Steven. It hasn't been working for a long time." The truth was heartbreaking, something she should have said years ago, but she'd been too much of a coward. "We've been friends for so long, the best of friends…" She expected him to protest, to try to stop her, but he only looked at her, his face pained but no longer confused.

"I know," he whispered.

She choked on a sob, muffling the sound with her hand. Because in all of her life, she would never have expected this response. In all her dreams, she should have never expected him to understand.

He closed his eyes, visibly snuffing out his own emotion. "Expecting you to follow me in my career was like caging a wild bird." He opened his eyes and looked directly into hers, as though seeing her for the first time. "I couldn't bear to let you go, and that was selfish. Keeping you by my side was what I always wanted, but that doesn't mean it was right."

Her nose began to burn, but she let the tears come. Because a long time ago, her mother had told her never to apologize for being emotional. To never feel weak because of shed tear, because showing your heart was a sign of strength. For the first time, she wasn't ashamed of them. For the first time she knew exactly what her mother meant.

A couple of people were standing outside now, gawking at them in a way that made her feel protective. She adjusted her back, blocking their view of Steven, and took his hands. "I'm so sorry. I should've never broken up with you in such a careless way. I should have—"

But he shook his head, stopping her. "Don't."

Tears were flowing from her eyes, and she brushed them away with her fingers. For all his faults, there was so much good in him. He just wasn't want she needed. "I've always loved you; I need you to know that. Just not in the way you wanted me to."

He sat down beside her again, leaning against her, offering his shoulder for her to cry on. "I think I've always known that. I hoped it would be different, but…" His words trailed off, and they both sat in silence for a minute before he continued. "I held on too long, even when I knew we were both going in different directions. My only hope is that it's not too late to be friends."

She turned into his chest, and he wrapped his arms around her. "Of course we can. Always."

They stayed there, just like that, for a good twenty minutes. With his arm wrapped around her, them both mourning the end of their relationship, before he finally called a Taxi to head back to the airport. Because even though they were not each other's future, they were each other's past. A past filled with memories, laughter, and friendship. And that was hard to let go of, for anyone.

CHAPTER TWENTY-NINE

IT WAS ALMOST EVENING when Samantha knocked on the door of Renee's hotel room. A mixture of sorrow, regret, and nausea rolled in her stomach as she glanced down to her phone. She'd been trying to get hold of Tristan all afternoon, to explain what happened, but he still hadn't answered any of her texts. Hadn't answered her phone calls, or even his door when she'd gone there earlier. His message was clear: he didn't want to talk to her, and there was a part of her that didn't blame him.

The door opened, and Samantha quickly put her phone away as she looked up to her best friend. Renee stood in the doorway, her eyes puffy and swollen, making Samantha's heart clench even harder. "Is he here?"

Renee only glanced up and down, taking in the tattered shorts Samantha had changed back into after the rehearsal, and turned to head back into the room. "Nope." But she left the door open, which was the only invitation Samantha needed to walk into the room.

Samantha twisted her fingers as she following the trail of tissues into Renee's bedroom, where she found her buried deep under a pile of blankets in the dark, lonely bed. *The Notebook* was playing on the television, and Samantha crawled in beside her and rested her head on the top of Renee's shoulder.

She pulled in a shaky breath, realizing *she* should be the shoulder to cry on, the arms of support at a time like this. Instead, she was the bearer of deceit, the one to cause her best friend to crumble.

"I'm sorry," she whispered, her voice breaking with each word. It was a feeble effort to make things right, but it was all she could muster at the moment.

Renee squeezed her eyes shut, struggling with her own emotions as she pulled a tissue from the box. "My father isn't coming. Tristan will be walking me down the aisle."

Samantha suspected as much, but it was still heartbreaking to hear it from her best friend's lips. She handed Renee a tissue. Because she knew the hopes and dreams Renee had always carried. She knew about Renee's dream of a fairy tale wedding, which always included her father walking her down the aisle in every one.

Renee blotted her eyes, turning toward Samantha to search her face. But she didn't look angry, she looked heartbroken.

"Everyone thinks he's unbreakable, but he's not."

Samantha nodded, her chin beginning to quiver as she tried to pull herself together—because she knew Renee was talking about Tristan. Unbreakable Montgomery. The Rock of West Valley high school.

"I went to his room, but he wasn't there. I've tried calling —" But her words came out on a sob, and she couldn't finish.

Renee threw the covers from her body, her cheeks flushed with anger. "Why didn't you tell me?" she yelled. "Why is everyone keeping secrets from me?" She stood at the side of the bed, her hair was an unbrushed mess, and Samantha had no idea what to tell her.

She pulled up to her knees, trying to come up with something to say. "I don't know." She shook her head. "I should have said something, but it was your wedding, your big day, and I didn't want to take anything away from you."

Renee spun around. "That's bullshit!" she yelled, gripping the balled-up tissue in her fist.

Samantha turned toward the darkened window, trying without success to pull herself together. "You're right." She choked. "I didn't tell you because I was scared. I didn't tell you for a lot of reasons… Because my feelings were so big. Because it was all happening so fast."

"You think I can't handle big? I'm a fucking adult, Sam. Things happen. Don't you think I know that?"

Samantha swallowed and looked back to her friend. "I didn't want to share it, Ren. Not even with you. Because sharing things with you always makes them real." It was the honest to God truth. The completely selfish truth of a girl who didn't trust her own heart. She took another tissue from the box, her shoulders shaking. Then she felt Renee move beside her on the bed, smoothing the hair from her eyes and cheeks.

Samantha looked up, tears rolling down her face.

"Do you love him?" Renee whispered, her face just as tear-streaked as Samantha's.

She didn't hesitate before answering, because she wanted the words spoken more than anything. "Yes. I love him. I love him so much."

Renee pulled her into her arms, and they both collapsed into each other's embrace. "Then you have to tell him."

Samantha's words were barely audible as she nodded her head. "I know."

CHAPTER THIRTY

THE NEXT MORNING went by in a blur. There were hair appointments, nail appointments, and makeup from the moment she opened her eyes. And Tristan was still nowhere to be found. She was sure he was with the guys, doing all the wedding things he was supposed to, but the fact that she hadn't seen or spoken to him since the rehearsal left her stomach in knots.

She stood on the step, waiting for her best friend to walk down the aisle, and glanced over the crowd of people, knowing they waited with bated breath, just as she did. But for a different reason. Because they were waiting for their bride, her best friend for all eternity, while she was waiting for Tristan.

The door opened at the back of the room, and the crowd turned and rose out of their chairs. Renee stood at the open doorway, the "Bridal Chorus" playing softly from the piano in the background. Her dress was off-white, with a lace bodice and delicate sleeves that hung off her shoulders like lace ivy. Her head was high, her skirt simple, draping elegantly all the way to the floor—showing bits of her long legs as she took step after step.

But Samantha barely noticed her, because it was Tristan that made all the air expel from her throat. He was dressed in a tan tuxedo. An off white button-up shirt fastened at his tanned throat, but it was his eyes that memorized her most. They were full of emotion, with bits of gray darkening their depths. He looked, emotional—because he was taking on the role that should have been his father's. Taking on the role of a person who was far too selfish to be there today.

Tristan pulled in a deep breath and squeezed his sister's hand in a transfer of strength. Samantha's eyes moved down to her feet, because as emotional as this was to witness, it must have been ten times more emotional for the pair. They had fought like cats and dogs for most of their lives, but seeing them now, watching them walk side by side, nobody would ever know it. Together they were a harbor of strength, a unit of love and an example of what family was supposed to be. They were crossing the hurdle of a broken family, of a deadbeat father, with their heads held high as though no one was the wiser.

They stopped just below the stairs, where Phin waited with tears in his eyes to fetch his future bride. He shook Tristan's hand, and they both hugged, exchanging a few words before breaking apart.

The minister stepped forward with a soft smile as he looked from Tristan to Renee. "Who presents this woman to be married to this man?"

Tristan cleared his throat, then clasped his hands together in front of his body. "Her mother and I do." It was both heart-breaking and heartwarming at the same time. Because those were words which normally came from a father—yet Tristan, barely twenty-five, said them with more pride, more emotion than anyone else ever could.

There was a hush amongst the crowd, as the minister nodded, and Renee climbed the stairs with Phin. Tristan moved to the end of the row of groomsmen, glancing up to the wooden arbor where Renee and Phin would say their vows, and ignored Samantha completely.

Samantha tried to pay attention, to stay present and listen to every word that was spoken, but it was impossible. Because inside, her heart was breaking. Inside, she was struggling to keep herself upright.

Tristan hadn't even looked at her. Didn't acknowledge her for the entire service, and all her fears and insecurities came bubbling to the surface. She wanted to scream. To jump up and down, just to get his attention. To have him talk to her, even if the words he said were to tell her it was over, because his silence was unbearable. His silence was like a double-edged sword, slicing through every vulnerable crevice of her body, her mind—her soul.

She somehow made it through the ceremony, a smile on her lips as she walked out toward the gardens. The guests were ushered toward the open bar, while the bridal party was whisked away by the photographer. Samantha was hardly present for any of it. Her body was living, while her mind and heart protected themselves in a proverbial hole. When the wedding party was released from the photographer, everyone headed back toward the waiting reception.

Samantha caught up with Tristan just before he entered the building. She pulled at the hem of his sleeve, forcing him to turn around. His eyes were distant and dark, so different from the man she'd gotten to know over the past week.

"What's wrong with you?" she whispered. "Why haven't you called me back? Why are you ignoring me?"

He licked his lips, seeing her, but not really looking. "I don't know what you mean."

She stared at him, wanting to shake him out of whatever had taken him, because this was not the man she'd grown to love. "Tristan, I'm sorry."

His eyes closed, and he gripped the bridge of his nose in an effort to control his emotion. "I thought you broke up with him."

She shook her head, tears falling down her cheeks with the relief of finally getting through to him. "I couldn't just—"

But he cut her off. "Why was he here? Why was he holding you in his fucking arms?" His words were quiet, but were spit from his mouth with all the venom she deserved.

She looked into his eyes, seeing all the hurt and hatred that lived there. Guests were walking by, looking her up and down as they entered the reception room, and all she could do was tell the truth. "We'd been together for six years, I couldn't—"

But he didn't listen. "That's what I thought." He turned on his heels, not allowing her to finish, and entered the reception room.

She stumbled forward, left in the doorway with her heart in her throat as she watched him walk away. There were people all around her, laughing, smiling, and celebrating—while she struggled to keep herself upright. She walked into the ballroom dressed in a beautiful gown, her hair done up like a princess, yet feeling more alone and undesired than she'd ever felt in her entire life. Needing some sense of solitude, she shuffled through the crowd and pushed through the door to the restroom. She plucked a box of tissues from the closest table then sat down on the toilet and started to cry.

She knew she'd messed up, knew he was right to be angry, but he wouldn't even listen to her. He wouldn't even allow her to finish a sentence.

The door to the restroom opened again, and she held her breath, not wanting anyone to hear her crying. The last thing she needed was to cause a big scene at her best friend's wedding. She heard the stall door close beside her, then a moment later Renee's head was poking over the stall door by the ceiling.

"Hi," Renee whispered.

Samantha half sobbed, half laughed at the sight of her best friend. "What are you doing here?" she whispered, her chin wobbling. "You're supposed to be taking pictures."

Renee shook her head. "We already took plenty. But I can't go on, knowing you're in here dying inside."

Samantha closed her eyes, hating the fact she'd done this to her best friend. That Renee was in the bathroom offering her comfort when she should be out there with her new husband.

"I locked the door. Will you come out and talk to me?" Renee pleaded.

Samantha immediately nodded, knowing it was the least she could do. She crumpled up her soggy tissue, threw it in the trash, and unlocked her stall.

Renee was sitting on a chaise lounge, fiddling with her dress, but glanced up when she saw Samantha. She patted the spot beside her on the cushion. "Sit."

Samantha did as she was told, grabbing hold of Renee's offered hands.

The emotion of the day was etched all over Renee's face. Emotion about her father, her brother, the wedding. "Remember when I left to go visit Tristan a few years ago?" She began. "When you were in that awful English class and had the midterm load from hell?"

Samantha nodded, but her throat tightened uncomfortably because she knew what this was about. Renee was going to tell her about the accident, about Tristan's shoulder. Samantha had heard the story only days before, but for some reason she remained quiet. She'd heard it from Tristan, but now she wanted to hear it from Renee.

"Tristan was in a bad accident. He had a concussion, his rotator cuff was torn, bone ripped from its socket...among other things. He was a mess. He underwent emergency surgery to repair what they could, but he was told right away he'd never play ball again. As you can imagine, football was his life, his identity, and I can still remember the look on his face when he was given the news."

Renee's eyes brimmed with unshed tears as she looked at Samantha. "But what I remember most, was that he immediately looked to my father. Tristan idolized him, always had, and when he saw the disappointment in my father's eyes, it crushed him. And instead of being a support to his son, my father lectured him. It hurt Tristan more than his injury, more than the loss of his favorite sport…"

She turned to the box of tissues and plucked one from the box, her voice shredding. "Tristan argued with the doctors for over an hour after that, trying to convince them to do more, to give him another chance, but they couldn't." Renee's eyes bored into Samantha's, needing her to understand. "Tristan hates letting people down. He can't handle not being enough. As hard as this whole thing has been for me—it's been harder for my brother. Because the man he'd always tried to prove himself to has shown that maybe he's not the person to look up to."

She wiped at the corner of her eyes as though trying not to ruin her makeup. "Tristan carries the world on his shoulders. He always has. It was unfair of my mom to give him that secret. To make it his responsibility to handle the communication with my father… But like always, Tristan took on the role of making everyone else happy. When my father didn't even show up…" She cleared her throat, trying to continue. "I think Tristan feels both like a failure, and rejected at the same time."

She sniffed softly into her tissue and looked down to their joined hands. "I think seeing you with Steven was the last thing he could take. All his insecurities, all his fears came rushing out—"

Samantha plucked a tissue from the box and blew her nose. "Steven didn't know what happened. I had to—"

But Renee stopped her. "I know you did. And Tristan will understand, too, when you explain."

"But he—"

Renee gave Samantha's shoulder a squeeze. "Listen to me. When I saw Tristan walk into the lobby that first day with you, I was relieved. Because I hadn't seen him smile like that in years. I didn't know what had changed in him, but I realize now—it was you. You brought something out in him, Samantha. Something I haven't seen since before he was injured."

Samantha frowned, trying to comprehend what her friend was trying to tell her.

"He's pushing you away, can't you see that? He's pushing us all away."

Samantha shook her head, feeling a thousand bricks land on her shoulders. "What do you want me to do? He won't look at me; he won't even talk to me," she said, her voice choked with emotion.

"Then make him listen. He may take his time to hear you, but he always does." Tears spilled from Samantha's eyes, and Renee grabbed another tissue and continued to talk while she attempted to salvage her friend's makeup. "I don't know if Tristan has ever felt loved. Really loved, aside from me and my mother... But he needs more than us. He's been loved for his looks, loved for his body and what he can do with it, loved for so many other things, but I think it's hard for him to see that it can be unconditional. That he can be himself and still have value. That people aren't perfect, and that doesn't mean love ends."

Renee rose to her feet, smoothing the silk of her skirt down her legs. "He's pushing you away on purpose. And if you really love him, Sam, you won't let him do it."

IT WAS JUST a half hour later when Samantha pulled herself together enough to rejoin the reception. She had cried for a long while. Trying to process all that Renee had told her. It was heartbreaking and awful, but still, she had no idea how to get through to someone who wouldn't even look at her. Everyone was seated at their tables, being served their chosen meal of prime rib or lobster, and she took a seat next to Mark. He immediately poured her a glass of Chardonnay and pushed it across the table. "I was about to send out a search party. Where'd you disappear to?"

She took a large gulp of the offered drink. "The restroom," she answered with a tight voice.

He glanced over to Tristan on the other side of the room. "Trouble in paradise?"

She nodded and pulled in a deep breath, but only glanced up for a moment, because she was afraid if she looked longer than that the tears would come again. "Can we talk about something else? I'm not feeling up to this right now."

His brow furrowed, but he nodded and began cutting his steak. They continued eating their meals in silence, time passing as though she was in a fog, and before she knew it, her sculpture was being rolled out into the middle of the dance floor.

She knew it was coming, but at the same time she wasn't ready. Wasn't ready to stand in front of all Renee's friends and family. Wasn't ready for a thousand eyes to be watching her. But the DJ called her out on the dance floor, and she turned to Mark. "I don't want to do this." She whispered, but she rose from her seat anyway and collected the microphone from the podium.

She looked into the faces of all the guests. People she barely knew, but were about to see her at her most vulnerable. She turned around to face all of them, then glanced over to Renee, deciding she didn't care what any of the guests thought. She was doing it for her best friend, her salt of the earth friend whose heart was bigger than anyone else's.

Renee watched her, eyes and body at attention, waiting for her to speak. Samantha's chest tightened, and all the tears she'd been holding rushed up to clog in her throat. She ran her hand along the length of the microphone cord, hoping energy or strength would miraculously enter her body. She owed Renee this. If nothing else, Renee deserved a speech from her maid of honor.

Samantha closed her eyes, letting out a deep breath before pulling the drape from the sculpture. The fabric fell to the ground, revealing a plethora of green, blue, and earth toned colors.

She turned back to Renee, meeting her best friend's eyes as she took in the sculpture for the first time. It was of a ballerina, tall and beautiful, though it's legs were twisted, fabricated into roots stuck deep into a ball of soil. Her arms were long, held over her head and growing up to the sky like limbs, covered in tiny, intricate leaves in a myriad of colors.

Samantha turned toward the audience and pulled in a breath. "I still remember the day I met Renee," she began, staring through tear brimmed eyes to look at all the faces. "Her hair was up in one of those tight ballerina buns she wore all throughout grade school, and Ricky Jones had just stepped on her fingers. I instantly felt a connection." She smiled softly, stretching out her hand to examine her knuckles. "I'm pretty sure I still have the scars from when he stepped on my hand only the day before."

The crowd chuckled, and Renee's lips curved in a soft smile. "But Renee was always different than me. Because, instead of worrying about herself, she helped Ricky up to his feet when he fell." Her voice grew husky with emotion. "She's always been like that. A harbor of strength. A sheltering tree to all those lucky enough to be loved by her. But she's kind of crazy, too." She nodded, causing the whole crowd to mumble with shock.

She glanced over to the seat she'd seen Tristan sitting in not five minutes earlier and found it empty, which caused her stomach to drop a few inches. She took a calming breath, turning to Renee again and straightening her shoulders.

"A few months ago, Renee called at midnight to tell me about a guy." She raised her brows, indicating she wasn't happy about being woken up so late. "He was wonderful, and perfect, and she was going out on a date with him. But four weeks later, after many phone calls in between, she told me she loved him." The crowd began to chuckle, and Samantha cracked a tiny grin. "Quite frankly I was shocked, but who was I to judge?" She paused for a moment, shaking her head. "Then she told me she was going to marry him." Samantha looked down, her heart so raw and open she may as well have been lying on an operating table. "I thought she was having one of her crazy moments—like literally had lost her mind. Because I'd spent six years with a man, and my heart still wasn't open to the idea of forever."

She looked up then, glancing around the crowd who had suddenly gone completely quiet. "How, in such a short time, did she know that she loved him?"

Everyone around her began adjusting in their seats, whispering, but she didn't stop.

"You see, Renee and I are the same age. Born only two weeks apart. We've done everything together. Shared the same birthday parties, the same friends, same graduation. How could she be so frivolous with her heart to marry a man after such a short time?"

Gasps could be heard throughout the hall, and she looked into Renee's eyes, her lips quivering with the tears she held onto so desperately. "But six days ago, I realized that Renee had it right the whole time. Because time isn't a factor in matters of the heart. I can see now she's given her whole heart to Phin. That she's shown him her flaws, and let him really see her." She looked toward the ground. "Because that's how love works. That's what I want. I don't want perfect. I want flaws, and I want passion. I want someone to give me everything without holding back. Even the ugly pieces. Even the pieces hidden from everyone else."

The audience hushed, and Samantha turned back to face them again, knowing Tristan was out there amongst them. Somewhere. "Love is about being vulnerable. It's about doing things that scare you. Like giving your heart to someone after a few weeks, or a few days. When you find the right person, time stops." She nodded and smiled at her best friend. "That's what happened to Renee and Phin." She placed the microphone back on the podium and whispered, "And that's what happened to me."

The crowd went silent, and she lifted her glass above her head. "To the bride and groom, and to love that is timeless."

Everyone cheered and clinked their glasses. Mark stood up, then lowered his head in a nod of respect. She could see he was proud of her, and frankly, she was proud of herself, too. Because she would have never done this a week ago. She wasn't strong enough then.

Mark came toward the podium, placing his hand on her shoulder before whispering in her ear. "Good job, kid. The ball's in his court." He then relieved her from the spotlight, and had the whole room laughing before she made it to the bottom step.

She weaved between the tables, not intending to stick around. Because every last drop of her strength had been used up on that stage, and she needed to get out of there. First, she focused on getting to her table, then, gathering her things, putting one foot in front of the other, breathing in and out. Because if she tried to focus on more than that, it was too overwhelming. She made it to her table without anyone noticing her, took a couple sips of wine as she gathered her things, but before she could turn away, an elderly man came forward to block her path.

"Is that piece yours?" he asked. His voice low and eloquent. He looked to be in his sixties, elegantly dressed, with a kind face.

Samantha glanced back to the sculpture near the dance floor and nodded her head. Light was bouncing off the tiny leaves and a few people had gathered around to examine it. "Yes," she answered, trying to move around him again.

He stepped in front of her, eyeing her up and down curiously. He held out his hand in introduction. "My name is Henry Covington. I own a gallery downtown."

She swallowed quickly, glancing up into his face in a daze.

He adjusted his stance, then took a sip of his dark drink and tilted his head. "Pieces like yours are exactly what I've been looking for, miss...?"

The wind left her lungs and she forgot how to speak—everything. Even her own name. This had been the darkest day of her entire life, and now this man stood in front of her, offering her a candle of hope. Tears brimmed her eyes and she looked down to her feet.

A woman with dark, silvery curls came to stand by his side and took hold of his arm.

"Dear, this is the young artist who made the sculpture," he said, lowering his head to whisper in her ear like Samantha wasn't right in front of them. They held a conversation about the detail, the artistry, and Samantha finally found her voice again.

"Samantha Smiles," she cut in, holding out her hand. "It's nice to meet you both."

The older woman took her offered fingers, squeezing them softly. "It's stunning, dear." she confessed, "Simply stunning."

Her husband placed a card into Samantha's palm, then curled her fingers around the sharp edges. "It's been a pleasure, Miss Smiles. Please call me, I'd love to chat." He patted the top of her closed hand and turned to his wife. "I do look forward to your phone call, but if you'll excuse me, I'd like to dance with my wife." He then nodded his head once more and escorted Mrs. Covington to the dance floor.

Samantha returned quickly to the table, unable to process anything but goodbyes as she tucked the card away in her clutch.

She walked down the long hall to her room with her head held high, praying to God that Tristan had heard her, that maybe he was waiting for her at her room, but the closer she got, the more it became clear that he wasn't.

She entered the dark room alone, where she slipped off her gown, letting it land as a puddle of fabric onto the floor. She crawled into bed with pins still in her hair and let the tears flow. Tomorrow she would go back to LA, she promised, and try to forget about the man who took her heart while she wasn't paying attention. But tonight, she would allow herself to grieve. She would cry until her mouth went dry, until all her tears were spent, and hopefully when it was over, her heart wouldn't hurt quite so badly.

CHAPTER THIRTY-ONE

THE NEXT AFTERNOON Samantha ran the business card over and over again against her palm. She'd called Mr. Covington early that morning, and he was flying to Los Angeles the next week to look at her collection—he wanted all of it. Every single piece, purchased unseen, simply because he liked her style.

It was surreal. To realize life could change so quickly. That love could enter, then be ripped away in the blink of an eye. That a career at rock bottom could flourish, simply by being in the right place at the right time.

She fastened the card back away in her wallet, then added the last of her belongings in her overstuffed suitcase. She'd already called the front desk to check out of the room, but glanced around it one last time. The curtains were drawn open, revealing the beautiful day ahead of her, and the empty suite she had to leave behind. But she was leaving behind so much—she was leaving Tristan, who still was nowhere to be found. And a best friend, who she wasn't sure she'd see for a long time.

She wanted to stop by Tristan's door one last time to see if he was there, but pride wouldn't allow her to chase him anymore. Like Mark said, the ball was in his court now. What she needed to say was said last night. She loved him. Unconditionally. It was up to him what he did with the information.

She grabbed her backpack from the top of the desk, and slung it over one shoulder before setting her keycard on the dresser and heading out of the room. She took the elevator all the way to the garage floor, where she could continue on past the valet and out into the city streets. But when she got there, Tristan was propped against the side of his Mustang in one of the stalls. She swallowed hard, wanting to ignore his aviator shielded face, and his feet crossed at the ankles, but her eyes instantly filled with tears. Even though she told herself she wasn't going to cry for him anymore. Even though she thought every drop of tears had been shed last night.

She tried to rush past him, not wanting him to see her in this condition, but he stepped in front of her, blocking her exit.

He pulled his glasses from his face, revealing tired, dark circles. "Can I talk to you?" he asked, emotion turning his voice to gravel.

She looked up at him, swallowing hard as she gripped onto her backpack for dear life. "Now? Now you want to talk to me? I've called you a thousand times. I stood up there in front of all of those people—"

"I know—"

She turned on her heels, feeling emotion try to consume her. Her heart was beating wildly, trampled by a thousand horses, and she needed to get away.

He stepped in front of her again. "I was scared! Dammit, will you listen to me?"

She froze, because she'd never heard him yell before. Or seen him look so tortured. Tears brimmed his eyes, and he used the backs of his hands to brush them away. "I was shitty to you; I know that. I was vulnerable, and instead of letting you in, I closed you out." He was visibly struggling to keep himself together, and she almost wanted to take him in her arms, but she couldn't. She needed to hear what he was going to say.

"To my father," he began, "vulnerably was a sign of weakness. When I cried he told me I was soft, when I fell he told me to get up. It was part of being a man. I learned at an early age to give him what he wanted, and in return he was proud of me. I still can't figure out if I played so hard because I loved the game or because he did, but when my football career ended, he lost interest. I couldn't even persuade him to come to his own daughter's wedding."

Samantha's heart throbbed in her chest. She ached to hold him, to argue that his father had been so very wrong, but she stayed silent and allowed him to continue.

"When I gave people what they wanted, they were happy, but no matter how hard I tried, how hard I played the game, at some point I couldn't hold the ball any longer. When I found out about my father's infidelity, I stopped trying. I was gruff, and I said what I wanted, and I scared people off. I tried it with you, but for some reason you've always looked at me differently. You see me, even through all the walls I put up around myself." He stepped closer. "It scared the crap out of me."

He looked into her eyes, not hiding his emotion, but struggling to control it. "When I saw you with Steven, with his arms around you, it was the last thing I could take. All these insecurities started pouring out of me. He'd had you for six years; I'd been with you for only a few days. Eventually I would drop the ball and you'd see me. Maybe not then, maybe not tomorrow, but some day. So I convinced myself that choosing to walk away earlier wouldn't hurt as much as later. That you'd be better off with someone else."

Samantha struggled to stand, tears running down her cheeks. "Tristan—"

He widened his stance, clenching his jaw. "Let me finish."

She searched his stormy eyes, waiting for him to speak.

"Last night I left the wedding and sat in my room with a bottle of whisky. I started thinking about everything. About my father, my family. And I realized I was being a coward. That I was letting everything with my dad control me again. Because of all that happened, I was pushing you away."

He hesitated, biting his lip as though searching for the right words.

"But time stops when I'm with you too," he said, finding her eyes again. "It stopped when I was with you all those years ago, and it did again the moment you got into my car in Los Angeles. And I realized if I pushed you away I'd be giving up the best thing that has ever happened to me, because of fear."

He glanced down to their joined hands, then back up again before continuing. "I'm in love with you, Samantha. I love the way you challenge me, I love your mind, I love the way you look at me, I love your body and soul. I don't know where this road will lead us, but I'm not ready to get off. I've had more fun with you in the past week than I've ever had in my life, and I want a do over. Every single moment of it." The tiniest hopeful twinkle glittered in his eyes and he gave her hand a squeeze. "Let's get in my car, forget about our past, not worry about the future, and just drive. Wherever the road leads us. You and me, just us."

Her eyes overflowed with tears, and she glanced over at the Mustang filled with luggage and pillows and a large bag filled with chips.

"Say yes," he whispered. "Say yes, and I'll spend the rest of my life making sure you never regret it."

She walked into his embrace, where he squeezed her so tight she felt her bones crack. When she threw her arms around his neck, he hoisted her up, cradling her against his chest.

She kissed his lips, sobbed against them, her whole body shaking with emotion. "Yes," she whispered. "Yes."

ONE YEAR LATER

IT WAS early morning when Samantha opened her eyes for the first time, letting in only a fraction of light before quickly snapping them shut again. She still had a headache, and her throat felt like a tractor had tilled back and forth over the tender flesh. The windows were open, and wafting in from the bakery below was the scent of fresh baked bread.

She smiled, even though the action caused shards of glass to scrape down her neck. She couldn't help it. Even though she was sicker than a dog, she was still happier than she'd been in a long time. She was in Paris for the first time in her life—with the man she loved more than anything in the world. The Devil had knocked on her door, bringing strep throat with him, but nothing could get her down these days. She had everything she ever wanted. A man who not only adored her, but who had become her travel companion and best friend.

She heard the click-screech of their front door opening, then rolled to her side to see Tristan walk into the room with the bags he'd collected at market. He sat on the side of the bed and pressed his lips to her forehead before setting them down beside her on the mattress. "No fever. How are you feeling?"

"Better," she croaked. "What did you bring me?"

He furrowed his brow and opened the bag. "Well let's see…" He pulled out three bottles of juices, ranging from red to orange. "I wasn't sure which one you'd like, so I got orange, passion fruit, and I'm not sure what this one is." He grinned. "She tried to tell me, but…"

Samantha grinned, propping herself up to kiss his nose. "Thank you. You're the sweetest."

"Ahhh… But that's not all." He stuck his hand in the bag and pulled out a Styrofoam cup and a loaf of crusty bread. "It's only bone broth, but I thought if you were hungry—"

Her eyes began to water, and he stopped talking, setting the broth on the table to move closer. "Are you okay? Is it your throat?"

"No," she said shaking her head. "It's you." She wiped at the corner of her eye and hugged him. Gripping his body to hers with all the strength she could muster. "How did I get so lucky? How is it possible I found someone to love me this much?"

He hugged her back, all his muscles tightening around her at once. "I'm the lucky one."

Eventually they sat side-by-side, tearing off pieces of the delicious bread and soaking them up in the warm broth as they watched a movie. It wasn't the ideal thing to do on vacation in Paris, but they still had three weeks left, and she couldn't think of anything else she'd rather be doing.

When the movie was over, she peeled herself from the mound of blankets and took a shower. She washed her hair for the first time in a couple of days, and when she got out, she felt practically like a new woman. Clean, fed, loved.

She found Tristan over by the window, looking out at their spectacular view of the city. Her hair was tied up in a towel, and she wore one of his threadbare old t-shirts that smelled just like him. She walked toward him, because even a year later, she still craved to be near him. She set her hand on his shoulder, and rested her face against his muscular back. "Do you know what today is?" she whispered.

"No. What?"

"Your sister's one year anniversary." She moved to his side, and he draped his arm around her shoulders pulling her closer. "Do you think it's a good time to call?"

He smiled down at her, then moved the short distance to the table to fetch his phone. "Let's find out."

"Hello," Renee answered on the first ring. She was on speakerphone, held in Samantha's palm as they looked out the window.

"Hey Ren." Samantha smiled. "Your brother and I just wanted to call and wish you a happy anniversary."

Renee laughed. "You're in Paris on vacation and remembered my anniversary? Don't you have anything better to do?"

Tristan took the phone from Samantha and started laughing "Samantha's sick, so we're just hanging out, waiting for her to get better."

"Aww... Well that sucks. I thought she sounded different."

Samantha grinned, and Tristan handed her the phone again. He then moved behind her, and began massaging her lower back with firm fingers. "Could be worse," she said softly.

The two friends then went on to chat about the normal things. Work, life, and all the strange things only a best friend would care about. But before long, Phin could be heard in the background, and Renee was getting off the phone.

"Well, we're about to go out to dinner, and I can't find my shoes. I'll tell Phin you called, and I'll expect a whole rundown of your trip when you get home."

"Sounds good," Samantha whispered.

They all said their goodbyes, and then Samantha turned around, to rest her cheek on Tristan's chest.

He hugged her tightly, peppering kisses along the side of her neck, "Do you know what else today is?" he whispered.

She only grinned, feeling herself getting turned on even in her state of weakness. "What?" she asked.

He kissed her again. "The anniversary of the day you first told me you loved me."

She turned around, tears brimming her eyes in surprise. "It is, isn't it?"

He nodded. "The best day of my entire life."

She tilted her head, squinting up at him. "The best? Because I remember that day, and it felt more like a slow, endless torture."

He brushed his knuckles over her cheek and looked into her eyes, as if the realization still pained him. Very much. He then lowered his hands to the small of her back and closed his eyes for a moment. "It was torture for me, too." He took a deep breath, then opened his eyes allowing her to see all the emotion that lived inside of him. "I watched you walk out of the reception that night, thinking it was the last time I'd ever see you, and it—" But he shook his head, unable to continue, as though he didn't want to relive the pain. He dropped his chin down to the crevice of her neck, as though he needed her closer, needed her as much as she needed him.

"Alone in my room that night, I realized a few things. That I trusted you completely." He kissed her collarbone, and she could feel him shudder beneath her fingers "I also realized that if I was going to love you, I needed to allow myself to fall. Without a net, without a mask, because if I was going to be with you, you were the type of woman who deserved everything."

She wiped the corners of her eyes, but then he took her hands in his, needing to say more.

"It wasn't until you almost walked out of my life that I knew I had to take the risk, that I had to push away what I'd always been taught, and go with what I felt in my gut. To go after what I wanted." He moved closer, his lips hovering over hers, breathing the same breaths, breathing the same air. "Because somewhere in the darkest moments, beauty lives. Waiting for you to take hold of it and run. I didn't sleep at all that night. I went to the hotel lobby and bought every flavor of chips I could find." He kissed her lips then, though only barely. "It was the best day of my life, because it was the day I decided to go after you."

Sobs were jolting from her body, and she couldn't take it any longer. She gripped him to her chest, hugging him harder than she thought possible. "I love you, Tristan Montgomery. I love you so much."

"And I love you, Samantha Elizabeth Smiles." He then carried her to their bed, where she convinced him to make love to her even though she was sick. Because try as he may, the Devil could bring sickness, but he could never prevent them from loving each other. Even without a net to catch them.

THE END

ACKNOWLEDGMENTS

I want to give thanks to my family and friends, especially my husband. Without whose love and support none of this would be possible.

To my editor Bree, who goes above and beyond on a daily basis! I can't thank you enough. Your support, and constant willingness to help is priceless.

To my author friends, who are always there to listen to me talk about my fictional troubles, and help me sort things out in my head. I love you!

ABOUT THE AUTHOR

Taylor is mom of three young (or not so young) children she loves more than life. She runs them around endlessly, hoping she looks presentable enough to be out in public, and day dreams about fictional characters. Maybe she's crazy, or maybe she craves the barbie games she played as a little girl a little too much, but that's where her stories are born. It's where they blossom, and grow, and eventually breath life on the page of her stories.

She resides in Los Angeles with the love of her life, and three constantly growing children. She becomes giddy with excitement every time she hears from a fan, and would love to hear from YOU!

If you never want to miss one of her stories, make sure to join her news letter! http://eepurl.com/bqiWSX

Find Taylor on social media!
taylorsullivanauthor.com
taylorsullivan.author@gmail.com

Made in the USA
Middletown, DE
24 July 2018